Fever

Fever

Linda Dominique Grosvenor

sepia

BET BOOKS

BET Publications, LLC

SEPIA BOOKS are published by

BET Publications, LLC
c/o BET BOOKS
One BET Plaza
1900 W Place NE
Washington, DC 20018-1211

ISBN 0-7394-3241-9

Printed in the United States of America

ACKNOWLEDGMENTS

I haven't figured out how to include everyone who has touched this project but here it goes. . . . I'd like to thank God, not just in passing, but in living, for it is He who guides me and shelters me in this rat race we call life. I'd like to shower some praise on my husband, John Riddick, Jr., who himself has picked up his pen and can now see and appreciate all the hard work that goes into creating a written work. To my son, whom I not only tell that anything is possible, but in addition take the time to lead him by example. Claudia Menza, you are the best! To Tanya Marie Lewis, *"Ain't nothing like the real thing!"* Pastor Mark Spell and the DOCM family, I love you. To my Momma Gloria, sisters, brother, Tonia, Hicks, my new publicist, Aska Covington, and my loyal readership, I'd like to thank you for your continued and unwavering support. It is you that I write for. Enjoy!

"The only abnormality is the incapacity to love."

—Anäis Nin

1

Tim

Oversize palm trees hugged the veranda, and the freshly shaven lawn left no evidence of footprints or other trespasses, just a colorful squeeze toy waiting to squeal as it played hide-and-seek with bare feet. The tall weather-beaten fence couldn't keep out the sun or tame the brisk wind long enough to still the wind chime. The flower bed still made him sneeze as the succulence of ripe pollen tangled and overwhelmed.

Monet, an incourrigible golden retriever pup, despite his unbreakable habit of chewing on anything bite-sized, was cozying up now and becoming Tim's best friend. Tim gladly obliged Monet as his mind endeavored to define this as anything other than an exaggerated Hallmark moment full of tears that never dried, only paused to replenish. He never imagined a time in his life as pregnant with possibilities. We all have something to be thankful for, he reassured himself, trying not to be sappy.

He stood back and admired his elongated suit jacket and matching black pants that hung there on a thick smooth wooden hanger. They always complemented him as his broad shoulders and well-defined back normally conjured images of him beating his chest like an African tribesman in New Guinea. Tim flicked lint from his iris linen shirt and draped it across his bed. He put on, then adjusted his glasses.

There was something more distinguished about him now. Not just the tortoiseshell frames, the way they made him appear well read, the high shine of his shoes that sat pensive in the corner, or the furrowed brow that was always contemplating new thoughts more prolific than the last. More so, it was the way he spoke with a confidence in something other than himself, a thirst that was only quenched by the actualization of his ideas. Thankfully he hadn't burned all his bridges. There were still people who called, cared, and wondered and hoped he'd make it. And he would make it. Determination was something he wouldn't soon lack.

Tim stepped in front of the wide television that was as verbose as a yapping dog who only wanted to play fetch long after midnight had settled everyone into their routines of slumber. He searched around for the remote control. Right now individuals on a news program were debating a topic too trivial to engage the television in. He muted it, respecting Sunday morning rituals. He reached in his rack and pulled out a jazz CD. Craig Crawford always mellowed him.

Pulling the sliding glass door open, Tim strolled into his yard holding a glass of mango nectar, squinting slightly with his slippers in tow slapping his heels, and reliving the past month vividly over and over again in his head. Steady stride and destination still somewhat uncertain, like many other things in his life Monet blindsided him, sending him and his drink grazing the manicured lawn and the lounge chair toppling on top of them both. Monet licked the juice off of Tim's face apologetically while Tim tussled with the chair that was now dented and permanently leaning to the side.

Tim sat in the chair anyway, bracing himself with his right foot, and separating the sections of the Sunday newspaper like an orange shared by four. He had just begun working with the dialogue for his next script and was completing the rewrites on the former. Although the gloss of the business had dulled slightly, he knew that this was what he had been waiting his whole life to achieve. Acclaim. Low hundreds as a payday for his first film was a start. Anything that parted the curtains of his mind and drew out his dreams validating them instead of rendering them a falsehood was Robin Hood in his book.

It was then that Nina did what she had always done, tiptoed into his mind unsuspectingly and shook him. He thought back to their conversation that night. She had called inquiring whether he had found a church yet. He was looking and hadn't felt led anywhere in particular but he had a feeling about where he was going this evening. It might just be his final destination. Someplace he could venture on a regular basis. He didn't like lukewarm coffee, people, or churches, but something just told him that when he found a church it'd feel like welcome home.

He may not have always been, but thankful was something that he was lately. At Tim's feet Monet sat bathing his toes with his huge slobbery tongue. Tim's cordless phone, still snuggling in the grass from last night, was ringing. His laughter caught Nina off guard.

"Having fun?"

"Well, as a matter of fact, I'm not." He chuckled, pushing his feet into damp slippers that were now masquerading as a bone. "How's your momma?" he inquired, self-assured that his curiosity wouldn't always get the better of him.

"She's hanging in there."

"And your dad?" he asked.

"Oh, he's hanging in there too." She paused.

"And Troi?"

"She's surviving."

"I hear that."

"And you, Tim? How busy is work keeping you? I mean, do you have time to relax and unwind?" She covered up her question with involuntary laughter that still left him sensing that she was feeling him out.

"In this business, time doesn't come, you have to seize it. Be it moments, minutes, or milliseconds," he preached.

"You sound relaxed though."

"I am." His lips curled into a mischievous grin as he recalled when last his lips were pressed on hers. Now that relaxed him. He wanted to extend a heartfelt invitation to her so that she could see for herself the legendary smog that appeared to be eating the city in the distance, and observe the obscure bridge that was nothing to brag about even on a clear day. But she had Momma, Daddy, and sister issues to attend to and he didn't care very much for shotgun.

"You know what I can use right now?" she asked, momentarily interrupted by short, sharp barking noises on Tim's end.

"Sorry, you were saying?" he fumbled.

"I said, what I want most in the world is to lie back for a couple of days and do absolutely nothing, a little vacation or something. You know what I mean?"

"Tim . . ." a perky familiar voice interjected on his end, dragging out the one syllable in his name like a song.

He silenced the unexpected guest by muffling the phone with his hand, then put his finger to his lips.

"What was that again? I'm sorry," he apologized.

"I wasn't saying anything. Let me not keep you, I have to go anyway. I have a dozen things to do." Nina spoke calmly so as not to let on she was frowning. The heat rose in her cheeks.

"No, come on, tell me," Tim protested.

He thought that at least after all this time they were tighter than blue jeans in the rain or the effort it took to get them off. Whatever happened between them was fate. He couldn't blame the woman with bad timing.

Tim knew he cared about Nina but he couldn't allow his emotions to dictate. He had to be rational. Detached yet cordial. And although he ached like a knee skinned down to the bone to be near her, he pretended that it didn't matter one way or the other. He never wanted to be the bad guy. He knew that hurting Nina was like killing an angel, then plucking off the wings.

She said she had to go. He responded in kind. He closed his eyes and thought, a little harmless petting would do.

"So when am I gonna hear from you again?" He stroked his face and imagined this conversation possibly being their last for a good while.

"I'll be in touch," she offered.

"Are you still afraid of airplanes?" Tim hesitated.

"I can't tell, still haven't been on one."

"Would you fly if I sent you a ticket?"

"One never knows what they'd do if the opportunity presented itself," she said, hardly moving her lips.

Tim was mentally whipping himself. Never could curb his tongue. He had to learn just to say good-bye and leave it at that. He didn't know why he was always dragging things out or trying to buff every situation in his life to a car-wash shine. Tim cupped the phone with the palm of his hand, whispering to the woman who had reentered his space, knowing that as predictable as women were, Nina was probably straining to capture every word.

Visions of Nina shivering slightly as he played in her hair, and quivering as he moved in closer to her neck, came back to his remembrance. That's the way he would always remember her. Eyes closed, pouting and enjoying what he offered her. Part of him wanted to say, "Don't go, stay," or "Don't stay there, come here." He looked toward his floor at the neutral-colored carpeting instead, lowered his voice, and said, "Hey, Nina, I'll talk to you soon."

That's the way he wanted to remember his life, gloriously fulfilling as someone he dug was digging him just as much, throwing caution to the wind and allowing themselves to revel in the moment. A handful of years and a marriage ceremony later, things were different between Nina and Tim. Church only occasionally and a romance that had cooled to the touch. The communication between them was an unfeeling hollowness and he couldn't make heads or tails of it. They had both stopped making time for the little things, dinner, affectionate conversation, and lovemaking that went on for hours. They had given in to the nonchalance of everyday existence and now here they were, trying to sort out a bunch of odds and ends that wouldn't permit them to discern love right there in the palm of their hands.

Tim had guarded his heart his entire life, sifting through a maze of feminine warheads for someone who was willing to help him feed his dream of being a successful filmmaker, and now this. Women always made promises in exchange for marriage. Promises they knew they couldn't keep. They vowed that they would remain the epitome of beauty and understanding, for as long as it took to get their feet warm, and that almighty band of gold snuggly on their finger.

Tim put every breath he had into his films. All he was asking for in life was a woman to have his back. Catch him when he fell. Listen without judging. Make a marriage work without putting him on the spot demanding constant validation. Show a brother some love and appreciation. Be his wife, and then some.

Maybe Nina wasn't who he thought she was, maybe he no longer wanted what he had or needed her love the way he used to. It could be that the novelty of their affection for each other was gone and that the everyday things like watching her hair transform from a greasy head rag to tight curls falling around her face no longer impressed him. Being married, coming home to dutiful inquiries, boredom separating them into their own worlds. Needs changed. Yeah, lots of things changed, he just didn't know what he'd do to rectify it all. The boredom had consumed him and he didn't know if he even wanted to fix their broken love now or ever.

2

Nina

Nina had listened attentively as Tim spoke of his new life that didn't include her. A new life where she was nothing more than a voice on the answering machine, and she'd cry herself to sleep every other night because she missed him. She fought not to say she craved him.

It sounded tempting and unclean, but she did. His voice made her think about peanut butter and jelly, the third grade, initials carved into an unsuspecting tree, and her first kiss all those years ago on a red toy fire engine in the rain. She knew their worlds had changed. His was moving in a more enlightening and self-discovering manner while she just existed, becoming increasingly more absorbed in nocturnal thoughts of Tim.

He knew where he was going and had his head on straight. Nina was still consumed with issues from her past and it wasn't fair to drag him into her life, then use their time together to sort through her mess. She had to have something to bring to the table. It wasn't just about getting the man, but about keeping him. In her mind she had finally come to the realization that although she found him entertaining, it was more than that. She looked at her face in the mirror and confirmed out loud that she was doing exactly what she vowed she'd never do, open up, again.

Opening up wasn't so bad. It was just all the effort it took to get there and everything you had to relinquish that had her going. Cleaning house. She was learning to do that with an old-fashioned broom. That meant that everything negative had to go. There were things that needed to increase in her life too. Tolerance. She was sure working on that. And love? Well, as of late, it had her over a barrel. All she needed to do was believe that what's yours is for you and what isn't, well, God always makes a way of escape.

Tim and Nina. Two predestined souls, God-timed births, and an orchestrated location. If she believed all of that, why was she sipping coffee now and pondering why love isn't convenient? Tim was preoccupied with whatever the significance was for that woman being in his apartment. The woman he muffled the phone over, trying his best not to let Nina hear. He hadn't even insisted that the woman wasn't important. There was a time when Nina felt like a priority to him, but not at the moment. Not anymore. Humiliation wasn't a garment that she would wear for anybody. Him in California and her in New York? A way of escape? She nodded. Maybe this was hers.

Nina was cautiously reflecting on her life. She had sold her overpriced Brooklyn brownstone, picked up, and relocated her life to California to be with Tim. She and Tim had taken the leap, jumped the broom, got hitched. The "until death do you part" thing. They planned an intimate ceremony exclusively for close family and friends. Pastel flowers, a three-tier cake with butter cream icing, no bridesmaids, his-and-her Greek wedding bands on loan from a local jeweler. Her heart bought the fact that he wanted to marry her on the summer solstice because she loved him. "It's the longest day of the year," he said. But now after the hype had died down in their airy house, and all the thank-you notes had been written, here she was at home, alone. All by herself. No sign of a husband anywhere. She didn't want to tip her mental scale with philosophical banter so she ignored the night breeze, kicked off her slippers, and snuggled up on the couch with the remote control again tonight. Monet was curled up in a furry ball at Nina's feet, wagging his tail to an unsung rhythm as she ruffled the scruff of his neck.

Tim was on location somewhere north of San Bernardino with the streets blocked off, annoying the neighbors with bright lights and filming late into the night. Nina didn't quite understand how the fairy tales had duped her into believing in happily ever after in a world where that hardly ever happens. Surely she thought she was more realistic than that. She was a rational woman, most of the time. When she moved to the West Coast, things were certainly going well for Tim. He had begun to make a name for himself in film and was coined a "fresh young talent" by *Filmmaker* magazine. In her mind she imagined accompanying Tim to those glitzy premieres with roped-off velvet VIP areas, gliding across red indoor-outdoor carpeting, dodging the flashbulbs that blanched the night, she and Tim arm in arm basking in the praise of his hard work.

But it was only like that on television and now here she was moping around their home. The bamboo dinette set, wicker lawn furniture, and the mud-cloth throw pillows were all she had to show for the familiar life she had given up for her husband. Once able to fend for herself and meet her own needs, now she assumed her role as the compliant wife. She sat around in their comfy little spread bored to utter oblivion. Nina's only major dilemma besides paper or plastic was ironing out dinner's ultimate challenge—fresh mashed potatoes with herbs, butter, and garlic, baked macaroni with three cheeses, or both.

Both was what had gotten her in the shape she was in now. Hips riding her like a saddle, thighs slapping each other as she walked, and her face trying to give birth to a second chin. Dieting and the gym were nowhere in sight. The Marriage Twenty, that was what it was. The twenty pounds you gained after marriage. In her case, more like forty. She was wearing the bliss of it all on every curve of her body. Nina had debated back and forth with her neighbor Francesca about the actuality that the Marriage Twenty even existed.

"It comes with the contentment of being married," Nina said, enlightening her friend.

Francesca sat in Nina's kitchen tossing water chestnuts into her salad and shaking her head, not believing a word of it. Francesca rested her hands on the hips of her thin frame, looked Nina right in the eyes, and said, "The Marriage Twenty is a myth perpetuated by lazy East Coast women who need an out for having over thirty percent body fat." It wasn't entirely true.

She appreciated her friends and their little gabfests, but being married and lonely was worse in Nina's mind than being single with no one calling and leaving messages on her machine.

Sitting across from your own reflection at the dinner table, tossing sweet peas around on your plate, facing an empty chair, no one else there to partake of your culinary goodness, not a pleasant feeling.

Aside from their brief honeymoon in Cancun several years ago overlooking the green mossy lagoon, Nina couldn't remember the last time she and Tim had done something intimate together, just them, without his nappy-headed friends tagging along or thoughts of editing, filming, and reshooting scenes filling his head the entire time. Even the much anticipated Valentine's Day and all its fervor that she had come to depend on for a morsel of red lacy affection had failed her. Tim had left her a bottle of cheap wine and a box of stale chocolates with a note resting on the wire shelf in the fridge that said *Sorry, baby I had to work.* She hadn't had a drink since they had grinned and toasted each other at their wedding ceremony.

The wine, however, proved one thing finally, that after almost five years of marriage, Tim hardly knew her at all. Trying to get him to open up and talk and appreciate the love they supposedly had was like nailing Jell-O to the wall. How disappointing that was. So disappointing, in fact, that Nina turned up the volume on the television, sat in front of it, and ate an entire box of chocolates that were turning white around the edges, before the second set of commercials aired. She refused to cry about how things weren't going her way. She would learn, as she always had, just to make do and not give the situation the satisfaction of her complaining.

"I'm doing this for us," Tim would say, going on and on about work and his career.

Us? It wasn't feeling like *us* to Nina. She honestly didn't care about fame and all the perks, like free business dinners and the celebrity mingling that went along with it. At this point in her life she just wanted to rediscover that feeling that came shortly after dusk when traffic slowed down and the kids in the neighborhood went inside for their family meal. In the beginning Tim had always used those times to stir warm spine-tingling emotions deep down inside her soul. She wanted it back. She wanted his breath on her. She wanted his hands . . . she needed them. She wanted the hands that made her hum little tunes in her head, and the passion that took root in the corridors of her being and made her want to marry him in the first place. She wanted his love at home right next to her at night. Her head on his shoulder as he typed, edited, and read his dialogue out loud so she could tell him how realistic it sounded.

She'd watch his lips convince her that fables were facts. He could tell her mind anything when their love was hot like that. She shook her head. She wasn't whining; she just wanted a real ironclad marriage where both partners meant every syllable they uttered in their wedding vows and then spent a lifetime and a half proving it.

Nina didn't like spending the little fragments of time that they managed to scrape together worrying about how many rolls of toilet tissue they had left or wondering whether or not there was enough milk for cereal or coffee in the morning. If they both managed to be in the same room for longer than thirty minutes, her every impulse would be to tap him. Get down deep enough inside his mind to find out where he stored the love he had promised her. The love he had given her a peek at and had now tucked safely away where she couldn't get at it. Where was the ripe unadulterated passion that had had them both tossing around in the bedsheets until 10:00 A.M., skipping breakfast, the morning news, and sometimes work.

In her mind she knew that Tim should be giving her much more than he was, but who was she to complain? Was she giving all that she could? Or was she sitting back taking notes and making a mental checklist of his shortcomings as if he were the only one? Even more than that, if she challenged him, pushed too hard, or pried, he could do what all men do when they don't feel that their wives are being supportive; he'd talk about needing space and wanting to find himself. Flat out, he could leave.

She hadn't been much to look at lately. Out in public his eyes often wandered and left her blaming herself for how he responded to her. She had done the spa thing with Francesca but even when she glamorized the outside, the response from Tim was still the same: silent standoffishness. Her insides ached for the closeness that they once had back in New York on those familiar streets late at night sipping coffee in those dimly lit cafés. Walks in the park, the Staten Island ferry, festive jazz sets, and sitting sprawled out in the yard out back, impressed by the luminescent seduction of the stars and their brilliant array that twinkled across the sky. All of that was gone now. The chase was over and she was here, sitting on the sofa with *his* dog waiting for him to come home.

If Nina hadn't married Tim she figured that she'd be back in her brownstone on that tree-lined Brooklyn street stretched out on her cool parquet floor in the stillness of the night gleaning all the culture that emanated from those overactive city streets. Steel drums, block parties, boys kissing overeager girls, dads taking their sons shopping for back-to-school shoes, the aroma of fried fish wafting down the street on a Friday night, making people quicken their paces, hurry home to rummage through their own fridge. She'd be single and yearning but she'd be content knowing that no one was calling, no one was coming over, and no one was thinking about her. Then she could go on pretending that once she was married it would be perfect. Bliss. Elusive idealism.

Nina adjusted herself on the sofa pillows as Monet bolted from the sofa and stood by the front door wagging his tail. Monet's keen ears knew the sound of Tim's car pulling into the driveway, the jingle of his keys finding the lock, and the low, never excited "Down, boy" that was always the first thing out of his mouth.

Tim was unexpected but he was home. Nina made her way up off the sofa slowly and cautiously.

Knee-high Monet's tail slapped Nina's leg and his muzzle nudged her out of the way for Tim's attention.

"Hey." Tim nodded in Nina's direction and brushed by her into their home.

He headed for the kitchen and stood in front of the fridge with the door open, leaning over surveying the shelves and letting the cold out.

"I didn't know you were coming home early." Nina rested her back against the entranceway to the kitchen and tried not to make it sound like a question.

"I didn't know either," Tim mumbled, pushing his face under the aluminum foil, eating the last piece of blueberry pie from the plate.

"So how was it?" Nina wrapped her robe tightly around her waist and followed Tim through the kitchen and into the bedroom where he sat on the side of the bed and pushed off each of his shoes heel first.

"Got the rewrites almost done," he mumbled with his mouth full, then swallowed.

"That's a good thing, right?"

"Have to reshoot two scenes."

"Really?" She hesitated.

"An exhausting day," he mused.

Her mouth was full too. Full of words that wouldn't come out. She had so much she needed to say to Tim. Revelations. Things that she wanted him to understand, needed him to justify for her. The first question on her lips: *Would it always be like this? So impersonal? A love that had them burning to get at each other, ultimately uniting them in holy matrimony, now feeling so separate and divided? Cast off? Shed like dead skin? How slowly their love had decomposed.*

"I still have work to do." He unbuttoned his chambray shirt and slipped it off his shoulders and draped it on the corner of the bedpost. He unzipped and stepped out of his black slacks, his belt clanging to the floor. He reached for his tattered gray sweatpants and headed into the bathroom.

Nina's mind was racing.

We're gonna talk tonight. I have some things I need to say, Tim. I'm tired of feeling like this. You're ignoring me like I'm a piece of furniture. Leaving me here all day, alone. I have needs. Sexually. Mentally. When's the last time you touched me, Tim? Or talked to me? It's not just about you, you know. Coming and going and leaving me to fend for myself. I have dreams. You can't deny me that. I won't let you deny me that.

Nina removed her robe and shimmied into a nylon gown. She lifted the comforter and slid into her side of the bed wanting to be next to Tim. Hoping to be next to him. Close to his body's warmth, near to his love. She heard him in the bathroom turning off the tap and moments later a jingle from the lever as he flushed the toilet. Tim emerged from the bathroom, made himself comfortable in their bed too, then reached down to the side of the bed for his laptop.

"You're gonna work in bed again tonight?" Nina sat up facing him.

"I have to get these final changes done, Nina." He looked over at her, then plugged in the cord on his side of the bed, flipped the switch on, and began typing.

All the words she wanted to say, hoped to say, were arrested, then dissolved in an instant, one by one, like bubbles bursting leaving no evidence that they were ever there. Her feelings were trapped inside her, down in the pit of her stomach where the fear always was, wanting to come out but never having the courage to overcome what could happen if she said too much. The biting feelings she had about his lack of interest in her lingered around them until he no longer noticed her glaring at him out of the corner of her eyes.

Nina rolled over, her back to him, and faced the wall. No kiss good night, nothing. She'd stare at the clock on the nightstand and watch the numbers flip over every minute until her eyes got heavy and she fell asleep.

That's the way it was almost every night. Then when she woke up, he'd be gone. No trace of his love anywhere to be found.

This was a different life. It was supposed to be better. Dishwashers, central air, a half-acre cul-de-sac. How utterly deceitful of Tim to fly her to the West Coast, leave half of her things behind, put the rest of her things in storage, promise to love her, and then blatantly do the opposite! Dinners with studio execs and their wives whose small talk about the senseless films their husbands made that they conveniently didn't see degraded the very proud women they were thought to be.

Part of her hated Tim for being able to go on with his dream. He had welcomed her into his world here in California but that was exactly what it was. His world. Nothing around this place had her name on it. Not one stitch of furniture, not one pot, one pan, or one fabric blend, aside from the vinyl shower curtains that he allowed her to pick out when she first came down, said that she lived there. Even the dark-colored masculine sheets said manly. The place gave no hint of femininity or that a woman even frequented it. Nothing around them said that they were married except the ring on his finger, and the set of silverware they had received as a wedding gift that was now packed away deep in the hall closet. His old tapes and CDs were piled in the corner, a constant eyesore that he never minded. His African masks lining the walls still.

She wondered if Tim thought he was still single. She wondered if he thought that it was okay to forgo a beautiful day at the park to sit home and edit his scripts, nibble on snacks in between, and just leave her to her own devices, not caring one iota what she did or how it got done. There was no way to get around in this lifestyle she wasn't used to. Everything too far for her to walk, Tim driving the only car they had.

There were things about him that she didn't get. She had come into his life and had satisfied everything that he needed her to be to him but he hadn't always satisfied her needs. She was tired of everyone always saying that she should be glad that she was married. Everyone telling her that they were still looking and that they wished they had found someone as nice as Tim. *He's not always nice,* she thought.

They didn't understand. In the beginning when it was about wooing her at the fancy restaurants and showing her off to his friends and coworkers, she had felt like a queen. Wandering into department stores, him asking her, "You like that?" and pulling out his wallet at a time when it seemed money was no object. Lately she felt dethroned. There was nothing in his eyes that made her feel that she was special. Nothing that reminded her how proud he was to have her here with him.

Most of the time she felt like an intruder in his life. He'd come home and walk through the front door and look up as if he wasn't expecting to see her there. If he had asked her if she had seen his things, anything, and her reply was no, in her mind she'd know what he was thinking. He would be thinking that before she came and brought her clutter and feminine products with her, he knew where everything was. Now here she came and rearranged everything and he couldn't find squat.

Attention. It was all that she wanted. Any remnant of time he had left when he was done perfecting his craft was spent doing anything that had absolutely nothing to do with her. Watching movies and catching up on the latest sports stats. "I'm dissecting the scenes," he said. Although his eyes always told a different story. She saw desire in them. Not for her though. For the scantily clad women in music videos and movies whose legs were toned to perfection and whose tummies made them more desirable than Nina and her love handles ever would.

Love fools you most of the time. Nothing about the hot, passionate love she had for Tim had prepared her for this lukewarm affection that he'd throw her way every now and then. Nothing in her wildest dreams could have told her that being married would sometimes feel as if she were single again. Married but still alone. It didn't compute. And so she kept on trying to fill her days with anything that would give her the satisfaction of having accomplished something without him. She read books, watched television, spent the day at the market, and tagged along to the places that Francesca needed to go. Ate pie. Cheese. Bread. More pie. Nothing filled her up.

She wanted her own joy. She needed it to be so abundant that she could bottle it and make it hers, able to unscrew the top and delight in it at will. She couldn't take the way he was. The way they were with each other. There was nothing compassionate about him anymore. He was almost emotionally unrecognizable to her. She couldn't see the man she married. Not with her eyes or her heart. All she knew was that in the past year, everything had diminished. There was no love, no desire, and no fever. She knew what she had done, exactly what women always said that you should never do. She had willingly given up her individuality for a man. Now the man still had a life, a wife, was coming and going and accomplishing things that were on his destiny's to-do list, and she was the one displaced, in desperate need of something of her own. Something and someplace that she could call home, finally.

3

Carla and Sam

Carla stood in the mirror disregarding her reflection, wondering when she had become so disinterested. She brushed her hair back into a ponytail and then flipped it over and pinned the sections down into a neat bun like Troi had taught her. She pushed the top off of the sleek bottle with her thumb and sprayed the fragrant oil sheen in her hand, rubbed her hands together, and smoothed it in on her head in a backward motion.

She and her best friend, Troi, had each married the most sought-after Singleton men and she was still doing what she said she loved doing for a living, teaching. She was happy. Sort of. She loved Sam. She just couldn't put her finger on what was wrong. She peered at those familiar eyes of hers glaring back at her in the mirror. She straightened out the frown on her forehead and the displeased wrinkle around her mouth, but it came right back willingly. Her shoulders sagged. She had a furrowed forehead and a sarcastic smirk on her lips, the epitome of unhappiness.

The years had found Carla and Sam still holding strong to what they had vowed to be to each other. He was always impulsive, full of surprises, made time, wanting to sit down and hear about her day with the kids and what she had taught them. He never brought up his first wife, ever, or the things they had done together, and deep down she was glad that he and his ex hadn't had any children together because she knew that she couldn't tolerate another woman coming into her house negotiating visitation rights with her husband.

Carla had had her pick of suitors but it was the divorced Sam that was the much-prized conquest. He had made a pledge to himself to enjoy the departure of his first wife and that was what he had been doing until Carla came breezing into his life like a love song being sung from an apartment window by a lovesick man who had been bitten by the possibilities of second chances. He couldn't ignore her no matter how hard he tried. She was in his mind just calling him, serenading him with the promise of forever.

In the beginning, before they were married, Carla had listened to all the pros and cons about taking a man's last name. She loved him a whole bunch but she wasn't about to give up her identity for any-body so she inserted the hyphen and let it ride. Sam was never too thrilled about that.

"You too good for my last name?" he kidded.

"I took your name, Sam." Carla smirked.

"You added my name. It's not the same." A seriousness covered his face.

That was probably part of the problem. She could admit that she wasn't the ideal wife if he'd admit that he wasn't always the type of husband that fixed things that needed to be done around the house, but they were both sorry for so many things. Always apologizing. After a heated argument they were always remorseful.

"Morning, Ma." Ashley's chipper voice resounded throughout the bedroom as she circled her seven-year-old arms around her mother's waist.

Carla flinched from her daughter's touch and smiled weakly.

"You coming with us today, Ma?" Ashley climbed onto her mother's unmade bed.

"Cmon, Ashley, Mommy doesn't feel well." Sam came in and ush-ered her out of the bedroom.

"Is Mommy going?" Ashley's wide eyes pleaded.

"Not today. Next time she'll come," Sam said.

"Where are we going, Daddy?" She took his hand.

"That kids' place you like. The one with the colorful balls and the twisty fries."

"What's wrong with Mommy?"

Carla watched as Ashley's sad eyes searched his for the answer to the most-asked question in their home lately.

"I don't know, sweetheart." He shook his head.

Sam walked out of their bedroom without ever acknowledging his wife. He begrudgingly walked back into the room without the child and spoke only as if it were his job to do so.

"What do you want to eat tonight?" He stood with his hands balled up deep in the pockets of his blue jeans, looking off to the left.

"Fish is fine, or Chinese." A softness coated Carla's voice.

She blinked slowly and when she looked up and focused on the room and everything in it all she saw was the back of his teal polo shirt and his snug-fitting jeans heading out of their bedroom door.

Carla couldn't deal with these thoughts now. She sat on the bed and listened as their father-daughter laughter faded out the front door and spilled onto the street in front of their house. Carla eased off of the bed, moved around the room slowly, and scooped up the cordless phone, punched the memory button and the number three, and pressed the phone to the side of her face. She watched through the window as Sam removed a rag from the hatchback and wiped down his shiny black utility vehicle.

"Troi?"

"Hey, how's it going, sis?"

"Fine, you?"

"I'm good, and the baby?"

"She's seven now, child. Hardly a baby; went out with her father to have lunch and window-shop."

"Just like her momma, ain't she?"

"I suppose." Carla almost regretted making the call.

"And what you doing moping around the house?"

"I'm not moping, just taking a little *me* break. How's Dakoda?"

"She's doing well, especially in school, considering . . ."

"Cut her some slack now, you know how we were in school."

"Yes, I know, but she's there to learn, not—"

"Kids know that, Troi, but they want to fit in while they're there too. Peer pressure is a powerful thing. You taught her well. She won't stray far from that."

"Speaking of straying, when are you gonna come on by and start rehearsing with us again? We need your voice."

"Rehearse what?" Carla frowned.

She didn't want to hear about church. Those backbiting people would use their last breath to talk about her instead of asking for forgiveness. It wasn't her fault, it really wasn't. Things happened. When her postpartum depression had seemed to last way into a year, the doctors wanted to do some additional tests, take blood, and examine her further. Her husband had tried doing everything the doctor said, giving her time and space and listening to her go on about nothing in particular. He did the best he knew how but it wasn't nearly enough. Carla had barely enough energy to give to her job, so when she came home she was spent. Sam said over and over if he could take back the events on that particular day he would lock them away forever. The day that their heated debate grew fangs, escalated, and seemingly changed their lives forever.

"*All I ever asked was that you try, Carla.*"

"*You think I don't try? Just because you don't get what you want doesn't mean I'm not trying!*" she lashed out.

"*Funny how you never have a problem when it comes to anybody else. Only me, Carla! Only me!*"

"*What's that supposed to mean?*" A frown distorted her face.

"*You're the one who cheated on me when we were engaged, not vice versa,*" he spat.

"*Am I ever gonna live that down? Or is that something you're gonna remind me of from now until we feed the trees?*"

"*I'm just stating the obvious. You need to take time with your own family and stop spending your energy on everyone else outside this house.*"

"*Don't bring the kids into it. I love to teach. I was teaching since before I met you, so don't start!*"

"*You were single before you met me too. Are you still single now?*" he said sarcastically.

"*I'm not gonna do this with you, Sam.*" She turned away from him.

"*Yes, you are, Carla, stop running. . . .*" He grabbed her arm and held it tightly in his grasp.

"*No, Sam. . . .*" She pulled away.

"*Yes, we're gonna do this, right here, right now!*"

"*Sam, stop . . . you're hurting me!*"

"*I won't stop. We need to get to the bottom of this! I can't live through another failed marriage! First you love me, now I can't even touch you? My momma's practically raising our baby! What are you giving me, Carla?*"

"*Sam, I can't do this. . . .*"

"*You will do this! Right here and right now, Carla!*" He wrestled her hands.

"*Sam—*"

"*No, Carla, I don't want to hear it!*" He raised his hand.

"*Sam—*"

"*You don't respect me as a man,*" he growled.

"*Sam, I . . .*"

Sam turned around and watched Carla collapse and then curl up into a fetal position on the cold kitchen floor.

The color left Sam's face and his eyes got wide. He snatched up the phone as he kneeled down on the floor and held her head in his lap and frantically dialed his momma, Troi, and then their primary doctor.

"Sounds like a breakdown," the doctor said. "Has she been under any undue stress or major changes in her life?"

"Some . . ." Sam said as he vowed he'd spend the rest of his life trying to make it up to her.

He never meant to back her into a corner or push her over the edge. He just had questions that he needed answers to. She wasn't giving him any logical reason for the way they were and he didn't know how to help her if she wouldn't let him in and at least tell him what the problem was.

They hadn't been intimate in over a year. She had enforced a look-but-don't-touch policy and Sam had gone along, not wanting to rock the boat, because after the breakdown anything could set her off. A man satisfying himself wasn't the same as making love and he honestly didn't think he should have to resort to that especially when he'd rather be pressed up against his wife, nuzzling the nape of her neck and smelling her hair at night. They were married and he was meeting all of his wife's needs; all he needed was for her to meet a couple of his. Two or three. Maybe even one.

"I'm not ready to start singing again," Carla told Troi. "Besides, they all still think I'm crazy. They don't want me on their uppity little choir."

"You have to do what you've been called to do. Stop worrying about people letting you fit in. You as a teacher should know better than that."

"Yeah, well, I was just calling to see how you and Dakoda were." Carla's whole demeanor shifted.

"Okay." Troi allowed Carla to change the subject.

"I'll give you a call soon. I promise," Carla added as an afterthought and hung up the phone without allowing Troi to get to the bottom of what was wrong.

She wanted to be alone. Craved her single. Didn't want people around forcing her to talk and communicate something that none of them would ever understand.

There was nothing on television, nothing in the fridge that she felt like eating, and the mail hadn't come yet. Carla decided to take a long, hot shower and try to wash some of the things she was dwelling on down the drain. Life shouldn't have had her feeling as miserable as it did. Always smiling on the outside and hurting down deep where it really mattered. She wouldn't let life win.

She went into the bathroom and turned on the shower. She disrobed and stepped inside the tub and closed her eyes and tried to enjoy the silky bubbles gliding across her skin. Her imagination was at a standstill. She tried to be calm but her mind still wasn't letting her be free. She didn't think that she could forgive Sam if he had been the one having an affair. She didn't even know exactly when that other guy had gotten her attention. He had proven to be just like the rest, only wanting one thing, passing through; they always were.

But his eyes were curious and his words slick. There she was, in the corner being herself and ignoring him, her scarf tied neatly around her neck, rearranging the Bibles. She had to have been a target from the onset. A conquest. His goal. They had started off with cordial conversations about school, him feigning an interest in the education system and how children today needed people who cared about them, not just someone after a biweekly paycheck and summers off. Then late-night rehearsals became "I'll drop you off, it's no problem" or "Let's get a bite to eat." Next thing she knew, despite the engagement ring sparkling on her finger, she was held up in his car some nights until eleven, groping and filling herself on every ounce of passion he afforded her. Enjoying every minute of the seduction, then calling and telling Sam that she'd lost track of time when she finally arrived home and got his frantic messages.

One evening, she and the guy were at their usual spot on Riverside Drive parked under the highway's overpass when the heavy petting and light carresses turned into car seats being reclined, music turned up loud, and in an instant he was all over her, shoving his hands between her legs, pushing his face between her breasts and pulling her panties off, ignoring her screams.

"You wouldn't be here if you didn't want this," he said, his fingers intruding into her private places, his sizable body taking advantage of hers. Not listening to her when she said over and over again that he was hurting her.

She was pushing him away but he was determined to indulge in her that night. Pulling her hair and balling it up in his fist and forcing her to submit to every lustful desire he had. The mild-mannered alto from the Zion Jubilee Choir became an ugly mess that night as he had his way with her never exuding one ounce of tenderness, showing no restraint and no remorse. He used her up, deposited his offering, and dropped her off in front of her building like a pile of garbage to be picked up early tomorrow morning with the rest of the waste.

It was late, almost 12:45, when it was all said and done, but she buttoned up her sweater, counted only one missing, and straightened out her skirt. She closed her eyes, didn't want to cry, readjusted her scarf, then took the train ride to Jersey anyway and landed on Sam's doorstep sobbing, wanting to tell him what had happened. Needing to tell him. Praying that he would understand what she was telling him.

"What were you doing there with him?"

"We were talking." Carla spoke cautiously.

"Nobody sits in a car at eleven o'clock at night talking." Sam's anger was borderline rage.

"Okay, I'll tell you . . ."

"Tell me what?" Sam's eyes bore into her as her mouth hung open and the words made their way to her lips one at a time.

"He didn't mean anything to me, Sam, honestly."

"Who is *he?*" Sam demanded.

Carla made up a name and left it at that. The thought of a church scandal was the least desirable thing she was willing to be engaged in right now.

"Did you have sex with him?"

"You know you're the only man who means anything to me, Sam." The tears streamed down her face.

"I'm not asking that." He shook his head. "I asked you if you had sex with him!"

She wiped her nose in her sweater sleeve and looked at him helplessly.

"Carla, yes or no, I'm too old for games! Sex, did you have sex?"

"Yes. . . ."

"Yes?" His eyes grew wide. "Did you just say yes?"

"Yes." She nodded. "But—"

"No but. . . . Where did you sleep with him?"

"I don't want to talk about it—"

"Where, Carla!" his voice bellowed.

"In his car." She lowered her eyelids and refused to look at Sam.

"You had sex with him in his car?" He rubbed his face in utter disbelief.

"I said no, Sam, I did, but he wouldn't stop," she cried. "I said it over and over again." She sobbed on his shoulder and swore him to secrecy between breaths. He reluctantly embraced her and tried to give her some comfort.

She never could go back into that place they called a church or sing another note to a God who would allow such a thing to happen to her. She and Sam got through the incident the best they could, by never talking about it, and then they married that same summer. She moved into his house in Jersey and he vowed he'd protect her from everybody. Sam and Carla put the entire episode in the car that night behind her. It was a long, tough struggle to trust people in Sam's absence. Even after the nervous breakdown, things started to pick up. Days seemed a little brighter and time off from work gave her the opportunity to think clearly about what she wanted to do with her life.

She started back teaching the kids in the fall of the following year. Aside from her not being thrilled with the commute from Jersey to the city, life was wonderful. Things were good. She was doing what she loved. Now here she was reflecting on the past.

Carla eyed the clock and wondered when Sam and Ashley would be back, then eased into bed and curled up tight with the wool blankets wrapped around her and thought seriously for a moment as she tried not to drift off to sleep. Then she put her finger on it. She knew what was bothering her all this time, all these years. There was something that she really needed to do once and for all before it hung around and ruined the rest of her life as well. She needed to tell Sam the absolute truth.

Sam and Ashley hadn't been gone that long when Sam's key in the door jarred Carla from semiconsciousness. She knew she probably did needed to appreciate him, Ashley, and their life together. She couldn't live life treating her husband as if he didn't matter; nothing gave her that right. She wiped the corner of her eyes and listened intently for the voice she always heard pattering through the house calling her name.

"Mommy . . . Mommy . . . Mommy . . ." Ashley ran into her bedroom.

"How was your day?" Carla smiled and lifted her little girl up onto her lap.

"We went to the park and to Chuck E. Cheese and then I got this shirt, Mom." She pulled at her glittery top and got down off of her mother's lap and went running out of the room.

"I rented some movies," Sam said, coming into the room and placing the thin pile of DVDs down on their bed. "We can watch those later if you want."

"Okay." Carla eased the word out of her mouth and nodded.

"I went by the pasta place you like and got you some grilled garlic salmon with fettucini too."

"Sounds good." Guilt wrote itself all over her as she afforded him a feeble smile.

Sam never stopped trying. He'd give her blood if that was what it took to make things right between them again.

Carla clenched her thick robe around her in a fist, eased past the armoire, and headed down the hall for the living room. Sam stopped her midway.

"I love you, Carla," his lips said, eyes pleading for an ounce of mercy.

"I know you do," was all she said.

He moved in closer to her and held her shoulders, searching her eyes, making a futile attempt to discern her mood.

I can do this, Carla thought, closing her eyes tight. *I know I can.*

Sam backed her into their bedroom, pressed the door shut behind him, and locked it. His lips found her cheeks, her neck, and her mouth. He pressed himself to her body, peeled down her robe from her shoulder, and planted soft kisses up the curve of her neck thinking that tonight was surely it. She was enjoying the moment, gazing straight into his eyes now as he untied her robe and left warmth every place his lips touched.

"You have the best body . . ." He bubbled in overeager laughter.

Carla didn't make a sound. She closed her eyes tight again as if she was waiting for it all to be over.

His lips traced the contour of her hips, lips, breasts, then earlobes. He needed to be one with her. Fitting perfectly like a mold, each other an impression of itself. Fourteen months. An eternity. He took his time, slowly, cautiously, begging every step of the way for a minute or maybe three, four, ten, fifteen. He closed his eyes now too, finally, pleasure his tonight. Loving the feeling and the slow easing, knowing it had been so long since he had felt his wife like this. Unnaturally long. The excitement indescribable, wanting each minute to last a minute longer as he throbbed with passion for the woman he had married. The moment bordering on ecstacy, within a second of him giving her everything he had. All of his seeds. All of his love. A new beginning.

Sam didn't immediately hear her raising her voice. He didn't feel her beating his chest, pleading for him to stop.

"Get off me, I said!" She gave him one hard shove. The rage in her eyes ugly, harsh, and unforgiving.

Sam glared at her, not believing for an instant that she had stolen this moment from him. This tender moment that he'd been waiting over a year for. Fourteen months. He raised himself off of the bed without hesitation and lifted his jeans back onto his hips, then fastened them around his waist and did his belt.

Sam spoke with an unbelieving softness, fighting not to let his voice tremble. "It's been fourteen months." He cleared his throat. "I'm not asking for a sensual escapade, Carla, just flat-out sex. You don't even have to look at me after if you don't want to, but I'm a man. Just give me something."

Carla watched her husband walk out of their bedroom with a dull look on his face for the second time today.

Scented candlesticks in the bedroom, navy satin sheets, and potpourri sitting around in brass dishes on the night table. Despite all of that Carla still wasn't feeling the romance or the love. She never equated *wife* with all this that was going on around her. Human frailty. That's what they called it. The quality or state of being frail. A fault due to weakness, especially of moral character. A sinner. Unworthy. She shook her head and tried not to think about it, but even though she had overcome all of the horrible things in her childhood, that didn't stop the past from crossing her mind occasionally.

She was sorry for never being in the mood to please her husband anymore. He had spent so many nights making attempts to woo her. He hadn't always been as vocal about her rejection of him, but tonight was different. She saw something in his eyes as he spoke that hadn't been there before: distance. She thought of his muscular frame and his warm supple lips, but the past wouldn't let her go. Her mind was telling her that she didn't deserve him and that there were other women who would appreciate him more.

Just let him go, her mind said.

He did lots of things just because he was being understanding of his wife. Her out-of-the-blue desire not to want to attend Zion Missionary wasn't an issue at all. He gave up his position as a junior deacon and began attending church less, then not at all. For her he had nothing left to give. She had it all and didn't want any of it. The truth. It was begging her to tell it. Clear the air, purify her thoughts, and uncover those hidden demons. The evil that eats away at you until you no longer are.

The heavy sun was done brightening the day and was setting. The clock said 6:37. The phone intruded upon her contemplative thoughts. As she dismissed the ring, she wondered only for a moment who it was. Sam must have gotten it. She listened as his hushed tone must have soothed whoever was on the line. In a moment he came back into their bedroom fully dressed, had his work shoes on, and was buttoning the top button on his dress shirt.

She wanted to apologize but the look on his face bade her to let him speak first.

He looked in her eyes and spoke calmly, as he almost always did.

"I need to go show a home to a couple and after that I dunno, so don't wait up."

Carla looked away, not wanting to hear any of it. Not liking the part of her that wouldn't tell him.

"And just so you know," he said, "I'm not gonna wait forever, Carla. It's not that I can't, I just won't."

The minute he closed the door behind him she collapsed onto the bed and lay there in the stillness of their bedroom squeezing a pillow, rocking herself, and wondering what would become of them, what would become of her and their life as she listened to him start up the truck and drive off into the early evening. The tears in her eyes were merely demanding that she do one thing after all this time, they were urging her just to tell the damn truth.

4

Troi

Life never said that it would come with promises or guarantees. People just thought it did and tried to understand the meaning of life, drawing their own conclusions in the process and learning through trial and error. Troi knew that all too well. The storms that came in her life one after the other, testing her willpower, also made her relentless, seeing things through, despite wanting to toss in the towel on more than one occasion.

Troi had stood by her husband faithfully until he passed away in late December of AIDS complications. He had gotten eerily thin and his mom and dad had been there but they didn't want to talk about it, just pray, although that was fine by her. It wasn't snowing the day that Vaughn died but it was cold enough to make your knuckles bleed if you weren't wearing gloves and tried to make tight fists. That in itself should have told her that death was coming soon. She had sat by him in the hospice for almost seven months trying to make his last days bearable. Every day she'd come and make small talk knowing that he couldn't hear her, wouldn't hear her, and wanted no part of hearing her. His face ashen, body ravished, free will immobilized. He had asked her to stop coming a while ago. He didn't want anyone seeing him that way. She never listened.

She had sat in the blue polyester chair for the greater part of each day with a drawer full of cotton-tip applicators, gauze, and boxes of powder-free synthetic exam gloves behind her. The last coherent word he had spoken was "Dakoda." Now his suffering was over finally.

Vaughn had bounced from job to job until he fell ill and his condition rapidly deteriorated. Even though Troi was still doing hair and trying to pay bills she still made sure her husband was taken care of, regardless of how many times people told her that they wouldn't have put up with what he had done to her. Troi loved him and she put up with it all, no matter what people said. She didn't mind sticking by Vaughn. Yes, he had had a homosexual tryst that left her feeling more embarrassed than anything but they stuck it out for their child, for their love. They both loved Dakoda enough to put their personal matters aside and at least try, and those who didn't get it didn't matter.

She hadn't been single long but after six and a half diligent years of night classes Troi finally had something in her life to smile about again. She got her degree in business. Her brainchild was to create and market a black hair care product. Carrot extract, shea butter, and other natural ingredients mixed into a thick spreadable paste that would bring out a black woman's natural beauty. Troi had forgone the initial notion of reopening her salon, Shangrila, after the fire that had totally destroyed it so many years back. Dakoda was thirteen now and Troi knew that without a father she needed to be there for her. She wanted to make a living doing something from home. So she set her plans in motion to take care of her baby girl and make a living in the process.

Troi had been selling a crudely packaged version of the product she'd concocted to her regular customers who had still been coming by the house years after the shop burned and forced her to set up her services at home. They didn't trust anybody else with their hair, they said.

The idea for Hair Joy illuminated her mind like a flash while she was sitting up in the hospital with Vaughn flipping through a women's magazine one afternoon. Hair because that was what it would be used for and Joy because it gave her joy even to contemplate taking the next step with an idea as grand as that. Hair products made billions of dollars each year. Something as well thought out as her product should be able to get just a sliver of that financial pie and put her baby girl through college and allow her to live the remainder of her life in some medium level of comfort.

Dakoda had gotten her gorgeous complexion from her dad. She came dragging into the room, clad in her tattered jeans and black army boots. No good afternoon, no good evening, no smile, no nothing. Just a headful of stubborn hair.

"Who was that?" Dakoda asked.

"That what?"

"On the phone, earlier."

"That was Carla. . . ."

"Oh."

"Good afternoon, Dakoda." Troi glared at the teen.

"Good afternoon, Ma."

"You just waking up?"

"No, I been up. Since about one."

"Carla said hello," Troi said, busying herself in filling her jars with her hair product.

"Tell her hi."

Troi couldn't discern her friend's mood. Lately it seemed that Carla was letting any obstacle that presented itself become a permanent fixture in her life. She couldn't figure her child's mood either. Once so gleeful, now it seemed as if Dakoda didn't have a blessed thing to be thankful for. Always frowning, always going, never staying to sit, talk, and share about her day or her life.

"I'll be back."

"Dakoda—"

"I'll be back, Ma."

"Where are you going?"

"To the store. At the corner."

"Bring your mother some orange juice. And a paper." Troi handed her a five-dollar bill and eyed her child as she watched her hurry out the front door.

Troi looked around the place and could still feel her sister in every nook and cranny of the brownstone that she had sold her. She still couldn't believe she was living here, owning her own place, enough spare rooms to do hair without ending up pulling synthetic hair out from between the sofa cushions years later.

Troi put some coffee on and tried to clear her head. After all these years she still ground her coffee beans fresh. Her sister had given her a Cuisinart coffeemaker. Some things didn't change. Vanilla bean with a hint of amaretto.

She was contemplating her new business idea. Her degree in business hadn't prepared her for the real world. She didn't know where to start, apart from getting a business license. She'd give Sam a call before the end of the week. He'd been selling homes for years now; surely he could give her some insight on her next course of action, and enlighten her about the change in her best friend in the process.

Before Troi could gather herself in her own space, Dakoda rushed back into the house rattling a box of breath mints and handed her mother the daily paper.

"Where's the orange juice, Dakoda?"

"Oops, I forgot."

"What were you doing that you forgot?"

"I was talking to my friends." She sighed deeply.

Troi examined her child and looked her in the eyes. "So you've taken up smoking now?"

"I don't know what you're talking about. . . ."

"You don't know what I'm talking about?" Troi glared at her daughter.

"No." Dakoda looked to the floor.

"You smell like a chimney and you come in here shaking a box of Tic Tacs and I'm supposed to be fooled?"

"Cmon, Ma . . ."

"Cmon what? You trying to kill yourself too?"

"Can I go?" Dakoda put her hand on her hip.

"You're all I have left, Dakoda."

"Ma, please . . ."

"Please what?"

"Never mind." Dakoda folded her arms.

"Never mind, always never mind." Troi waved her hand, dismissing her child without another word.

She watched in disgust as Dakoda stomped off to her room. Couldn't tell her anything. Just like her father. Always wanting it his way or no way at all. She didn't know how her child would fare in life with that type of attitude.

Troi shook her head. Tried to think business. Tried to think about her future. When it came to business Troi didn't expect any preferential treatment. She knew that she'd encounter the usual pair of isms, sexism and racism. She was prepared. Anything she ever wanted she had to fight for, so she gloved herself for this match as well. She needed something to keep her afloat. *God doesn't always give you money; sometimes He gives you ideas.* That was fine by Troi.

Troi worked hard. Her whole life she had been preparing to have her own. Her own family, business, and way of doing things. She just hadn't planned on single-handedly raising a thirteen-year-old. Her heart not fully healed, she kept interested suitors at bay. Her purpose wasn't to replace Vaughn or his love but just to exist on her own until joining herself together with someone else later down the line seemed a pleasing option.

Pie. Troi woke up this morning in the mood for pie. Yam pie, pecan pie, and maybe apple. Cooking was different now. Strange, even. Dakoda had foods that were her favorites. Her favorites differed from her dad's so Troi enjoyed cooking different things. There were foods that were Vaughn's favorites that she still made on occasion out of habit. Her child liked macaroni and cheese, hated all green vegetables, and didn't really care for meat. Troi would whip up something to put a smile on her girl's face.

Troi put the macaroni on to boil, grated the cheese in the food processor, and washed the dishes in the sink before she put the chicken in it to clean. She plucked stray feathers, rinsed the chicken with lemon juice, and turned the flames on to burn the remaining hairs jutting out of the wings. She dumped all of the chicken in a big green mixing bowl and seasoned it heavily with the spices that Nina had taught her to use, then transferred them to a casserole dish and put them in the oven to bake.

Troi rinsed the flat snow peas between her fingers, shook off her hands, and put them aside in a bowl on the countertop while she drained the macaroni, rinsed the pot, and put on the yams to boil. She could hear Dakoda's footsteps pacing the room overhead, smelling the food cooking, wanting to come down but allowing her pride to rule her. More than anything she thought she had taught her daughter that she could talk to her. Troi had never had that option with her own mother so she was dead-set on extending it to her own flesh and blood.

"Dakoda?" Troi stood with her hands on her hips and yelled up to her child.

"I'm on the phone, Ma," she yelled downstairs.

"When you're finished."

"Okay. . . ."

Troi mixed up the butter-and-flour paste with the milk and the melted cheddar and mozerella cheese in the macaroni, put it in a baking dish, and slid it into the searing oven right next to the chicken. She pulled down two boxes of Jiffy and set a bowl aside to mix the corn bread. Troi poked the yams with a fork before she went and sat down in the living room.

Dakoda came bouncing downstairs and sat between her mom's legs. Another routine that neither of them would soon part from.

"It'll make your hair manageable and smell good," Troi said.

"What's it called?" Her slanted eyes looked up at her mother.

Dakoada knew her mom was always mixing up something. She also knew that sitting at her momma's feet meant talking.

"Hair Joy, maybe."

Dakoda stuck her nose in the jar and smiled as she inhaled. "Does smell good. You should sell it."

"Let me ask you a question. . . ."

"Okay." Dakoda looked down at the floor.

Dakoda's mood was different. Must've been a boy on the phone. Troi tried not to let her stern tone drip through as she asked the question.

"Why are you smoking those nasty cigarettes that you know are no good for you?"

Dakoda hesitated and then said, "Everybody's smoking, Ma."

"Everybody's doing a lot of things. Is that what your father and I taught you? I thought we taught you, if nothing else, to think for yourself?"

"I am. . . ."

"Not following everybody else, you're not."

"Ma . . ."

Troi turned her daughter around to face her and spoke to her like a concerned friend would.

"Dakoda, your dad is gone. You are all I have besides my sister. I have no idea where my father ran off to and what woman he took with him. I don't know what happened to my momma or the house we grew up in. She's gone too. All I'm asking is that we be here for each other. Is that too much to ask?"

"Not really." She shrugged.

"Guess what I'm cooking?" Troi's voice became more playful.

"Macaroni and cheese, yam pie, barbecue chicken, and corn bread."

"How'd you guess that?"

"I can smell it, Ma. And the box of corn bread is sitting right there." She pointed to the countertop.

"We'll eat in a minute, okay?"

"Okay."

"Dakoda . . ."

"Huh?"

"I hope you don't think I'm being hard on you. Really, there's just too much stuff out there that can hurt you . . . and I don't want to see you hurt. If you go following friends with one thing, they'll have you out there doing something else even more dangerous."

"My friends aren't like that, Ma."

Dakoda's naive eyes were wide enough for her to believe it herself.

"Dakoda, you're old enough, you know what happened to your father. Just be careful. That's all I'm saying."

"Uh-huh." Dadoka aimed the remote at the television and consumed herself in one of her favorite programs.

Just talking about family again stirred memories and hurt Troi deep to the core of her being. She missed her sister. Troi didn't like being so far away from her especially after they had grown up like best friends, knowing each other's secrets and shortcomings. But she knew that people's lives consisted of daily routines that pushed them further away from their friends and families than distance ever could.

Now her sister had Tim, and Tim was her world. It didn't mean that she didn't care about Troi, it just meant that Tim was right there in front of her, a daily reminder of things she needed to take care of with him and for him.

Troi pulled open the oven door, and the heat greeted her face. She tested the corn bread with a toothpick, then pulled out the rack and added the barbecue sauce to the baking chicken. She closed the oven, pulled out a frying pan that she would use to toss the snow peas around in with some butter, Spike, and minced garlic, smelling up the house good.

"We ready to eat yet, Ma?"

"Yes, c'mon and help me."

Dakoda set the table for three. Her mother had told her that her daddy was with them even if he wasn't visibly here.

Troi brought the dishes to the table and Dakoda helped.

"I can do it myself," Dakoda said.

Dakoda made her mother sit down in the chair and served her the dinner that she was thoughtful enough to cook even though Dakoda knew that she needed to say she was sorry because she was too young to be walking around with an attitude.

"Oh, Dakoda, you're so heavy-handed with the food."

Troi's eyes got wide as the child scooped a hefty helping of macaroni and cheese and spooned it onto the plate.

They grinned at each other as they took each other's hands to say grace. Dakoda closed her eyes and spoke softly.

"Lord, I'm thankful for my mother even though I don't always show it. Watch over my dad please, Lord, and I ask you to bless us and have us be what you want us to be. I thank you for this food that we are about to receive. Bless the hands that prepared it and make it fit nourishment for our bodies. Amen."

Troi nodded. "Amen."

Dakoda eyed her mother as they ate in silence, taking their time but finishing almost everything on their plates.

"You know that nothing in the world meant more to your father than you."

"I know," Dakoda said, "but can we talk about something else please, Ma?"

"Okay," Troi relented.

They took their time eating second helpings, talked about how Dakoda was doing in school and how Troi prayed that Hair Joy would make her rich. Then they cleared the table.

Dakoda piled all of the plates and serving dishes in the sink and helped her mother wrap up the leftovers and made room for them in the fridge.

"You wanna watch TV?" Dakoda asked her mother.

"In a minute. Let me make a quick call." Troi smiled.

Troi stood in the kitchen pressing the numbers into the key pad, hoping that there was an answer, hoping she wasn't interrupting something private. Something that didn't include her.

On the other end, the ringing and intermittent pauses, a familiar hello. Troi couldn't help but grin, and the smile spread magically across her face.

"Hey, Nina . . ."

"Troi!" Nina squealed.

They fell into their old way of doing things. Troi clutched the receiver. They gabbed about old times, new times, sad times, bad times. Everything they had been missing about each other came tumbling out anxiously.

"Remember when you got mad because Daddy didn't come to your graduation? And you started throwing food?" Troi asked.

"Yeah, I remember that." Nina could still see it all so vividly.

"What about my wedding? Do you still have the bouquet?" Nina asked her sister.

"You're my sister; any bouquet I catch at your wedding is mine for life!" she kidded.

"You ever think you'll remarry?"

"I can't say," Troi said softly.

"Any cute guys coming around?" Nina inquired. "You know how you kept them coming when you were younger."

"Not hardly. Especially not with Dakoda here."

"Girl, you know how to kiss when nobody's looking. You did that even with Daddy leaving the light on for you and everything." Nina giggled.

At almost eleven o'clock, too late for company, Troi's doorbell chimed softly.

Troi covered the mouthpiece with her hand. She opened the door. Sam was standing there. Tall, a little beaten down, and a sad countenance. Still Sam.

"I need to talk to you about Carla." He stood with his hands shoved into his pockets.

"Nina, somebody's at my door. Can I call you later?"

"Sure. . . ."

"Okay, sis. Love you. Bye."

5

Tim and Nina

Nina got up earlier than even Tim had expected. He was still home, hadn't gone off to work yet. She had spent a few minutes on the phone with her sister last night. They had so much catching up to do. But nevertheless she was up with the sun and raring to go, began cooking a king-size breakfast that she knew he didn't have time for but she hoped the smell would entice him to at least take a nibble.

"You're up early," he said as he retrieved the morning paper from the front yard.

"Couldn't sleep." Nina scrambled the eggs around in the pan with the spatula.

"Why? What's going on?" Tim sat at the table and sipped his coffee.

"Shelby's coming to visit. . . ."

"What? Just like that, Shelby?" He frowned.

"Yeah, why?" She shrugged.

"Thanks for informing me. I mean, this *is* my house too, Nina." He reached over and snatched up a piece of toast from the plate in the center of the table.

"Well, what am I supposed to do with you working all the time? You put every second into your work. What about me sitting home here?"

"What about you?" Tim raised his eyebrow.

"Exactly!" Nina tossed a spoon in the sink.

"What's your problem?" He looked at her disbelievingly.

"What's *your* problem?" She put her hands on her hips. "I can't have a friend over? You'd rather me have some kind of addiction?"

"I'm not saying that and I don't want to argue."

"Who's arguing? I'm just saying something. Every time I say something you call it arguing."

"You know how I am. I don't need you stressing me on top of everything else," he said.

"Okay, now I'm stressing you by telling you Shelby's coming?"

"She'll be compromising our space."

"*My* space. You're never here, remember?"

"So is that how it's gonna be? You doing whatever you want and not consulting me?"

"I need something to do when you're not here. Is that so wrong?"

"I'm not saying it's right or wrong. I'm just saying that I'm your husband and that means that we need to communicate."

"Don't make me laugh, Tim. Your idea of communicating is waltzing in here past midnight and grunting at me while you're look-ing for something in the fridge. That's not love, that's not marriage or communicating, those are leftovers you're throwing me. You spend all of your energy doing and being the blossoming filmmaker and I get what's left: scraps. That's not what you promised me. So ei-ther you lied or you don't really know what you want." She twisted her neck.

"Okay, here we go again. The I'm-not-acting-like-a-husband speech."

"Well, you're not. You come and go as you please and we don't do anything together. For Valentine's Day you put wine and choco-lates in the fridge and I'm supposed to be happy about that? *I don't even drink wine!*"

"Valentine's Day was four months ago! Why are you bringing it up now? If you don't get something you complain; when you do get something you complain. I just can't win around here!" Tim slammed the paper down on the table and pushed his chair back.

"Whatever happened to moonlight and soft kisses, Tim? Is it so wrong to want that back?" She moved toward him.

"When *I'm* the only one working to keep a roof over our heads, yes!"

"First you tell me that I don't need to work; now you're throwing it up in my face because I stay at home? I had a job when I met you, you just remember that!"

"A lot of good that's doing us now. The job you used to have can't pay the bills we have now."

"You know, if I was the type of woman who nagged you day in and day out you'd probably worship the ground I walk on."

"If? What do you call all this back and forth? It's nagging, Nina. You are nagging me."

"When you came home last night I didn't say a word. You lay in bed working. Our bed is an extension of your office now but I didn't utter a syllable."

"What's your point?"

"When's the last time we made love in our own bed? That's my point!"

"Nina, don't start."

"I'm asking because I want to know."

"Months."

"And?"

"And what? I don't have time, Nina. I'm sorry I can't perform for you whenever you get the urge."

"And you never get the urge? Or do you handle your business elsewhere?"

"Are you insinuating that—"

"I'm not insinuating anything. Answer the question." She put her hand on her hip.

"Why do I have to let you know my every move? Just to soothe your insecurities? Don't you understand, we all worked hard on this film. If I don't get it completed and distributed, it's history. This house is history, our life . . . is history!"

"So what!"

"So what? So, you need to find something to do instead of sitting around waiting for me to be everything to you. Filmmaking takes dedication. That means that I won't always be here to hold your hand. Do you know how many sisters wish they didn't have to work and could sit home all day and chill?"

"If you're so worried about how many sisters out there want you, go find them!"

"Look, just stop yelling!"

"*You* stop yelling! I sit home and baby-sit your dog all day long and do I get any thanks for it? No!"

"Who asked you to do that? He can take care of himself."

"Yeah, whatever you say. He chews up my leather shoes, Tim!"

"Day in and day out I'm slaving, trying to make ends meet for us. I put up with white men who won't even take my work seriously;

then I have to come home to a wife that wants me to entertain her friends, have sex at the drop of a hat, live in this posh part of town that we can't afford, and then for the icing on the cake she wants me to curl up at her feet like the family pet. I don't need this. Make up your mind, Nina. What do you want?"

"I want you, Tim, that's all. I want you. That's all I've ever wanted."

"I've gotta go."

"Don't. . . ."

"You're trying so hard to be what I want you to be, think for yourself. Wasn't your mother just like—"

"Leave my mother out of it!"

"Listen, I've got to go before I say something that will have you packing up everything you own and booking a one-way flight back to New York by morning."

"Well, maybe you should leave then. . . ." She folded her arms.

"Precisely."

"You ain't my daddy, Tim."

"Your daddy ain't much of a daddy either, so don't go bragging on him." He shoved the newspaper into his leather knapsack.

"Well, at least . . ."

Tim turned and faced her wearing a look of shock. "Go on and say it. At least what? At least you got a daddy? Is that what you were gonna say?"

"Nothing." Nina lowered her head.

Tim walked out and slammed the door shut behind him.

Nina's stomach twisted. This was making her sick. She knew that that was the way he wanted her. Bare feet, dress too big hanging off of her shoulders, hips swinging around, rushing to the market, Lamaaz classes, and play dates for her kids, never backtalking him.

She was nervous and angry, didn't feel like much of anything as she scraped the entire eggs, grits, and bacon breakfast down the garbage disposal in a huff. She stuffed the toast down the disposal with a fork and hadn't even soaped up the rag to wash the breakfast dishes when someone was tapping on the door lightly.

"Knock, knock, anybody home?"

"Hey, Francesca." Nina looked up momentarily.

"I just saw Tim drive off."

"Yeah." Nina twisted up her lips.

"What flew up *your* butt?"

"Nothing. We had it out this morning, that's all." She sighed.

"You mean you finally said something?"

"Yeah."

"What brought that about?"

"Shelby, my girlfriend from New York. She's coming for a visit."

"That's good."

"Yeah, I thought it was too. He says we don't have the room to put her up."

"With all this space?" Francesca looked around. "Maybe he just doesn't like her."

"She was at the wedding. He didn't mind then."

"Who can figure men?"

"Francesca, can you do me a *huge* favor?"

"Sure. What?"

"Tim took the car and Shelby's flying in at three."

"Not a problem."

"Thanks a bunch."

"That's what next-door neighbors are for."

Francesca pulled up in front of the LAX curbside in her red drop-top convertible. Shelby had been off the plane all of five minutes and she was already hassling the airport security staff about preferential treatment. She lifted her shades on top of her head and headed out through the automatic sliding glass doors with them hot on her heels. Nina couldn't have missed such a flamboyant sight.

"Heyyyyy!" Shelby's arms were outstretched, the baggage boy making futile efforts to manage all of Shelby's luggage without them toppling over.

"You look good, Shelby!"

"And you gained weight." Shelby raised her brow and pointed at Nina.

"Thanks for the insight. Shelby, this is my neighbor Francesca. Francesca, this is Shelby."

The two women embraced and kissed the air.

"It's so muggy here," Shelby said, motioning for the baggage boy to place her luggage in the trunk.

"We have good days and bad days," Nina said.

"Any bistros where we can have lunch and gab a bit?"

"There's this place I know, the food's incredible but it's a man-trap," Francesca interjected.

"Just my cup of tea. Shall we, ladies?"

"I'm not really in the mood for men fawning and making chitchat. I mean, I don't need a man to validate my womanhood, never have," Francesca said flatly.

"Neither do I but it's sure fun when they're trying."

Francesca got behind the wheel and Nina eyed Shelby and tried to determine if she was going to talk the entire ride.

"I forgot how beautiful the homes were out here." Shelby pointed out the terra-cotta roofing. "I'm definitely in the market."

"You know my sister's friend Carla? Her husband sells real estate in New York. I'll find his card and you can give him a call." Nina smirked sarcastically. "I'm sure he can find you something quite nice, *back in New York,*" she emphasized.

Shelby sat back in the seat, the wind in her hair, taking in the sights. "Yes, you do that."

Francesca kept her eyes on the road. "The interesting thing is," she said, "that men are exactly like the weather; good day or bad, men will always be men . . . unpredictable."

Shelby grinned. "Yes, and I've made his acquaintance. As unpredictable as he wants to be but he's a pure visual delight. A fine specimen."

"Who?" Nina asked.

"Sam," Shelby cooed.

"Sam is a married specimen, Shelby." Nina shot her a glance.

"Nina, honestly, I get your point but he's eye candy, for sure." She waved her hand.

"Men like when you look at them. They revel in that. It makes them feel like they've still got it," Francesca said.

"I thought we were avoiding the men topic?" Nina asked. "You two have one-track minds, you know."

"Not necessarily. . . ." Francesca glanced from the corner of her eye. "It's research. You've got to take a look at history, learn how to predict the male species' every move."

"You keep your eyes on the road and *I'll* handle the men." Shelby pursed her lips at Francesca. "Take it from me, Nina, there are some things that you just don't know about men." She opened her compact and leaned back in the car.

"So the fact that I have a husband and neither of you do doesn't mean anything?" Nina frowned at them.

"Take it easy. Stop letting men make you so uptight."

"Not men, you, Shelby. You're the one making me uptight."

"Doesn't bother me a bit." Francesca pulled up in front of the glitzy restaurant with the gold and black awning and put the car in park for the valet.

In no time flat Shelby had dropped their girlish conversation and was already curbside leaning on the silver late-model Porsche dining with a tall, masculine, mocha culinary experience.

Francesca pulled open the door, greeted the hostess by name, and glanced around the airy restaurant looking for her favorite table.

"Table for three?"

"Yes." Nina nodded.

"Four," Shelby interjected, pulling up to the women, hanging on the arm of her newly acquired accessory.

Francesca eyed Nina. Nina eyed Shelby. Shelby brushed past them both and followed the hostess to their table holding on tight to his bulging bicep the entire way. She made herself comfortable in the maple cane-back chair and ordered the toasted ravioli and a bottle of red wine and then proceeded to give one hundred percent of her attention to the debonair-looking man in the beige linen suit.

6

Carla and Sam

Hunan House. His favorite place. Fish wrapped in an old Chinese newspaper, takeout too, the best the Orient had to offer. Sam was a chili head. Loved hot sauce and spicy foods, a truly harmless vice. So Carla spooned the pepper steak into the pan and let it mix with the butter to create the ultimate taste sensation that had Sam bragging on his wife from day one. She doctored it up and tossed in some yellow peppers, a squirt of lemon juice. Fortune cookies in a bowl at the center of the table, chopsticks, and white rice.

Going in to work had done Carla good today. Three people had asked her what was wrong and the enlightening thing was that she had no idea. She had no real reason to feel the way she did. Any of the women at school she was sure would be eager to trade places with her in a heartbeat. Giving up their doldrums for what they believed were nights full of passion with Sam. She had decided before she got off at three to go downtown and get fish for dinner. Salmon. When school let out she was well on her way, fighting rush hour to get his favorite cut of fish, the freshest she had ever bought in New York City, down at the Fulton Fish Market on her days off. She ended up shooting over to Hunan House and ordering pepper steak off the menu instead.

She wanted everything perfect, back to the way it was between her and Sam before she had done the unthinkable and put herself in the position where saying no to another man's sexual advances wasn't an option.

She wanted to make Ashley something special too. A little mommy's-been-rotten-lately treat. She'd bake her her favorite flower-shaped sugar cookies with pink and white sprinkles. *Pack some to take for class tomorrow,* she thought when the phone rang with must-answer urgency. Before Carla could get her bearings, her hands covered with cookie dough, no place to wipe them, not wanting to stop what she was doing to take the time, she snatched up the phone.

"Hello." Carla held the cordless phone with her fingertips.

"Can I speak with Sam?" The woman spoke directly, not really a question.

"He's not in. Can I help you?"

"No, I'll call back." The phone went dead in her ear.

Carla stared at the phone before replacing it on the hook. She wouldn't let a phone call worry her.

The peppers were smelling up the place and making her hungry but she would wait. Carla, Ashley, and Sam eating as a family again was something that she missed and would make all attempts to cherish wholeheartedly tonight.

The meal was prepared with a pristine care. Plates laid out on the table, napkins folded like birds. Carla looked around the room, tried to add the finishing touches. A carton of Chinese dumplings, egg-drop soup, and stir-fry vegetables warming on the stove.

Carla took the opportunity to change into something less scholarly. It hadn't taken her long to slip out of her slacks and striped knit sweater. She helped herself to a dumpling, then two. She really didn't like them because they always stuck to her teeth when she bit into them.

She couldn't wait to see the look on his face, the look of surprise, pleasure, and contentment when he walked through the door and realized that she had put so much care and effort into dinner. She needed to see that, feel that, to know those things he felt were still there somewhere just waiting to resurface. She wanted him to know that she was sorry.

Carla sat in the kitchen chair counting the minutes that turned into hours as she played with spoons and forks, unfolded napkins, and then refolded them again.

At nine o'clock, Carla sat nodding off in the chair waiting up for her husband and child. It wasn't like Sam not to call or leave a message saying that he'd be late. Did Ashley get sick at school and they forgot to call her? A car accident? Worry never changed a thing.

Nine thirty-five, 10:15, 10:45. Carla heard Sam's deep voice as he wiggled the key in the lock.

"You go on to bed," he told Ashley as he kissed her forehead;

then she marched into her room, sleep already riding her back like the devil.

Sam laid his keys down on the table by the door and sifted through the mail piled up there. He hadn't even made eye contact with Carla.

"I made dinner," Carla spoke up.

Sam's eyes made their way to Carla's voice. "We ate already." He continued to shuffle through the mail.

"I didn't know you were eating out," she said.

"Parent-teacher's night."

"Oh, I forgot." She patted herself on the forehead.

Sam eyed her disbelievingly.

"Look, honey, I'm sorry. . . ."

"I'm sorry too," Sam said. "Sorry that our marriage doesn't mean as much to you as it does me."

"What do you want from me, Sam? I'm trying, you've got to know that."

"Troi and my brother Vaughn went to marriage counseling. Troi's sister Nina went too, just because. There are people who would rather try to talk to someone than sit down and pretend that there's nothing wrong with their life."

"I'm not going to counseling. There's nothing wrong with me!"

Sam removed his jacket, rested it on the back of the chair. He sat at the table fingering the bowl of fortune cookies with a disgusted look all over his face.

"Some woman called here for you," she said.

"Work or personal?" He fiddled with the wrapper, pinching the corners and pulling it open.

"Don't you use your cell phone for business?"

"You know I do. Why are you asking me that?"

"So it was personal, I'm guessing." She shrugged.

"Did she leave a number?" He cracked open the fortune cookie and pulled out the sliver of paper.

"No, said she'd call back."

"Listen." He sighed. "I'm tired and I'm going to bed."

He picked up his jacket and moved away from the table and headed for the bedroom. He froze in his steps as his cell phone lit up and vibrated on his hip.

Carla didn't know how she was going to get past this hurdle in her life but she imagined she'd do it just as she had done with all the other issues in her life, with a fight. Carla reached across the table and picked up Sam's fortune. The red words clearly printed on the strip of white paper read *Romance moves you in a new direction.*

She tore the paper up into teeny tiny pieces and threw them in the trash along with the crumbled-up fortune cookie and the Chinese dumplings. Silly superstitions.

Sam said he had an early morning meeting with the boss. His boss had called right before he had gone to bed growling into the phone that he wanted him in his office first thing in the morning. Sam had learned a long time ago not to question his boss so he dropped Ashley off at school, picked up breakfast, and then headed for the office with his guard up and ready for the confrontation.

The office was brightly lit and humming with agents running credit checks, sending and receiving faxes, collecting escrow, and making appointments to show homes.

"He's in there waiting for you," his coworker said before Sam could rest his container of coffee down at his desk.

Sam walked into his boss's office and sat down in the empty chair across from him.

"Good morning," Sam said.

"Close the door, will you?"

Sam closed the door and made himself comfortable in the chair again.

"Let me teach you something, son," his boss said arrogantly. "That socialite woman you showed a home to a couple of days ago, on Chandler Way?"

"What about her?"

"What does she do for a living?"

"She's an event planner, I think. I forget. Something like that."

"Her father is one of our exclusive clients. She does nothing but spend his money and she does it very well. He owns several homes in the Westchester area and is on the town council. He's thinking about running for some government office next year and it would behoove us to be on his family's good side."

"That's impressive, but what does that have to do with me?" Sam asked.

"Doesn't it seem odd to you that she was very certain about what she wanted but left here without a good solid lead on a home?"

"What are you saying?"

"Mid-six-figure range? Isn't that what she wanted?"

"Yes. . . ."

"Her credit checked out?"

"Yes, but—"

"But is beside the point."

"What are you saying?"

"Make her your personal project, Sam."

"You've got to be kidding me!"

"I'm not kidding. So you just show her something, anything, everything, schedule as many appointments as you need to until we close a deal."

"In all honesty, the woman was coming on to me. She wasn't interested in buying a house at all. . . ."

"How do you know that's what she was after; maybe she was just overly friendly." His boss shrugged coyly.

"She put her hands on me. I tried to ignore her but she just wouldn't let up. Then when I got home, my wife said a woman called the house last night. It had to be her."

"What your wife doesn't know won't hurt her. The client comes first. Now get her on the phone, show her a house, and make a sale!" he yelled.

"I'm sorry." Sam waved his hands. "I'm not going to jeopardize my marriage for a sale."

"So you'll jeopardize your job instead?" His boss opened his office door and stood staring at Sam incredulously.

"So you expect me to cater to some rich kid to keep my job?"

"Business is business, Sam."

"And the law is the law!"

"Let's not make this a legal matter. Besides, do you know what kind of men complain about rich, beautiful, successful women coming on to them?"

"No," Sam grunted.

"None. A real man would never complain."

7

Troi

Troi was making peach cobbler. It wasn't a secret that it was Sam's favorite. She remembered that all she had to do was hint at peaches or thumb-pressed pastry crust and he'd come running, paying special visits and complimenting her the entire time. He was helping himself to seconds.

What Sam had said last night hurt her heart.

"You're her closest friend and I don't know who else to tell," he said.

"Carla and I don't talk much anymore, Sam. I called her the other day but she was evasive. She's been that way lately."

"And . . . with the breakdown, I don't want to put any more pressure on her. . . ."

"Right. I understand. You okay?" She looked in his face.

"Yes. I was just thinking we'd be closer by now."

"You mean like in the beginning?" Troi felt as if she were pulling teeth.

"No. Especially not in the beginning." He eyed her for an indication of knowledge and secrets that sisters share but there was none. "You really don't know, huh?"

"Know what?" Troi asked.

"About Carla and that guy from Zion."

"What guy, Sam?"

"She had an ongoing thing with him."

"No, she never told me."

"She said it wasn't physical at first; then one night he wanted her to make good on her promises. He wanted more. She said she re-fused so he took it by force. She landed on my doorstep visibly shaken. I didn't know what to do. She asked me not to say anything or tell anyone so I didn't."

Troi was horrified. "She didn't say who he was?"

"No. She gave me some made-up name. I checked, and they never heard of him. Then she just stopped singing in the choir altogether and stopped going to rehearsals."

"Sounds like she needs to talk to somebody. No wonder the woman had a nervous breakdown. Keeping a secret that big while trying to be a wife, mother, and work too?"

"She's not going to see a counselor. She adamantly refused."

"Why?"

"Some of us are more open-minded than others and understand that having someone professional to talk to and seek a means to clear the air doesn't mean you're crazy . . ."

"I know. Vaughn and I—"

"I know," Sam said.

"So how are you holding up?" Troi asked.

"Not good. We fight all the time. I mean, tell me if I'm crazy. We haven't been together-together in over a year."

"Together-together?"

"Yes, sexually."

"What? I had no idea, Sam."

As close as Troi and Carla were, Troi didn't fully understand why she wouldn't tell her, of all people, about the incident in the car. That did explain, however, why she didn't want to come back to Zion. That was why her deep-seated anger festered inside her at the mere mention of singing. Made sense why she turned away from Sam and her best friend too.

"Her trust is shaken. I mean I was the first one she ran to, and I forgave her on the spot for even contemplating anything with that guy, so she trusts me but that's probably as far as it goes."

"Does she know that you're here?"

"You think she cares where I am? I mean, yesterday I thought I was reading her. We were having a *moment* and I was beginning to feel like she was my wife again. Next thing I know she was clawing at me and screaming like I was trying to do her harm."

"You've got to give her time. . . ."

"It's been a year. Over a year. How much time does she need?"

"As long as it takes, Sam. You can't rush that. It's a physical and mental thing. It could have left her unable to fully trust anybody ever again. It had to have scarred her."

"You're so understanding, Troi. You really are. You know, sometimes I think things should have been different. Me never meeting Carla and you never meeting my brother and then maybe we—"

"Don't you even say that! You hear?"

Sam's looked away from Carla. His cheeks flushed.

"Can't think it, can't do it. Never gonna happen, Sam."

"I was just—"

"I know what you were doing." Troi lowered her voice. "We just can't fall into that. I have too much to look after here with Dakoda without complicating things for her."

"I'm sorry, Troi."

"I know. You were just thinking out loud. It's okay to think as long as that's all you're doing. Besides, it's late."

"Yeah. Okay. I'll give you a call or maybe stop by tomorrow." Sam made his way to the door.

Troi was all too glad for him to leave.

Too much time. She had stayed dutifully like the sun, in a marriage that wasn't even giving her the benefit of the doubt. She couldn't remember the last time she felt satisfied or the last time that someone had—

Never mind, she thought. Now she just waited as days passed, expecting nothing, getting nothing, giving nothing, and here came Sam with thoughts of *what if,* trying to steal what little sanity she had left.

She did it all for Vaughn, the laundry, the cooking, cleaning, wiping, and scrubbing when wiping wouldn't do. She dispensed the medications too. All these years and this was all she had to show.

Some memories were good and some painfully obvious. That was how it had become between Troi and Vaughn. Now with one comment and a night to ponder it alone, here she was, needing to be touched, held, talked to, and conversed with on various levels.

Sam said he *might* stop by. In her head that *might* was a definite but she forbade herself to daydream about it. Her job as a friend was to find an amicable solution for Carla and Sam, not to desire him.

Sam loved his wife and there was no doubt about that, and as long as Sam kept on loving Carla, any passing thought that Troi may have had about Sam would stay dormant. She drifted off to sleep in Nina's favorite chair thinking just that. Feelings like that needed to stay dormant below the surface. Never awakening, never making an appearance.

First thing in the morning Troi was puttering around in the kitchen. Before she could even brush her teeth Dakoda was calling her.

"Ma, Uncle Sam's here," Dakoda yelled to the kitchen.

Troi smoothed down her hair and hoped that he didn't mind leftovers.

"Something's smelling good in here. . . ."

"Where? Ain't nothing in here for you," Troi kidded, sipping a mouthful of her coffee.

"She made one especially for you, Uncle Sam." Dakoda smirked.

"How you know?" He tickled Dakoda.

"Because . . ." She grinned. "You like pie and Momma knows that."

"Dakoda, do Mommy a favor and go to the store and get me some milk to go with the pie."

"Aww, Ma, now I'm gonna be late for school." She turned away from her mother.

"That's not Dakoda sassin' her mother, is it?" Sam asked.

"No." Dakoda pouted unconvincingly, and did an about-face, heading out the door with a dollar in her hand.

"Half gallon," Troi yelled after her. "Kids." She rolled her eyes.

"Well, can a hardworking brother sample the pie in the meantime?" Sam grinned.

"I'll think about it." Troi toyed with a saucer.

"Troi, about yesterday, I didn't mean anything. It's just that—"

"Hush. . . ."

Troi dusted off her hands, retrieved a fork, and dug into the pie.

"Now open up." She balanced the fork.

She held the fork to his mouth and extended her other hand to catch the crumbs. He steadied her hand with his and eased the fork into his mouth.

"Mmmm, delicious." He smacked his lips.

"It's just pie, Sam."

He gave her a warm thank-you embrace and held on a little longer than he should have. Troi, already leery of the entire situation, broke the hold first. When he looked down into her eyes his smile disappeared as did hers. She knew he was seeing her feelings, reading her mind, perceiving her thoughts. In her gut she felt what was next. She knew what he was thinking.

Why did I pick the wrong friend?

And she knew she had to put up a fight.

"Ma, milk is a dollar forty-nine and—"

"Listen, I'm gonna leave." Sam's nervousness was showing.

Dakoda barged back into the room and looked at both of them. Troi smoothed over the situation nicely.

"Take your pie with you," Troi insisted. She wiped her hands on the hips of her housedress.

"I don't need the whole thing now. . . ."

"Go on and take it, Uncle Sam, she made it for you. We got another one in the fridge." Dakoda smiled with her hand on her hip.

Pie wrapped in foil, Sam inched toward the front door and smiled on the way out and stopped to hug Dakoda, telling her, "Mind your mother now."

"I will," she said, picking up her book bag, and looked at her mother, who waved at her to forget the milk, and headed out the door behind him.

That night Dakoda came to her momma sharing some childlike insight.

"He looks so much like Daddy."

"Who?" Troi asked.

"Uncle Sam," Dakoda said.

"You think so?"

"Yeah."

"Maybe there are some similarities. The eyes," Troi reminisced. "The stature."

"Ma . . ."

"Yes?"

"I think Uncle Sam likes you."

"Child, please." Her momma frowned, waving her away, knowing the child was absolutely right. The chemistry between them had filled the entire room this afternoon.

"Your uncle Sam is married. Married to my best friend. We don't do things like that. Friends are thicker than blood sometimes," she told the child before sending her off to bed.

Troi had been lying in bed alone for the past few hours now thinking, didn't she deserve some good? Hadn't she been faithful?

She had always been rational but she wasn't fully understanding how what she wanted and loved was gone and now here her friend was shunning her blessing and pushing it away with both hands. She shook off those thoughts. The mental evil that seeps in and blackens your heart with its perverted thoughts is what leads to lives being ruined. She wasn't about to let it happen to her without giving it some serious opposition, and prayer. No matter how much deep down inside she actually wanted it, Sam did not belong to her.

8

Nina and Tim

Nina was sitting down to a breakfast of vermicelli with olive garlic sauce and a Diet Coke. Her first thought was to top it all off with sharp cheddar cheese on Town House crackers but Shelby and Francesca were front and center eyeing her every move.

"Girl, don't let this man do this to you, you deserve more than this. Your Gold's Gym card is collecting dust. Move it or lose it!" Shelby informed her.

Francesca and Shelby sat around the breakfast table with Nina dishing advice in an impromptu "put your man in check" session.

Nina was mostly listening, having no advice to give.

"You need to add some flavor to your existence. What's boring you the most about your life here?" Shelby asked.

"The furniture, everything." Nina spun her pasta on her fork and hung her face down in her plate.

"If you don't feel this place is you, do what I do when I'm bored with the look of things. Redecorate!"

"Our cash flow isn't as liberal as yours, Shelby." Nina looked over at her.

"Open a charge account," Shelby said. "That will change your whole outlook and make you even feel better about yourself."

"I say get him to give you some on a daily basis," Francesca interjected. "It's the best workout there is. Then you'll trim some off the top and have a resting heart rate of ninety."

Nina looked at them disbelievingly. "Look, right now the high-light of my day is being followed up and down the food aisles in the local market by an Asian man who hopes I haven't come to steal something from his overpriced store."

"But it doesn't have to be. You are beautiful," Shelby said.

"Gorgeous," Francesca added, absconding with Nina's bowl of vermicelli and dumping it down the garbage disposal. "You need to change the way you eat."

"Tell me," Shelby asked, "what do you hate most about this room?" She marched into the living room and looked around at everything in it.

"The cheap paintings," Nina confessed.

"Those mud-cloth throw pillows have go to go too. They're too ethnic." Francesca motioned with a distasteful look on her face.

"You need some stylish pieces. Marble or something timeless like cast iron and beveled glass," Shelby instructed.

"Something to make the room scream romance when you walk into it. Something to make it more cozy. When Tim comes home from work he'll want to stop right in the middle of the living room and work some Kama Sutra on you right there on the spot!" Francesca grinned. "Get yourself a peck of oysters, some domestic beer, and a fresh key lime pie."

"Key lime pie?" Shelby frowned.

"For dessert." Francesca nudged her chin.

"Ahhh." Shelby smiled, nodding her head slowly.

"Dessert?" Nina shook her head. "I don't get it."

Nina was tired of living in a *Vogue* world where it wasn't cool to be who she was.

"She never *gets* it," Shelby said. "That's her problem."

"Go home, Shelby." Nina rolled her eyes.

"I'm going." She smiled at Nina. "Just thought I'd come and liven up Cali for a minute." She smirked.

"Trust me, Cali will live without you." Nina grinned.

"That's okay, I have things to do on the East Coast anyway."

"Like a man?" Nina smiled.

"Perhaps."

"What about the one you were clinging to the other afternoon at lunch?" Nina quizzed her.

"History. They all have a purpose until I'm done." Shelby pushed up her shades, poured a cup of coffee, and sipped it black and waited for her ride back to the airport.

*   *   *

Berg or Stein, my films will get made, Tim quipped.

All morning his errands had him running all over the other side of town. He had forgone his croissant and coffee from the makeshift stand on the corner. He was hand-delivering paperwork and following up on information already sent out regarding his film.

The editing was almost complete but the small production company was having difficulty raising enough money for promotion and an even more futile time getting one of the larger entities to back the film for distribution. After selling his first film and watching them hack it up as he stood by as a paid consultant, he was appalled that he had little or no say. But now he vowed that he would film his movie on a shoestring budget if he had to because he wasn't giving up his creative control to anyone ever again.

Tim walked into his normally junky office to find his desk spotless. He was disoriented for a second. Not a paper clip or a file strewn about. Just a candle flickering in front of what could have been lunch. Steam visibly escaping, aroma uncertain, maybe chicken or fish.

He smiled.

An apology, he thought, as the silk fabric took him from behind and tightened over his eyes obscuring his view but not the rest of his senses.

Feathery kisses planted all over his closely shaven face had his mind racing as he was pushed forcefully down into a chair.

"A seduction?" He chuckled out loud.

His hands were being held behind his back.

"Okay, I give . . . what's for lunch?"

"Wild rice and braised lamb chops," Michelle cooed.

Tim scrambled to his feet. "Michelle? What are you doing here?" He pulled at the blindfold.

"I missed you." Michelle's cherry lips pouted.

"I'm-m-married."

"I don't care." She grinned. "That's a minor detail. Very minor." She shrugged.

She poured the champagne into each of the two glasses, rested the bottle on the desk, and told him that they needed to celebrate.

"How did you get into my office?" Tim frowned.

"I have ways. . . ." She swiveled her hips around his desk.

"How did you know where I worked?"

"Let's see . . . you're black . . . and you're a filmmaker who has actually got a film funded. . . . That wasn't the hardest thing in the world to do."

"You need to go." He pushed her off of him.

"Throwing me out so soon? I'm only here to help."

"Help what?"

"A friend of my dad's can get your film distributed, no questions asked. Then you won't be limiting your film engagement and people will respect you and think you're serious about the business."

She got his attention.

"That's what you want, isn't it?" She sat back down on his lap. "Makes no sense at all to make movies that no one gets to see. So I'm here to help make you famous. Behind every great man . . ."

"Is a woman, I know."

Tim eyed Michelle. She was still beautiful enough to catch a man's full attention and keep it without much effort.

"And what's in it for you?"

"I just want you happy." She smiled coyly.

"That's it? My happiness?" He didn't believe a word she was saying.

"And make it like it was before," she added.

"And how was that?"

"Me needing you and you satisfying me and my needs. Whenever and wherever." She draped her arms around his neck and kissed his face softly.

"So if I sleep with you—"

"Exactly . . ." She paused momentarily.

"And if I don't?"

"Dozens of films go straight to video every month, Tim."

"I see." He lowered his head.

"I've got my Blockbuster card. I can rent your latest." She smirked and jumped up when she heard the footsteps approaching. His partner, Reese, tapped on the door and walked in.

"Sorry to interrupt, Tim . . ."

"You're not interrupting, she was just leaving." He motioned to Michelle.

"Gone but not forgotten," she said, skirting past him and his partner and winking at him on the way out.

"What do you need?" Tim rubbed his head and focused on his partner standing in front of him.

"Nothing. It can wait." Reese nodded.

"You sure?"

"Yeah."

"Cool."

"Uh, Reese?"

"Yeah?"

"Can you lock up for me?" Tim asked. "I need to take care of some things at home."

"Not a problem." Reese winked. "You gonna eat that?" Reese nudged his chin toward the lunch on the desk."

"No, have at it."

Tim tried to put Michelle out of his mind the entire drive home. Dodging traffic, his mind doing somersaults.

He came bearing a fistful of flowers that had long since bloomed to make up for his lack of concentration on his marriage, his wife, and her needs, but mostly to quiet the noise in his head.

"I'm married now," Tim mumbled to himself.

Walking in through the kitchen door he sniffed around but didn't smell a thing cooking. Made him think twice about what Michelle was offering him for lunch. The house was quiet, silent like someone who lacked even a heartbeat. No television. No radio. The dog was nowhere in sight. Tim walked toward the backyard and pulled the door open. Monet came charging out of nowhere.

"Down, boy!" He held Monet at bay, not wanting to crush the flowers.

"Where's Momma, huh?" he said to the dog and smoothed down its fur.

Tim stood up and caught a hint of fragrance in the air that made him turn around.

Nina was standing voluptuous and glistening. She greeted him in a black lacy negligee, dampness still clinging to her skin, her hair tied back, black high-heel slippers with fur that matched her lacy getup.

"Listen, baby . . . about the other morning. I'm sorry." He held the flowers down to his side.

"I'm sorry too." Nina held his face and pressed her lips to his and pulled him closer.

"I don't mean to make my work more important that you, I really don't," he said.

Nina sucked his lips and ran her tongue across them. She didn't want to let him go.

"I understand what your work means to you," she assured him, and thanked Francesca for the wonderful idea.

Nina would have sat around until midnight under the moon

dressed in next to nothing if she could be certain that this was the kind of reception she'd get every time she put on a little show for Tim.

"I want us to go someplace." He played with her hair and moved a strand away from her lips. "We really haven't been anywhere lately. Maybe when Shelby's gone we can—"

"Where?" She began unbuttoning his shirt one buttonhole at a time as he spoke.

"Belize."

"Really?"

"Yeah. A week. I think I can swing that. My great-grandmother is down there."

"Shelby left on a noon flight," Nina said, the joy all over her face. "Maybe we need a little bubbly to celebrate."

"But you don't drink." He smoothed down his goatee.

"The last time I had a sip it was another monumental occasion too." She eyed him and smiled. "I think I can fit another occasion in there somewhere."

"Okay." He pressed the flowers to her nose and grinned as she inhaled.

"Thank you." She beamed, wrapping her hands around the stems and drawing them closer to her.

"What kind of champagne do we have?" he asked.

"No. I'll get it," she protested and then sauntered into the kitchen with the flowers to retrieve the two glasses she had chilling. She rested the flowers down on the countertop and popped the cork on a bottle of celebratory bubbly that was cooling in the fridge and pushed it down in the wine chill.

Tim was pushing off his shirt and heading for the bedroom. Nina vowed to start using her creativity much more. She liked what she was feeling. Tingling. Desire. Passion. Wanting Tim badly. Aching for some of him. All night of him.

Nina reached under the sink and pulled out her seldom-used vase and filled it up with ice-cold tap water. She snipped the rubber band that held them all together and plunked the flowers into it. She spread the flowers out in the vase and took a long admiring look. She opened the fridge and pulled out some sharp cheddar, crackers, and seedless grapes without hesitation.

She rinsed the red grapes under the cool tap water, then the green grapes and dried them off, then positioned the bunches in the center of a platter. She surrounded the grapes with animal crackers because she had eaten all the Town House crackers and began slicing wedges of cheese.

Creatively she pushed the champagne flutes down into the wine chill with the bottle of champagne and managed that under one arm while she balanced the platter of cheese, crackers, and grapes with the other hand.

Nina backed into their bedroom and set everything down on the dresser, pulled out the champagne flutes, and set them on the dresser one at a time carefully pouring two glasses of champagne without spilling a drop. She was feeling better about her and Tim, about their relationship and the way that they were communicating; she had waited a long time for a night like tonight. She grinned before turning around with one glass in each hand.

"A toast." She frowned as she turned and looked down at Tim sprawled facedown on their bed, no shirt, no shoes, and fast asleep.

Nina sighed deeply and made herself comfortable on the bed next to him. She chased one glass of champagne down with the other and looked long and hard at him. *Something has to change,* she thought. She glanced over at the clock and tried to figure out what she could catch on television.

"Some surprise," she mumbled to herself, certain that she would spend the remainder of the night biting the heads off of animal crackers and eating cheese, knowing full well that she was sick and tired of playing grin and bear it.

9

Carla and Sam

Ashley sat at the breakfast table with her face buried in a bowl of sugary cereal.

"C'mon, we're gonna be late, Ashley," her father told her.

"But, Mommy always says don't eat too fast, Daddy."

"Well, today you can eat fast," he said, glancing over at Carla.

He could feel her coldness creeping and seething through her blood in a hush. Nothing like she was when he had first met her. His wife and her shapely hips and full breasts hadn't caught his eye until after they were already dating, made him think of passionate nights to come. Now here she was glaring at him as if it were all his fault.

"What time are you going to be home tonight?" she snapped.

"I dunno," he said.

"Where are you going?" She put her hands on her hips.

"Out." He adjusted the tie around his neck and pushed the knot up to his throat.

He lifted Ashley's book bag and headed for the door without so much as a kiss good-bye or a wave.

Sam was a junior deacon, had all his ducks in a row. Then Carla came. He had things he wanted to tell her to her face, stuff that made him mad enough to march out the door and think about never coming back, but because of the past and all it entailed he refrained from causing her any more *undue stress,* like the doctor said. He wanted so badly to tell her, "If you want this to work, you need help."

"You are my husband and I have a right to know where you're going, Sam." Her harsh words totally disregarded Ashley.

You are my wife and you do what I say, he almost said.

"Please don't forget to pick up Ashley after school," he said softly, refusing to yell in front of their child.

Ashley put her bowl in the sink and tagged along behind him.

"Yeah, Ma. If you leave me there, they put me in the after-school program. They don't really help you with your homework there." She trailed out the door after her father. "Bye, Ma."

Carla hated when Sam did that. Spoke to her as if nothing were wrong. Made her want to hit him, throw things, maybe even leave.

Sam couldn't breathe until he got out of the house. He was disappointed. Disappointed with what he and Carla were turning out to be. Between the disappointment and her emasculation of his manhood he made all attempts to hide his feelings. He dropped Ashley off at school and tried desperately not to pick up the phone just to see how Troi was doing. His interest in her was helpful but not always pure. He had never thought that his brother deserved her and now here she was a widow, nobody to take care of her, nobody to love her, and he knew his phone call wouldn't help, only add fuel to the fire, but he dialed her number anyway.

"Hello?"

"Troi, it's Sam. I'm going in to work late and I wanted to know if there was anything you needed me to do or if you needed me to stop by the market and get a few things . . ."

"I've honestly got everything I need. Thanks for the offer, Sam."

"A paper?"

"Just got back from the corner," she said.

He could tell she was smiling.

"All right, but if you need anything don't hesitate—"

"I won't, and I really think it's the best thing, Sam. Honestly."

"Okay," he said.

"Carla's been through so much, you know?"

"Yeah. I know," he said, wondering why everyone was always so worried about Carla when he had feelings too.

"Sam, I have a customer. Can I give you a call later?"

"Sure," he said, wanting so much more than a promise of later.

When Carla arrived at school she was in a mood that no teacher should be in. An irate state. It lasted till way after lunch and recess. It had been riding her all day like a hellhound. From the moment she had woken and there was no Sam next to her. That's when it had started. Then he appeared out of nowhere not saying where he'd been or where he was going. Making a habit out of not telling her the truth. She wondered just who he thought he was, if not her husband.

Carla spent the afternoon scribbling assignments on the board that she wanted her students to do before class was over.

With her back turned to the class everybody moaned, including the youngster wearing a blue dress today who was normally her favorite child in the whole class. Chalk dust all over her new sweater, she faced them with a frown.

"Ahh, c'mon, Mrs. Singleton—"

"When I need your opinion, Jeremiah, I'll ask for it." She waved the chalk at him.

"But this is too much. We're only in the third grade. . . ."

"If you continue to complain you'll be taking it up with the principal. Is that understood?" She glared at him.

He put his head down refusing to budge.

"I'm talking to you, Jeremiah."

The classroom was silent.

Jeremiah sat in his chair defiantly, arms folded, pencil rolling onto the floor.

"Okay, let's go." She motioned for him to get up.

He didn't budge.

"I said get up!" she yelled from the front of the class.

Carla walked over to the boy, the eyes of the entire class peeled on her. "I said get up right now!"

She grabbed both arms and snatched the boy up out of his chair and shook him. "Is that what your mother teaches you at home? To disobey your teacher?" She flung him about, tears streaming down his face.

"Noooo! Let me go!" he wailed. "Noooo . . ."

"I'm talking to you! Is that what your mother teaches you?"

The little girl in the navy blue plaid dress scrambled from her seat to the classroom next door to get the other teacher.

The teacher from the class next door stood in the doorway.

"Is everything okay in here, Carla?"

In a twist of fate Carla was the one who spent the remainder of the afternoon in the principal's office.

"What were you thinking?" he asked her.

"I—I wasn't thinking. . . ." She eyed the wooden-based plaques lining the wall behind him.

"As the principal I don't have that luxury, I have to think. You know what happens when that kid goes home and tells his mother what you did? She'll hire a lawyer and want to sue us for child endangerment. She'll say that she sends her son to school to get an education, not to get physically abused by a teacher."

"I know." She fingered the magnetic paper-clip holder on his desk.

"Well, if you know, why'd you do it?" He frowned.

Carla shrugged.

"What's wrong with you anyway? You used to love working with the kids. Now you seem so . . . different."

"I still love my job. I just have things going on and I'm adjusting."

"Are you sure everything is all right at home? How's Sam and—"

"Yes, things are fine." She cut him short. The last thing she needed was people feeling sorry for her.

"Okay, Carla." He raised his hands in protest and then handed her a sheet of paper with a list of places she could go.

"What's this?" She skimmed the list on the page.

"Counseling. Anger management. Call it what you want."

"But—"

"You need to attend this class and comply with the guidelines," he said.

"I'm not going to counseling." She put the paper back on his desk.

He picked up the paper and handed it to her again. "It's not counseling . . . it's more like a meeting. Women sitting around with different issues. Conducted by a therapist."

"Counseling," she said.

"Group therapy."

"And if I don't go?"

"Then you can't teach, Carla. You know the district and the school board have criteria that must be met. We're not about to jeopardize the entire school for your noncompliance."

"I thought—"

"I don't know what you thought but I do know that when that child's mother comes in here to see me tomorrow, and I know she will, we can tell her that we've complied."

Carla stood outside the principal's office with the paper she had crumpled up in her hand. She had no idea how her life had gotten so out of control but she'd get to the bottom of it. It was lunchtime but she didn't feel like eating.

One of the teacher's assistants stuck her head out of the lounge and motioned to her. "Carla? Telephone."

She walked into the teachers' lounge and grabbed the receiver. "Hello. . . ."

"Long time."

She looked down to the floor trying to shake the voice that was stuck inside her head and wouldn't get out.

"I need to see you," he said.

"When?"

"Right now."

"I can't. I'm at school and—"

"It's not a question, Carla." He slammed down the phone.

Sam met with the client anyway. His boss was determined to close a sale, even at the expense of Sam's marriage.

When he walked in she was standing peering out of the window of his office. She had just returned from out of town visiting friends she said, even though he hadn't asked for details. *Probably an old lover,* he thought. Determined not to let her money or her long legs sway him, he positioned himself on the other side of the room.

"Something in Westchester or out in Suffolk would suit me fine. Four bedrooms at least." She moved over to the chair, sat, and crossed her legs.

"Any particular style?"

"Colonial is rather boring. What would you suggest?"

"I dunno."

"Are you okay?" she asked. "You don't look too good." She smiled.

He nodded. He wasn't about to tell a strange woman that he and his wife were on the outs. But he played along as she changed the subject and listened to her sad song and her tired "I don't understand why men aren't attracted to me" routine.

"Maybe they're put off by your prestige; money can do that."

"You think?"

"It's possible. Some men just aren't secure when a woman has more money than he does."

"I never thought about it like that."

He wasn't believing the generational tricks that women passed down to their daughters to get men.

Nevertheless as the long day wore on he ended up there. A place he said he'd never go, doing something he thought he'd never do. Having lunch with a woman who wasn't his wife, knowing she didn't have the most hidden agenda. He killed some time. Spent the entire outing thinking about another woman who also wasn't his wife. For months denied the pleasure of soft thoughts, and now here he was contemplating the scarlet sin.

Troi was a secret that he wanted to cover up immediately but he had a yearning that wouldn't let him. He felt her sincerity in everything she did. He knew a love like that wouldn't last. Too much opposition. His late-night visits were a burden on her as well, he could tell. Her not wanting Dakoda to see, while fighting every ounce of morality running through her blood, knowing all the while she deserved better.

Do you have kids? How old? How long have you been married? Are you originally from Jersey? Where did you go to school?

He answered every question methodically and then walked the woman back to her car and saw to it that they scheduled an appointment when he was thinking more clearly.

He just wished that his wife would make him a priority; then he wouldn't find the need to entertain himself elsewhere. Ponder thoughts of things between him and Troi that he knew could never happen under any circumstances.

On his hip his cell phone was vibrating.

"Hello?"

"Sam?" Carla's voice cracked on the other end and she began to weep.

"Carla, what's wrong?" His mouth couldn't form the words fast enough.

"Can you please come home, Sam? I need you really bad."

10

Troi

Troi shook off the evening's lament. Sam's call hadn't helped. But she had no time to feel sorry for herself. There were enough women sneaking around with men who were someone else's husband as a full-time occupation without her having to join in and do it too.

The first thing Troi did this morning after Sam called was put on a pot of coffee; then she scooped up some change and walked to the corner store for her daily paper. She shook off the thought that she had lied to Sam about needing anything, but she just couldn't see him now. Where was all this coming from anyway? She closed her eyes and tried to remember if these feelings had been there even when Vaughn was alive. She couldn't remember. Didn't need to remember.

She opened her eyes, stared straight ahead, and enjoyed the quiet on the morning street. A man walking his dog. His dog sniffed around her feet until the owner yanked his chain and pulled him down the street behind him. The air was cool, almost like spring when it's about to rain.

Troi walked into the store and peered up at the bread shelf inspecting the expiration dates. She squeezed two loaves and then slid a loaf of bread onto the counter next to her paper, counted out some coins, and with a small bundle in her arms made her way back down the block to await the arrival of her first customer.

Before Troi could get in the front door good and yell up to Dakoda to get ready for school her customer had arrived with a bag of bobby pins, a photo she had clipped from a magazine, and "he say, she say" on her lips.

"You're early." Troi twisted her wrist checking the time.

"Chile, my neighbors were up bright and early this morning fussin' and carrying on. I heard she been looking for her husband 'cause he didn't come home last night. Found him in his car, two blocks over from home, drunk as a skunk, one woman in the front seat and one in the backseat. She knocked him upside his head all the way to their front door, then pushed the man down a flight of stairs when he got there and didn't do what she said. Broke his arm in two places. He cried like a baby. Sobered up though. The cops came to straighten out that mess and I came over here to straighten out mine." She took a deep breath.

"You awful chatty today," Troi said solemnly.

"So much going on, that's why. You mind if I turn on the soaps?" She pushed herself into the chair.

"Be my guest." Troi waved her hands and set the remote for the thirteen-inch television in her customer's lap.

Troi needed something that would put to rest the wanderlust in her heart. The dirty afternoon soaps could do just that. Silly ideas and insignificant facts popping into her head all the time. *I won't have to change my last name when Sam and I get together.* Shame covered her like a blanket. How could she think such a thought? Carla had been her friend since elementary school; now here she was contemplating an episode. *Just once. Nobody will know,* her mind tempted her.

"Can I light this?" her customer interrupted.

"Smoking is a sign of weakness." Troi spat, changing the whole atmosphere in the room. "You know I don't let you smoke in here. You can be weak out there but when you come in here, be strong."

Not a word passed between her and her customer for minutes, only a television commercial distracting them for a few. The after-effect of the comment hung heavy in the air.

"You doing okay?" her customer asked finally.

"Yeah, I'm fine. Just changes I'm going through." She busied herself in her customer's hair. "Just going through changes." She shook her head and sighed.

"That's okay, you can make it up to me."

"How?"

"You know I need that recipe for peach cobbler you make so good."

"I've got a whole one wrapped up in the fridge," Troi said smugly.

"Stop lyin'!"

"I ain't lying. . . ."

"Who can pass up your pie?" Her customer tossed the remote aside, vacated her chair, and headed for the kitchen.

Troi was glad to take a break. She hadn't really felt much like doing hair for years now. Today she just wasn't in the mood for hair or anything else at all. She had forgotten to do her morning devotions. Couldn't think of anything else but Sam all night. Tall, athletic build. Just like his brother. The warmth of him would be a welcomed experience. A man, a woman, that sort of thing. She had to pull in the reins on her feelings. Muster some courage to tell herself no.

"You know, a couple of folks asked me about that stuff you gave me to use in my hair."

"Hair Joy. . . ." Troi scooped up the crust and maneuvered it to a saucer without dripping any, then licked her fingers.

"Yeah. I've got a woman on my job who wants me to bring her some and my sister has a booth at a shop and she wants some to try out on her customers."

"How many?"

"Four or five, I'm guessing."

Troi smiled.

"I need another one too; mine is almost gone."

Troi was pleased. With orders coming in maybe she'd make a business out of it after all. "You want milk with the pie?"

"Oh, no . . . milk does me bad. Anything else you have is fine." She picked at the crust. "Mmm-hmm. You sure know how to make some pie." The woman licked her lips.

Troi pulled the fridge open and scanned the shelves. She poured two glasses of fruit punch.

"You hear about what happened to your friend the teacher over at the school?"

"You mean Carla?" Troi pressed the crumbs together with her fingers.

"Yeah. Beat some kid really bad over at the school. Left him unconscious."

"What?" Troi's eyes got wide.

Troi's saucer flipped over, startling them both, and she knelt down to brush the crumbs together and wipe up the chunks of sticky peaches.

"Yeah, I think they're bringing her up on charges. I thought you knew."

"No, I hadn't heard." Troi rested her palm on her hip and tried to figure what was going on.

After Troi released her customer back into the world looking halfway decent, she reached for the phone. She had this nagging feeling that what her customer was saying wasn't gossip, but fact. Carla hadn't been herself lately so anything was possible.

Troi frowned as the persistent busy signal vibrated in her ear.

She turned around toward the sound of her front door slamming shut. She glanced in the hall and listened as Dakoda stomped up to her room. Her feet moving up the stairs quickly.

"Dakoda!" Troi yelled, then inhaled deeply.

"Huh?"

"Come down here!"

Dakoda came down the stairs with as much enthusiasm as she had gone up them. Came dragging her book bag behind her.

"Huh?" Dakoda asked with a bothered look on her face.

"What's your problem?"

"Nothing. . . ."

"So you come busting in the house and stomp up the stairs for nothing?"

Dakoda shook her head no.

"And you don't say good afternoon to your own mother?"

"Sorry."

"What is it?" Troi lowered her voice.

"They changed our classes around." She folded her arms.

"And?"

"We have a third-grade teacher now and some of the kids were making fun of us calling us dummies."

"So what? Are you a dummy?"

"No."

"So why do you let what people say bother you?"

"I dunno."

"You shrug, you don't know. Are those the only words and gestures in your vocabulary?"

"No."

"Dakoda, as long as people have tongues they're gonna talk."

"But they were laughing."

"Are you less than you were before they started laughing?"

"Huh?"

"Did their words change who you are?"

"No."

"Okay then. You go to school and do what you're there to do, learn. I mean, it can't be that bad. Who's this teacher anyway?"

"Miss Carla."

11

Nina and Tim

Tim made it up to his wife for falling asleep last night. As the sun rose slowly over the horizon and mingled with the day that was about to begin he awakened her with wet kisses from her ankles up to the suppleness of everywhere that was skin. Her shoulders arched and behind her neck welcomed the thought of him. She was beautiful to him, lying there tangled in the sheets. She had been there supporting him from day one. Never thought about leaving and going back to the life she had had. She meant more to him at this point in his life than she'd ever know.

Despite the outburst they had had a couple of days ago, Tim's lips evoked passion that they had known all too infrequently. They made sweet slow love until he left her tingling, perspiring, and feeling as if she had had an aerobic workout. Then he got up. While she showered he made breakfast, putting the topping on their now domesticated bliss.

Tim sat at the table with his fork guarding his plate. Nina entered the room beaming like an overgrown sun and kissed his blushing face as he sat wrapped in her baby-blue terry cloth robe, reading the sports section.

"Baby, order airline tickets."

"When?"

"Today."

"Are you serious?"

"Yeah. Pack us some things. Doesn't have to be much. We can pick up some light things when we get down to Belize."

"Okay."

"We should have enough on one of the cards." He polished off his glass of orange juice and headed to the bedroom.

"I'll have Francesca keep an eye on the house for us." Nina followed him with her plate in hand.

"Good. I'm going to the office for a few hours and edit through lunch so Reese can get this process over with." He stepped into his slacks. "He can do without me for a few days. It won't kill him."

"And then we can go?"

"Yeah. Fly out tonight if they have seats available." He pulled on his shirt and stuffed it down inside his pants, then zipped them.

Tim held her back against the palm of his hand, pulled her close enough to inhale her femininity, and pressed his lips to hers.

"We're gonna be okay."

"Yes, Tim. We are."

He reached for a belt and fed it through the loops, then buckled it snugly around his waist.

Nina kissed Tim's lips and he embraced her tightly before heading out the door.

Nina closed the door behind him and walked into the bathroom.

Snatches of conversation replayed in her mind. She thought about her and her neighbor Martha back in Brooklyn. Martha had once made fun of those codependent married couples. Now Nina was one of them.

What does he want with me anyway? she asked herself and pulled out the scales and carefully stepped on and glared down at the numbers tipping past two hundred. She stepped off the scales and stepped back on. It said the same thing. There was no escaping the facts. She didn't even recognize herself anymore. All the hopes and dreams, shot. A measly vacation wouldn't change that. If she could shut up that little voice she'd be fine. Whenever things were going well, here came doubt surfacing and making her think less of herself than she already did.

"Nina?"

She heard Francesca calling.

Nina mentally pulled herself together and quickly splashed some water on her face.

Francesca was never fooled.

Nina pulled open the bathroom door.

"Nina, are you okay?"

"No." She told the truth for once.

"What's wrong?"

"Everything." She closed her eyes tightly.

"Okay, start at the beginning." Francesca pulled her out of the bathroom and pushed her into the living room. They sat facing each other on the sofa and Nina spoke slowly thinking through every word.

"Tim's a filmmaker. I have no career so that makes me the film-maker's wife. I don't have anything of my own. Before we got married I had a career. Now I have nothing. Making breakfast? Doing laundry? Buying groceries?"

"Well, you can still have your own career. What do you like to do?"

"Nothing."

"Listen, Tim loves you whether you have your own career or not. Just support him. Supporting him doesn't mean you have to be in his shadow. Maybe he needs a secretary or a personal assistant."

"He can barely get his films distributed; what's he gonna do with a secretary?"

"Help him get distributed."

"I don't know anything about film."

"Learn. It's what your husband does for a living."

"Yeah, but I don't know. I mean, what am I bringing to the table? What do I have to offer him?"

"Don't second-guess yourself like that. You think I do? Phil and I aren't married but he makes the money and I'm content writing checks and supervising the repairmen when they come out. Holding down a home *is* work."

"Not much."

"Maybe you should start seeing your therapist again."

"I don't need a therapist, I need a life."

"Well, get one. Stop sitting around feeling sorry for yourself. You have to add spice to your own life. No one's gonna do it for you."

"I know."

"Nina, I'm not being mean, I'm really not."

"I know that." Nina walked into the kitchen and poured two cups of coffee and came back into the living room.

"Prove that you know it. Take him lunch. Put on something sexy."

"I did that yesterday; besides, have you seen me in clothes lately?" Nina inched up to the coffee table balancing two cups.

"See, there you go again. When are you gonna stop weighing yourself down? Pardon the pun. You can't want people to like you if you don't like yourself."

"Okay, okay, but what do I wear?"

"Must I do everything?" Francesca smiled.

Nina stuffed the pine basket full of things that she and Tim both enjoyed. Spray cheese, butter crackers, tuna with capers on croissants, macaroni salad, sardines, seedless green grapes, Pop Tarts.

On second thought she'd leave the sardines and take two bottles of mineral water instead. After giving herself a nod of approval in the mirror she thought she looked rather impressive in her springy rayon dress, matching jacket, and sandals. Ignoring the shirtsleeves that were tight around her arms, she set the plan in motion. She dialed her neighbor quickly.

"You pack lunch?" Francesca asked.

"Yes. His favorites."

"He's going to be surprised," she said, wandering over from next door with the phone pressed to her ear still talking to Nina as she entered her home.

"You look stunning, girl." She placed the phone on the kitchen table.

"You think?" Nina turned around and modeled.

"I think? Of course. And just think of this as the first of many afternoon excursions."

"I think I can deal with that." Nina smiled.

Francesca dropped Nina off at Tim's office building. Nina was rather pleased with the way they had gotten over those hurdles. His apology and impromptu trip made her think that marriage wasn't as hard as people made it out to be. Surely the good times outweighed the bad and she was satisfied with that for now. She'd have a bite, then head back home to order the airline tickets for their little getaway.

Nina took the elevator up and rested the picnic basket on the floor between her legs. *I forgot the tablecloth.* She frowned and made her way off the elevator.

The building was pretty old and it smelled funny. Still had the old mail chutes that no one ever used anymore. Not many people moving about on the floor.

Nina tiptoed up to his department and opened the door slowly.

She looked around and didn't see anything. The door to the right was the only other office. That was where Reese normally was. Across from it was the rest room and she hoped he wasn't in there. The room on the left was Tim's office. She smoothed down her dress, held the basket out in front of her, turned the doorknob, and spoke softly.

"Hello?"

Nina's face turned to mass confusion as her eyes focused in on the woman with her hair all over the place straddling her husband in the chair with her skirt hiked up around her hips.

Nina hurled the basket at them both. Macaroni all over his desk, green seedless grapes rolling under his chair.

"It's not what you think, Nina." Tim backed away from his desk.

The woman tossed her panties on his desk.

"You don't even know what I'm thinking!"

"Calm down. . . ." He moved toward her.

"I'm tired of people telling me to calm down! You calm down!" Nina hurled the words at them like daggers.

"Tim?" The woman smiled coyly.

"Who's she?" Nina snapped and waved her hands.

The words wouldn't form in Tim's mouth fast enough.

"Oh, wait, don't tell me. She's your secretary?" Nina's facetiousness was clearly evident.

"I'm not the secretary. I just happen to be friends with some—"

"Shut up, Michelle!" Tim spat.

Michelle slowly lifted her panties from his desk with her fingers.

"You mean I'm not the only one you brought here from New York?" Nina raised her eyebrow.

"It's not like that at all. If you give me half a minute I can explain," Tim said.

"All the flowers and wanting to take a vacation to Belize was all about covering up your infidelities! Wasn't it?"

Nina reached for something heavy on top of his filing cabinet. Something she could throw and do some serious damage.

"Nina . . . wait!" His hands were outstretched.

"Wait what? Are you gonna tell me that she was horseback riding right before I walked in?"

Tim shook his head.

"And here I thought I had to do more and be more. I was beating myself up about not being enough for you when you obviously had your own agenda. Enjoy lunch, Tim." Nina kicked the shiny packets of Pop Tarts out of her way, stepped over some grapes, and slammed the door shut on her way out.

Tim eyed Michelle's slanted eyes as she made herself comfortable in his chair and smirked so hard he thought her face would crack. He was done with her a long time ago. He had chosen Nina over Michelle years back in his old apartment at that face-to-face confrontation. Her showing up here was a sign. She was definitely up to something. He just needed to be certain what.

12

Carla and Sam

Sam didn't know what was wrong with his wife but he was through fiddling around and feeling as if his marital status were "occupied and taking up space." Carla was lethargic and unenthused about everything that had to do with their marriage. He tried to shake out of his mind the thought that Carla was keeping something from him.

Kissing up to some rich man's kid certainly helped.

"He's from South Dakota, met her mom at the University of Michigan," his boss told him.

Details, details, Sam thought.

Arguing with his wife every morning before work wasn't helping. But he was determined to be calm and nonjudgmental this particular morning.

"They want me to go to an anger management type class, sort of like counseling."

"That might help," Sam told his wife.

"But I was just lashing out. When you stormed out of here the other morning I was irate. You know that. Besides, we can't afford counseling."

"What do you do with your money?" he asked her, knowing that as usual she'd offer no answer.

"You have to learn to separate your personal life from business. You can't go taking your attitude to school. Especially not now. People are watching how caretakers interact with their kids and they're watching them like hawks."

"They said that the children are scared of me so they switched me to another class."

"What grade?"

"Eighth."

Sam didn't know how much more of Carla he could take.

"Eighth graders are stronger, more spirited; maybe it's for the better."

"How can you say that? I love teaching third grade. They took that away from me."

"Look, do what you have to do. They'll probably switch you back when the new semester starts."

"I doubt it," Carla grumbled and stormed out of the room to get dressed.

Carla didn't want to talk to anybody. It was her life. She told Sam she'd go to one meeting and one meeting only. She called in to school and told them she had an appointment, then took her time getting dressed. She heard Ashley ask her father why he and Mommy always had fights. He told her the same thing he always did, "I don't know, sweetheart."

Carla arrived at the session ten minutes early. She inched into the room and looked around the place indiscreetly. A woman was setting up red plastic cups on the folding table in a row and hoisted liters of colorful sodas onto the table's top from a cardboard box. She smoothed out the plaid vinyl tablecloth that was probably used to make the atmosphere in their meetings more social and friendly. Then she untied the red and white string that bound the box of the bakery cookies. She arranged them on the plastic platter, taking a bite of one, and began humming something she must have heard on the radio before she left this morning and had stuck with her all day.

The walls were sweating, chipped tiles on the floor in the room hadn't been swept, and the overpainted chairs were in a semicircle.

Carla wasn't ready. Although the meetings were open to the public she imagined that not many ever showed. Just the same helpless souls reaching out week after week, desperate for any residue of understanding that their fellow man or woman would so kindly provide in the few hours where they were making confessions, passing a paper cup, and silently praying for a miracle that would reflect some goodness their way.

The weekly meetings were supposed to have an intimate feel with an informal setting that was nurturing, nonjudgmental, and open enough to hold the attendees blameless for finding themselves in the need to be here, the receptionist told her. The meetings were always held in the strictest of confidence, the woman added.

Those in attendance never had to sign their names in the dingy surplus book or reveal anything at all if they didn't want to. Carla was glad about that.

There were four people waiting alone with her now. Three of them must have been regulars because they were apologizing for not making it last week and a face was sitting off to the side alone, clothed in disdain for having to be present. The new girl. She must have been. The new girl remained just that until someone else came in and took her place; then the next one became the new one and the older one took on a different meaning.

By the time the women started opening up, Carla knew she didn't want to be there. One woman's complaint about not having any money left over after shopping for an elaborate Thanksgiving dinner to feed and impress his family and friends, to another woman's woes about why her husband couldn't give her more than a two-month break in between having babies before he knocked her up again . . . and why he wasn't affectionate . . . and why he hardly ever looked at her anymore except at night, in the dark when he wanted to relieve himself . . . and why they were on baby number six and counting.

"Make him compliment you. . . . Get yourself fixed up, sheer stockings and some nice perfume with those pheromones," the first woman told the second.

"I will, as soon as you put some of that money aside before you go food shopping to get your nappy head pressed," she snapped.

"Oh . . . I didn't mean anything by that." The first woman covered her mouth.

"It's okay, I'm just tired of people telling me stuff I done tried a while ago. It ain't work then and it ain't workin' now." She pushed a whole cookie in her mouth and chased it with sugary water and mashed up the paper cup in her hand, then rolled her eyes at everyone in the room.

The third woman sat with her head down, afraid to say anything, afraid of what her posture was saying about her, and afraid to comment on any problems that the other women had shared that she had long ago just accepted.

From the basement windows Carla could see sets of well-dressed feet rushing off to a late lunch, running errands, or maybe just window-shopping. The sun's radiance took on a dusty hue and faded into a sunset behind the dirty brick buildings. She got a chill as she heard the March gust blow through New York City and whip around the old shaky windows, rattling them. She imagined that folks would bundle up in thick itchy wool coats and quickly hurry through the boulevard never looking back or giving the brisk winds a chance to blow down their necks and chill them.

"See you all next week," the facilitator said as she climbed on top of a stack of chairs by the wall, reaching for the string to pull down the blinds.

Carla could empathize how hard it was for someone to open up to a roomful of total strangers with eyes peeled and prodding, trying to maneuver past the protective layers. Just to stand to their feet and say anything or sometimes sit with their heads down, fumbling with something of little importance in their hands as they struggled to get the pain out one forced word at a time. Some spat out the truth but by the same token they'd try not to feel the eyes penetrating their secrets and making attempts to reveal it faster than they could tell it. *There has to be something so freeing about exposing yourself,* Carla thought, but doubted that she could tell things about herself that she had buried way down but not deep enough for them not to occasionally graze the surface.

"Carla?" the woman called to her just as she was about to file out the door. She walked over to Carla and tried to lower her voice.

"Because you're fully employed we're going to have to determine a fee for your participation in these sessions."

"Don't worry, I won't be back." Carla shook her head.

"You don't think these sessions will help?"

"Not really. These people have trivial problems compared to mine."

"Sometimes all it takes to get you on the right track is to release some of what you have pent up inside."

"I suppose." Carla shrugged.

"Here." The woman handed Carla a card with her name on it. "If you ever want to talk to just me, call."

"Okay." Carla nodded before making her way out the door.

She took the long way home. She hoped that they didn't expect her to open up and tell them her life story. Heroine addicts for parents, no friends, finally got a husband, and things were slowly unraveling to a bitter end.

Sam was glad for the moment Carla walked in the door. His sarcasm this morning was only a product of his guilt. He had wanted so badly to ask how the meeting had gone. He didn't have the heart to ask. Late at night and his wife was struggling with her own demons, and here he was, thinking of giving himself to another. Planning it.

Reliving through his senses the thrill of what it would be like late one afternoon when he could slip away unnoticed. Feeling like a man again in the arms of a woman who adored him, if even just for the moment. His mind was getting caught up in what he expected was next. He supposed that it was just those kinds of thoughts that led to an affair.

He needed someone he could talk to. Communication had always been part of the issue between him and Carla. He needed someone who didn't only see the woman's side. No one had really ever listened to him but Troi, and he knew that that was the way it would probably always be.

13

Troi

The sun pressed through the sky this morning and it was leaving the same way it had come. Gradually. In the kitchen Troi was listening to her music and mixing up a batch of Hair Joy. If she could get it into the department stores and beauty salons she'd have it made. Something in this lifetime needed to work out in her best interest. Life had always been a respecter of persons, showing favoritism but not to her.

Dakoda came home from school and sat in the kitchen with a bored expression on her face. She rested on her elbows at the countertop with her legs propped on the stool.

"How was school today?" Troi mixed the ingredients, looking over at her daughter.

"Fine." She shrugged.

"Just fine?"

"We didn't do nothing."

"Anything. We didn't do anything."

Dakoda was in one of her moods.

"How's your new teacher?" Troi smiled.

"We had a substitute today. Miss Carla wasn't there." Dakoda lit into a pack of Oreos.

"Okay."

"Nobody did any work," she said, pouring a tall glass of milk. "Just threw things."

"I see."

"The boys in the class made paper airplanes and spit balls like they always do when the regular teacher isn't there."

"And what do the girls do?"

"They just sit there trying to look cute. Some of them put on lipstick."

"Nobody learned a thing today, huh?"

"Not today. They never do. Not with a substitute." Dakoda dropped a cookie into her milk and watched it sink to the bottom of the glass.

"So I'm assuming you don't have homework?"

Dakoda pulled open the utility drawer and rummaged through the forks for a spoon.

"Just some reading." She plunged her spoon into her glass to fish for her cookie.

"You need to get that out of the way, then, don't you?"

"I guess. I know it already though." She scooped up the soggy cookie and ate it off of the spoon.

"What subject?"

"History."

"Not my favorite." Troi shook her head.

"Its boring World War II stuff." Dakoda dropped another cookie in her milk.

"Just learn it, pass the test, and move on." Troi spooned the mixture she was making into the plastic jars.

"Ma, can I ask you something?"

"As long as it's not about going shopping or sleeping over." Troi smirked.

"It's about Daddy." Dakoda raised her glass and examined the crumbs in the bottom of her glass.

"What about him?" Troi sensed the nervousness befriending her.

"Why did he have to die? I mean, with all the medicines and stuff they're doing now, why couldn't they find something to save him?"

"I don't know, Dakoda."

"Did you love him still, Ma?"

"I always loved your father. From the moment I saw him looking at me in church to the way he got nervous asking me out on our first date."

"Why was Daddy nervous?"

"Because he wasn't sure how I'd respond to him. It makes men crazy when you don't pay them any mind. I saw him looking but I just ignored him. Made up in my mind that I wasn't gonna chase a man. If he wanted my time, he'd have to approach me nicely. Like a lady, with respect."

"And that's just what he did." Dakoda giggled.

"All the women that were after him, I guess he wanted me to be the same way. When I wasn't, that piqued his interest."

"Piqued his interest?"

"Made him stand up and take notice."

"Ma?"

Troi eyed her daughter.

"Do you ever think you'll get married to someone else?"

"If you're worrying about someone replacing your father, get that out of your head. I love him. Only him. No one is going to take his place."

"I'm just talking about loneliness. Don't you get lonely?"

Troi could only grin at her little girl asking a million and one questions. "Sometimes I do. But I deal with it the best way I know how."

"How's that?"

"Pray. When God's ready to send me someone He will."

"What if God sends someone but you don't know that he's the one God sent?"

"Child, you sure full of questions today." Troi nudged her. "If he's the one, I'll know. You always know."

Dakoda unzipped her backpack and pulled out her notebook and history book.

"Good, you can get your reading done while I run to the market."

"What you gonna get?"

"I don't know yet. What you feel like?"

"Pizza!"

"How about a real meal, Dakoda?" Troi raised her eyebrow.

"Chicken's fine." She nodded and smiled at her momma.

Troi hated going to the market in the evening. Everyone had come home from work and grabbed the quickest, most visible thing on the shelf for dinner. Meat was picked over, boxes of macaroni and cheese knocked down, and lines were long and backing up into the food aisles.

She made her way around the fruit and vegetable section, punched her thumbs in some overripe cantelope.

Three twenty-nine for that?

Troi grabbed some packaged chicken, a head of broccoli, and a box of shells and cheese and eased into the express line behind nine other people. She glanced over the glossy magazines with pretty women perched on the covers and wanted to push everyone out of the way when she heard thunder crack through the sky and release an impatient rain.

Everyone let out a slow moan. The young teen standing directly in front of her with new suede sneakers frowned and tossed the warm bottle of Pepsi into a nearby basket of shortbread cookies, then left the premises. Now there were eight of them in line.

The cashier had a void and then had an even more difficult time scanning a box of Berry Berry Kix. Troi tried not to think of the weather as the pelting washed the windows and put a chill in the air.

Soaking-wet fabric clinging to her body, two fists hanging on to plastic bags that weren't very heavy, she managed her way home past rude New Yorkers.

Nobody offering to help me in the rain, she thought

"Can I get that bag for you?"

A car pulled up next to her with the window down. Troi looked over at the car and smiled. "Sam. Don't you ever work? What are you doing over here?"

"I can't visit?" He steadied the car and Troi got in. Sam drove two blocks and then made a left.

"I've wet your seats up now." Troi wiped raindrops from her nose and shook off her fingers.

"It's okay." He grinned.

Troi watched Sam make his way up the stairs with her bags. She came through the door stumbling in on his heels. Dakoda eyed them both. Sam coming over almost every night. Troi could sense how things could get a little crazy even in a child's eyes.

"Listen, Sam. I'd invite you to stay but I'm sure your *wife* needs you."

"Everything's fine," he insisted.

Troi sighed as Dakoda rolled her eyes and voluntarily left the room.

"Sam, you can't keep doing this." Troi frowned, removing items from the bags one at a time. She put the package of chicken in the sink and put the head of broccoli and the box of shells and cheese on the counter, then folded the bag they were in.

"She's not meaning the same thing to me that she used to," Sam said.

"You have to do it . . . you have to be there for her regardless." Troi shoved the empty bags down in the cabinet.

"I can't." Sam locked eyes with her. He spoke each word with a finality that did nothing for her but evoke the intense and constant craving within her that she fought to keep dormant.

His eyes looked her over. Hair wet, thin fabric clinging to every curve.

"Can you excuse me?" She moved past him.

"Sure." He sat at the table and made himself at home.

Troi had to get out of those cold wet clothes. And Sam, his eyes and the desire in him, made no bones about delighting in every inch of her until she was completely out of sight.

14

Nina and Tim

"Are you sure about this? I mean really sure?"

"What do you mean am I sure?" she asked Francesca.

"I'm just saying, he didn't get a chance to explain, Nina." She maneuvered her car through the thick airport traffic and pulled to a stop behind another car.

"Explain what? Explain why some ex-girlfriend ended up here in California in his office straddling him on a chair?"

"Were his pants open or closed?"

"What difference does that make? She was there and I wasn't supposed to be."

"I'm not arguing with you, I'm just trying to rationalize things." Francesca turned down the radio.

"I don't need rational. I also don't need him trying to woo me with early morning sex and a promise of a vacation to Belize."

"So you think it was all a lie?"

"I don't know what it was but I know what I'm not."

"A fool?"

"That's right!"

Francesca hit the brakes and brought the car seconds short of hitting a pedestrian head-on.

Nina twisted in the car seat and faced her friend. "Thanks for doing this for me. I knew you'd probably be the only one who'd understand."

"No problem. Are you going to be okay?"

"I'll be fine once I get to New York." Nina nodded.

"Call me?"

"I will." Nina leaned over and hugged her friend, then unfolded herself out of the car and grabbed her carry-on from the backseat.

"Don't forget," Francesca said, motioning with her fingers to her ear.

"I won't forget. I'll call you when I get there." Nina smiled and made her way inside the terminal.

The plane ride wasn't as bad as she had anticipated. No unwanted conversation, no crying babies or annoying flight attendants pawning off Diet Coke.

The cab charged her sixty-five dollars to take her into Brooklyn. Aside from being robbed by a cab driver she relished being back in the old neighborhood. Seeing the local deli on the corner and people making midnight snack runs brought back old memories.

She stood on the curb in front of the place she knew she could always call home. Right back in New York City with her sister on that tree-lined Brooklyn street. Couldn't get more familiar than that. Same flowers wilted in the pot at the top of the steps. Most of them dead now. Troi never did have a green thumb.

Nina dragged her bag up to the front door. No lights, no movement. She'd bet all of her luggage that Troi was already sleeping. Nina rang the bell and held her breath. She had no choice. Even though she'd spoken with her sister at least once a month, she hadn't seen her since Vaughn died years ago.

Clad in a dull paisley-print robe, Troi pulled open the door and squinted into the darkness.

"Nina?"

"Hey!" Nina embraced her sister.

"What's wrong? What are you doing here?"

"Visiting. I can't visit my sister?" Nina made small talk.

"It's after midnight. Why didn't you tell me you were coming?"

"It wouldn't have been a surprise then."

"Come in. Come in." Troi waved.

Nina stepped into the place that was too familiar to be real. She liked what Troi had done with it. She hadn't changed it much but it was different.

"You want coffee?" Troi rubbed her eyes and headed for the kitchen.

"Sure. Thanks."

Nina made herself comfortable in a nearby chair.

"How's Dakoda?"

"She's fine. Keeping up in school. I'm proud of her," Nina said.
"I'm glad to hear that."

Nina examined the photographs on the wall behind her. A picture
of her and Troi in Cozumel. Vaughn. Dakoda's grade school picture.
A wedding picture of their mom and dad that was so old it was peeling and had a deep crack down the middle dividing them forever.

"I see you kept the bookcases."

"Yeah. I don't have as many books as you though."

"I see." Nina scanned the empty shelves.

Troi sat in the dimly lit room with her sister. "Okay, Nina. I know
you too well. Why are you really here? And don't tell me about visiting and seeing how I'm doing. Give me more credit than that."

"Nothing." Nina sipped her coffee.

"Nina?"

Nina lowered her cup and tried to stop her hands from trembling.
She closed her eyes and breathed slowly.

"What is it? You can tell me," her sister said.

"Just drama." Nina shook her head. "I'll be fine."

"It had to be Tim so tell me what he did. Besides, you know
drama was my major, so dish it."

"Tim, woman, sex."

"And?"

"And I left. I don't know how you do it but I can't. Won't."

Nina rested her cup on the coffee table. "You remember Michelle?"

"Yeah."

"Well, Tim and I had a beautiful morning, if you know what I
mean. I mean it hadn't been like that in months and I thought things
were changing. Getting better for us and we were moving on in life
together. He cooked breakfast, hung around the house a little later
than he usually does, and said he was going in to work just for a few
hours. Told me to order plane tickets because he was going to take
some time off from work and we were going to do a mini vacation
thing in Belize because we haven't been any place together since that
little thing I don't even want to call a honeymoon. After he left for
work I got on the scale and went through the whole 'Am I worthy?'
thing. Francesca, my neighbor, came by and cheered me up and convinced me to surprise Tim. Put some spice in my life. So I packed him
a picnic lunch and had my neighbor drop me off at his office. I walk
in trying to surprise him and there she is with him surprising me."

"Who?"

"Michelle. Her nasty panties on his desk. Him sitting in the chair with her legs wrapped around his lap."

"No!"

"Yes. And there I was in the middle of the street in downtown traffic flagging down a taxi. I get home, throw some things in a bag, snatch up the credit card, and run next door to convince Francesca to take me to the airport without a whole lot of questioning. She does and here I am. New York. Home."

"I know you're hurt, sis, and I'm so sorry about what Tim did, but this isn't home, Nina. You need to straighten this whole matter out with Tim."

"There's nothing to straighten out. I saw it with my own eyes."

"The two of you are amazing. Do you know how hard it is to find 'the one?' Life is hard enough and when we all cut through the pretenses it hastens the delivery of what was promised to us. The love of someone who'd come into your life and slide right into that vacancy and reside there."

"I know what you're doing, Troi, and it won't work."

"I'm not doing anything but telling the truth. You know you love him. You're gonna have to work through this, be it now or later."

"So you mean to tell me if Vaughn had done the same thing you'd forgive him?"

"He's gone, Nina. I'd do anything just to have him back. So if I had to forgive again and again I would. Some people never understand a love like that. They let pride get in the way. Love isn't a game of keeping score to see who's winning out over who. When you fall in love you have to put the pride aside."

"I don't think you're understanding what I'm going through, Troi."

"Oh, I don't understand? My husband tells me he's gay, moves in with his boyfriend, leaves me and my daughter to fend for ourselves, and I don't understand?"

"I'm not saying that. I'm saying that you didn't see it."

"Just because I didn't see it didn't mean it hurt any less."

"I know, sis. That's still not what I'm saying but I'm tired, so . . ."

"Just call him," Troi said, lifting Nina's bag.

"I will. Just not now. Maybe tomorrow. Maybe the day after or the day after that."

Nina followed Troi into the bedroom.

"Okay. If there's one thing I've learned is that I can't force you to do anything." Troi dropped the bag by the bed.

"You learn quick." Nina smiled.

"Not quick enough." Troi smacked Nina in the head with a pillow.

"I can't believe you did that!" Nina's eyes were wide. "You're gonna get it!"

She reached for the other pillow and swung it with all her might. They both collapsed on the bed in a heap with a chorus of childlike laughter, looking at each other because it had been so long since they had done anything fun together.

"Why did you do that?" Nina grinned.

"A minor distraction, sister dear, and you need one."

15

Carla and Sam

The day was young and beautiful and felt like greeting everyone, but Sam didn't. He walked into the room never making eye contact.

"Good morning," he grumbled.

"Morning, Daddy."

"Morning, sweetie." His mood changed slightly.

"You remember I have a trip tomorrow, Daddy?"

"Yes, I remember."

Carla glared across the room at Sam wondering where he had been all night and felt very nervous about what was happening around her. Sam was no pushover, she knew that. Forgiveness comes with a price and Carla knew that deep in the back of his mind he would never fully let her live down the affair.

Carla pounced on the phone when it rang.

"Hello?" She spoke sharply.

She eased into the bedroom leaving Sam in the living room going through his briefcase.

"I said never to call me here!" Carla was adamant. "I can't see you now." She eyed the doorway and walked over to the bedroom door and pushed it shut.

"Look, I don't have any money." She frowned. "In case you didn't notice I have a family to take care of," she huffed. "Get it from where?"

Sam turned the doorknob and pushed his way into their bedroom.

"I'll see what I can do." Carla clicked the phone off.

"Who was that?" Sam's question came out of nowhere.

"Nobody."

"Nobody?" He shook his head. "Okay, Carla."

"Okay what?"

"I've made some decisions. We need to discuss them tonight."

"I can't tonight. I . . ."

"After the meeting then, but we need to talk. It can't go on like this."

"What's the problem, Sam?"

"What do you mean what's the problem?"

"You're the one who never comes home. You don't talk to me. Why do you hate me so much?"

"I don't hate you," he said.

"Yes, you do. I can tell."

"I don't," he snapped.

"Daddy?" Ashley parted the door.

"Yes, sweetie?"

"We're gonna be late."

"I'm coming, honey." Sam eyed Carla.

"Can we finish this tonight?" he asked.

"Yeah, I guess."

Guilt found Sam every second he spent thinking about Troi. Their possibly ever getting together was a foolish notion. Something that a rational person wouldn't think about. He could already imagine the negative repercussions for her. People would say how horrible it was for her to take her best friend's man, but in essence Carla had sent him packing.

He canceled all of his appointments. His boss glanced in his office suspiciously. He had a mind to do something that he hadn't done in a long while and he set off to do just that. Sit alone in a bar and swallow down some spirits. He headed down the street, not far from his office. It was a cozy little place frequented by most of the businessmen in the surrounding office buildings. Spirits would lighten the load. All it had to do was call and he'd succumb. The same spirits that glazed over his eyes and wouldn't allow him to recognize an old client perched right on the seat next to him. The same reason Brenda had left him.

They exchanged hellos and then he must have sat in that bar for half the day watching the older woman two stools over.

Seconds after he watched her pull off in her late-model car he went by the meeting place and sat outside parked inconspicuously under a tree. He watched everyone file out into the night, exchanging chitchat. He watched as tall women, short women, old women, younger women said their good-byes and made their way home to their families . . . no Carla.

When he got home, the baby-sitter was up with Ashley.

"Did my wife call?"

"No, Mr. Singleton."

"Daddy, my trip is tomorrow," Ashley said.

"I remember." He hugged his little girl.

Sam reached in his pocket and pulled out two bills.

"Thank you, Mr. Singleton." The baby-sitter folded up the money and pushed it down in the pocket of her jeans.

Sam was quite capable so he put his daughter to bed and stayed with her until she was asleep. He tried not to doze off himself but he did, until he heard the door creak open and the careful way Carla was walking around the apartment trying to go undetected.

"Where were you tonight?" Sam appeared in the doorway startling her.

"I told you I had to go to one of those meetings."

"No, you didn't." Sam shook his head.

"Of course I did."

"You might have told me you had to go but you weren't there."

"I was."

"You're lying again, Carla. Where were you? And this is the last time I'm asking or I'm gone!"

"I went by . . . to see a friend."

"A friend? It's a man, huh?"

"Sam, it's not what you think."

"You're still seeing him, aren't you?"

"It's not like that at all."

"Is that his smell all over you?"

"Why are you doing this, Sam?" Carla held her clothes to her body.

"I can't get anything more than a handshake but he gets the goods, huh?"

"That's insane!"

"Were you or weren't you with him?"

"Lower your voice."

"I won't. Ashley deserves to know what kind of mother she has!"

"I was with him but it wasn't about anything."

"It wasn't about anything but it was something enough for you to lie to your husband about." He snatched up his jacket and headed for the door.

"Where are you going?"

"I don't think that's any of your business. When you make a conscious decision to sleep with someone else you forfeit that right." He slammed the door on the way out.

At 1:00 A.M. Sam was drawn to Troi instinctively as if he had nowhere else he could go.

He could hear her unlock the door and pull it open and look at him as if he were an alien.

"Can I come in?"

"No, Sam. What are you doing here?" She frowned.

"Why not?" He spoke softly.

"Because . . ."

"Because is not a reason," he said, mocking her.

Troi stepped aside and let him in anyway. He came in, poured himself a cup of coffee, and made himself comfortable in her kitchen.

Her pale blue nylon gown hugged her body. Her hair neatly away from her face gave him a much-desired view of her full lips.

"She's cheating on me." Sam lowered his head over his cup of coffee. "All this time I thought we were working things out and this is what I get? The short end."

"It won't always be like that," Troi said, consoling him. Brushed the palm of her hand up and down his shoulder.

His eyes could see her sincerity. "It's like that now. That's all that matters."

Sam stood up and towered over Troi but she hugged him anyway. He needed the comfort, she supposed, as he wept softly on her shoulder. Men did cry and he was proof.

Her body was smooth. Soft. Feminine. The nylon glided over her hips as he rubbed his hands across it. He pressed into her. His body took less than a second to respond.

He wanted to show her his appreciation. Show her once and for all that she was a woman. Make her feel like one. Take her mind on a flight. Give her something to dream about.

His hands lifted her gown and rubbed the back of her legs. The heat of his lips grew near hers. He wanted to be near her, with her, inside her.

"No, I can't Sam." She pulled the fabric back down over her hips.

"Why do you keep fighting it, Troi?"

"If I don't, who will?" She moved away from him.

"I need you, Troi."

"You're drunk, Sam."

"I'm not drunk."

"I can't." She shook her head. "Drunk or not, you need your wife, not me."

"Carla and I are over."

"You don't know that for sure."

"I know all I need to know," Sam said.

"Sam, I think you should go. It's late."

Sam looked in Troi's eyes trying to discern if she mean it. Did she really want him to go?

"It's late. Can I just sleep on the couch or something?"

"I don't think so." She shook her head.

"I'm really in no condition to drive right now."

"Okay," Troi relented. "Only because you've been drinking. But if you come anywhere near me, Sam, you'll be on the curb and I'm serious."

"Okay." He nodded.

"I want you gone before the sun comes up too. My sister's here and my baby girl is upstairs. She doesn't need to try to figure all this out in her head. This is grown folks' business."

"Troi, listen . . . I just—"

"Sam, I can't and you know I can't."

"But you haven't even—"

"I don't want to hear any justification. I can't do it, no matter how much I desire you. She's my friend."

"Most people would just—"

"I'm not most people, Sam."

She walked out of the kitchen leaving him knowing that for certain.

16

Troi

Troi was scolding herself because she knew that it was more than inappropriate to have her best friend's husband sleeping on her couch. *You know you wanted him in your bed,* her mind taunted. *And when he touched you, you almost caught on fire.*

Troi closed her eyes and said a silent prayer.

"Was that Sam I saw last night?" Nina pulled herself up to the table.

"You want sugar?" Troi asked, her mind drifting.

"Yes." Nina smiled. "Now answer my question."

"I told him he can't come here." Troi shrugged and busied herself.

"Why?" Nina stirred the sugar in her coffee.

"First off, he's Carla's husband. They're having trouble and I can't get in the middle of that. Secondly . . ." Troi sighed. "He's being too attentive lately."

"What you mean? Like touchy-feely attentive?"

"No, more like I-married-the-wrong-friend attentive." Troi rested her spoon on the table.

"Oooo! He said that?" Nina frowned.

"Might as well. He's been over here almost every night. Started off innocently enough. Him needing an ear about Carla and what they're going through and then before you know it . . ."

"Before you know it what?" Nina grinned. "Sex?"

"No, not sex. Just him showing up not calling first and asking me if I need anything all the time. He's been waiting on me hand and foot as if he were my husband. You know I've always been faithful, I'm not gonna stop being faithful now."

"Faithful to who, sis?" Nina had to ask.

Troi paused reflectively and eased down into the chair.

"Faithful to Carla," she said. "I've got to be true to me."

"I wish Tim thought like you." Nina stirred the sugar in her coffee.

"Hi, Mom, bye, Mom." Dakoda brushed by like a bullet.

"Wait a minute. Come back here. Is that the only person you see, child?"

"Hi, Aunt Nina."

"How you doing, Dakoda?"

"I'm fine." She embraced her

"And school?"

"It's fine."

"Okay." Nina smiled. "Go on, don't be late on my account."

Dakoda waved and headed on her way to school.

"Girl, you gotta keep these children in line. She came in here the other day smelling like smoke. Talking about 'everyone else is smoking.' She just doesn't know how easy she has it."

Troi held her cup with both hands and blew on her coffee.

"Kids are a full-time job. I don't know what I'd do if had a child and had to deal with this mess with Tim," Nina said.

"So what *are* you gonna do?" Troi asked.

"I dunno." Nina looked around the kitchen. "I'm still trying to figure that out."

"You love him, right?"

"With all my heart. He changed me. You remember how I used to be? Sitting around the house all day moping and feeling sorry for myself listening to Nina Simone."

"I remember," Troi said softly. "You feel better about you now, don't you?"

"Not really, but I knew that he really loved me; that's why I married him, and that helped a little. I just should have remembered how he used to be." Nina shook her head.

"I think you should give the man the benefit of the doubt."

"I think that's what *Troi* would do." Nina bit into a slice of toast. "I know what I saw," she mumbled with her mouth full.

"You're right."

"Not to change the subject but I've been meaning to ask you, Troi. Have you seen Daddy?"

"Not since he ran off with that number runner's ex-wife. What's her name again?"

"You asking the wrong person." Nina rolled her eyes. "I have no idea and don't care to know. I just don't know how he could run off and leave his family like that. We are everything he's ever known."

"Maybe, maybe not." Troi shrugged. "You don't know how long he's been seeing that woman. Then he tried getting on our good side. Wanting us to vouch for him to Momma. I'm the wrong person to come to with some adultery mess. The wrong person." Troi shook her head.

"What about Momma?"

"She's been in and out of detox. Lost the house we grew up in. Last time I passed by there it was boarded up, labeled blighted property. Do-not-enter stickers everywhere."

"Things were going so good before I left."

"Yeah. But the real issue at hand is, do you conquer your demons or do you let them conquer you?"

"What's happening to us?" Nina's blank expression gave away the fact that she honestly didn't know.

"Only what we let happen." Troi shrugged.

"That's what I'm saying. And I'm not about to let Tim treat me like this. I mean, it's bad enough that we never do anything or go anywhere together but to deal with infidelity? That's not gonna happen. For all I know he says he's working late, editing and whatnot, but maybe he's showing her the town. Dinner and dancing. Maybe that's why he can't take me anywhere. He comes home around midnight religiously, raids the fridge, falls asleep, then wakes up to repeat the pattern the other six days of the week."

"What about church?"

"No. He stopped going and I'm not going alone. It isn't right, especially when people know I'm married."

"You know you're not being fair, Nina."

"What do you mean fair? Have you always been that gullible? He's cheating, Troi."

"What do you mean gullible?" Troi put her hand on her hip. "Having faith in people and giving them the benefit of the doubt isn't gullible. It just gives you a chance to sift through your doubts and gives them enough rope to hang themselves."

"What would you do if you were in my shoes?" Nina asked.

"I'd sit down with him and let him explain exactly what it was that was going on back there in that office. I wouldn't leave town and go into hiding."

Nina shook her head. "I have nothing to say to him. Not now. I'm doing everything I can to soothe myself and I shouldn't have to do that."

"So you think it's his job to make you happy?"

"I'm his wife."

"You're still grown. You're still an individual."

"I know that. But he's the one who has me doubting myself and I shouldn't be doing that. When he's happy, then I am too. When he's burdened, then I feel that way too. My mood changes in tune with his. I lost my identity years ago. I don't know who I am anymore. I gave up my job, my house, and he doesn't seem always to be conscious of the sacrifices I've made to move to be there with him. I'm sitting home all day gaining weight; then this old girlfriend no bigger than a size eight comes out of nowhere back into his life after he swore they were through. I can't let that go. Francesca doesn't think I should either."

"I tell you what. Let's do lunch. Like old times."

"Like I need another meal." Nina giggled.

"One meal is not going to put an entire pound on you."

"One Fish Two Fish?"

Troi grinned and nodded her head. "Let's go."

Nina ordered her favorite fetuccini Alfredo with grilled salmon, a Caesar salad, and a Diet Coke. She took her time making her way through the food on her plate one rich bite at a time.

"I feel much better now. You know I could never think on an empty stomach." Nina indulged in half a loaf of garlic bread in spite of her better judgment.

"You know, we haven't been here in years." Troi pierced the lettuce with her fork.

"Yeah, well, you know, in New York there are rotating hot spots. Years ago this place used to be jam-packed on a Friday night. I remember the Columbia University crowd would make their way over here quite often."

"I bet you did. Lobster, crab cakes . . ."

"Wine." Nina giggled.

"Wine? Ooo, you're lucky Momma never caught you."

"I had to have some fun. My first time away from home."

"Yeah, I hear you." Troi gazed out the window.

The neighborhood was changing. Losing its luster and the enticement, the culture that made people proud to say they were from New York.

Troi watched as a shiny late-model car squeezed into a parking spot curbside. A pair of long legs emerged from the car and the familiar-looking woman draped her arms around the man's neck as he pressed coins into the parking meter and turned the knob. His back facing the window, the woman tossed her hair and made every effort to let onlookers know that the man was hers. Troi grinned. She thought she knew the woman.

"Umm, speaking of Columbia, Nina, is that who I think it is?"

"Oh, Lord, that's Shelby." Nina squinted through the glass. "The last thing I want to have to do is explain to her why I'm here in New York and Tim's not. She'll never let me live it down." Nina focused her eyes on her friend's latest victim.

"It's none of her business, Nina, friend or no friend."

"Is that Sam?" Nina asked.

"Oh, God. It sure is." Troi's face fell, sullen with displeasure.

"I thought you said his affections were set on you?"

"They were. . . . I don't know. He hasn't been getting any," Troi confessed to her sister. "Maybe that's what it was all about from the beginning."

"How do you know he hasn't been getting any?"

"He told me."

"So what, did he trade you in for Shelby now?"

"Maybe. But then again, that's Shelby and face it, she . . . well . . . you know."

"Yeah, she puts out."

"Exactly."

17

Nina and Tim

Nina's mind relived the whole incident in vivid detail. It was unusually quiet when she walked into Tim's office that afternoon. No one in the reception area. Doors closed. Lights on. Her mind told her that she needed to guard herself, and she held the basket close to her body, her fingers tight around the handle. That sixth sense was cautioning her, forcing her feet to hesitate. But she proceeded and turned the doorknob anyway because she was his wife and she had a legal right to be there. The woman's perfume was heavy in the air. She could smell it on her hand after she touched the doorknob. Deep down she prayed to herself that it wasn't what she thought. Her eyes focusing, deciphering, straining to understand why Tim had leaned back in his office chair, hardly putting up a struggle as the woman wrapped herself around him like a birthday present.

We've never done it on a chair.

Nina didn't know which angered her more. The fact that he was doing these things with another woman or the fact that there was another woman.

The shock on his face when he saw Nina standing there holding the basket of lunch was pure horror. As if someone had rammed a sickle through his heart. At the office was more than likely the last place he ever expected to see his wife. Francesca had told her to add some spice to her life. Even Nina knew that this was hardly what she meant.

"Can you ask her to call me, Troi? This is my third time calling and I mean, I know she's there."

"You're right, Tim, and I'll tell her."

Tim placed the receiver in the cradle and pounded his fist on the table.

As if he didn't have enough to worry about. Now here his wife was thinking she saw something but didn't actually see what she thought she saw.

Tim had no desire to touch a strand of hair on Michelle's silly head. She had proved herself nutty years ago and he wasn't trying to relive that whole episode with her. He wanted absolutely nothing from that woman except for maybe any assistance she could provide with him getting distribution for his films, but he wasn't about to forfeit his marriage for it. Her offer was bait, for sure, but how did he get what he needed to better his life with Nina without becoming intimate with this woman? Bluff, deceive, and swindle. It was certainly a start.

Michelle had sauntered into his office unannounced and forgone the "Guess what I'm not wearing" soliloquy, then crawled up on top of his lap ignoring his struggle and his persistent command for her to leave.

"You know you want me. Just like old times." She kissed his neck, smearing red lipstick on his collar and wrestling with him.

"Look, Michelle. I'm married."

"Yeah, I saw her. A man like you shouldn't have to settle." She pointed at him with her finger.

Nina had come into his office redecorating it with the contents of the basket she was carrying. By the time Tim reached their home, Nina had already rifled through the drawers, left a note, and was gone. He knew she'd gone back to New York because New York was the only place she felt truly safe. She said it often enough and even though she always accused him of not listening to her, he had heard that statement and filed it away in the back of his mind.

Francesca pretended not to know Nina's whereabouts, which was fine because it gave him ample opportunity to set a plan in motion.

His partner told him he was being foolish even contemplating Michelle.

"She's fire," Reese said.

"I know what I'm doing," Tim assured him. "If I finagle this right, all of our work will not have been in vain. I won't see this project killed."

"Yeah. I just hope you know what you're doing."

Tim knocked around the house and tried to figure out which approach would work best. He hated playing his old games. He had found a good woman and didn't want to blow that.

"My wife left me." Tim sat on the sofa and grinned into the receiver.

"Poor baby. What can I do?" Michelle ate it up like melted ice cream.

"I don't know, what can you do?"

"You must be hungry. Especially with no one to prepare you a home-cooked meal."

"Kind of."

"You can swing by here and I'll whip you something up," she cooed.

Her legs weren't the first thing he saw when he entered her place.

It hardly took any convincing at all before he was sitting in her hotel suite and she was calling down to order up room service.

"You think you can handle me?" Michelle smiled coyly.

Tim glanced around the suite and gave her a look that said, "What do you think?"

"What's wrong with you? You missing your wife or something?" Michelle frowned. "I can take your mind off of that if you are."

"I can't lie. I do, but I'll get over it. I don't think I was ready for marriage. The only thing is that now she'll probably get half of everything I own and that'll leave me with little or nothing unless I get my film distributed." He rubbed his chin.

"Stop worrying about film. Think about something else. Think about me." She sat on his lap. "I told you that I can help you with that. If I give them the go-ahead they'll pass your film right through and acquire it for distribution. People owe me favors. One hand washes the other in this business."

"There's nothing I like more than a powerful woman. A woman who can pull some strings." He flattered her.

Michelle grinned, tossing her hair out of her face, taking the bait.

Shopping made Nina feel better so that was what she had done. Browsed through the used furniture shops along Atlantic Avenue in Brooklyn like she always did. Like she used to do when she lived here. She didn't know what her next step would be, maybe one of those personal ads that Tim said his sister always had him browsing through.

Explore the possibilities. Witty, versatile, stylish, nice, fit, feminine, cute DBF loves music, travel, outdoors, roses, and movies, seeks handsome, considerate, honest, nonsmoking SBM. Drug-free, please.

Maybe she wasn't fit. To run a personal ad like that would be outrageous but Nina thought, *Whose life isn't an exaggeration?* An amalgamation in their minds of the things they desire to be in real life.

Between clients, Nina sat around eating tuna and crackers with her sister. Her mind tossed around the idea of occupying her sister's spare bedroom for an extended period of time since her marriage showed no signs of working out. Anything so she didn't have to think about what Tim had done.

Troi was putting the labels on her jars and unscrewing the caps.

"You know what I'm tired of?" Nina said.

Troi raised her eyebrow and glanced over at her sister.

"I'm tired of people saying that sisters don't allow this and sisters don't allow that when it comes to men. We aren't superhuman. Some of us let men walk all over us and some of us don't. Black is just the skin I'm in but the footprints all over me are the telltale signs of what Tim has done to me."

"Girl, don't do that."

"Do what?"

"Dog him like that. I'm telling you, it was all a misunderstanding. Remember when you two first got together? You came running into the kitchen and couldn't wait to tell me how happy you were. You've gotta think back on those things. Don't focus on the negative. You'll never get through it like that."

"I'm not thinking about getting through it. I'm thinking about living my life. I've been alone before so I'm fine with that."

"It's really not about being alone. It's about trusting. Before you walked into the office, how did you feel about Tim?"

"I loved him."

"Did you think he loved you?"

"Yes. I know he did. I can normally read what he's feeling."

"So what do you think now? You think all of that feeling is gone?"

"No, it's not just that. It's just—"

"You're doubting yourself again, right?"

"I guess."

"And you're comparing yourself to that other woman. And you're wondering what he's doing and whether or not he's with her since you're here in New York thousands of miles away."

"Yeah. I guess I am."

"So why don't you talk to him? You know he has some things to say. Listen. Listening to someone doesn't mean you agree. Just hear him out."

"Girl, you know too much." Nina nudged her sister. "I'm the big sister and I should be telling you that."

"It doesn't matter who shares the information as long as you get it." Troi nodded.

"I really love him, Troi."

"You think I don't know that? You're smiling and you're here but you're miserable!"

"Is it that obvious?"

"Call him."

"I will." Nina inhaled deeply.

What am I gonna say to him?

Nina dialed the number nervously. The phone rang and she bit her bottom lip, just listening for him to pick up. It was the first time hearing his voice since she had left California and it made her edgy. He picked up the phone and his deep "Hello" sent panic through her and made her instinctively hang up the phone.

"What's wrong?" Troi asked, looking at her sister.

"Nothing." Nina rubbed her hands together.

"You hung up on him, didn't you?" Troi put her hand on her hip.

"Yeah."

"You know you're too old for games."

"Well, what do you do when you're just so mad at the other person that you want to burst?"

"You forgive him, Nina. Just forgive."

"More Troi philosophy."

"No, just more truth," Troi said. "It will make you free."

18

Carla and Sam

The noisy group of kids filed out of the classroom like a swarm of bees. They left a trail of crumpled loose-leaf paper and bubble gum wrappers on the seats and in the desks.

Carla stacked the pile of tests neatly in the center of her desk and looked up to see Dakoda at the back of the class hugging her book bag.

"Dakoda? Are you okay?" Carla put the number-two pencils back into the utility cabinet.

"Yes."

"You don't sound okay. Come here."

Dakoda had always been too emotional for her own good. She was sniffling back tears already.

"Tell me what's wrong. You can talk to me, you know."

"Are you and Uncle Sam getting a divorce?" Her wide eyes looked up at Carla.

"What makes you ask a question like that?"

"Because last night I couldn't sleep and when I woke up early this morning, Uncle Sam was sleeping on the couch downstairs."

"Where was your mother?"

"I dunno. Someplace."

"No, we're not getting divorced, sugar. Now run along to your next class and don't worry about that. We'll be fine. Okay?"

"Okay." Dakoda moved listlessly out of the room.

Carla's lips tightened at the corners. She wanted so badly to barge right up into Sam's fantasies and arrest his mind and then turn around and dust every street in Brooklyn with Troi, who had been masquerading as her best friend for all these years. But she had several stops to make before she could finally confront him. A stop that would help her keep her job, put an end to all of the secrets finally, and another stop that would reclaim what was hers, for good.

He stood waiting on the corner like he always did. Leaning against a peeling red fire alarm box. His plaid shirt never tucked in his pants, old sneakers that had seen better days.

Carla walked past him discreetly and he in turn followed her into his building. That was the routine.

"How's my little girl? I bet she's looking more and more like her daddy every day. Got her daddy's eyes, doesn't she?" he asked proudly.

"Actually, she looks like me." Carla rolled her eyes.

"You got it." He leaned over and whispered in her ear as she walked up the steps to the building.

"What did I tell you?" Carla's frown was cutting deeply into her face.

"Feisty girl." He nudged her into the building.

"This is it." Carla threw two twenty-dollar bills and a ten at him and watched them spin to the floor.

"I say when this is it!" He put his finger in her face. "And I say it's not it, pretty black girl."

"Look, what do you want from me?"

"I haven't decided yet." He grimaced.

Carla looked up toward the ceiling in the hallway. She knew the neighbors must've known what was going on by now. Every week there she was standing in the hall, looking suspicious, as if she were making a drug transaction.

"Can I go now?" Carla sighed heavily.

"Not yet." He ran his hands down over her hips and squeezed her firm flesh by the handful. His erection pressing into her, unwanted, yet persistent.

"How do you know I won't tell Sam about you and everything that you're doing?" She glared at him with the hate consuming her.

"Because you want the fairy tale." He smirked.

She took a deep breath and exhaled slowly. He was right. She did want the fairy tale, and right now the truth was something that could possibly upset all of that.

"Why don't you come upstairs? Let's pretend you don't have the money for me this week." He smirked.

"I can't do that." Her eyes watered.

"For old times' sake." He slid his hands up her skirt. "You used to love when I did this to you. Remember?"

"No." Carla shook her head, tears falling away from her face.

"I've got your secret hidden safely in here." He pointed to his head. "I trust you'll do the right thing so that it stays there."

Carla knew when she was beat. She conceded and did what she had to do to keep her life that honestly hadn't felt like a fairy tale in a long while.

He followed Carla up the stairs. She knew the way. When things like Ashley's birthday and her and Sam's wedding anniversary tapped in to her funds and she didn't have the money to give him to keep his mouth shut, she always ended up making exchanges. Exchanges of favors that left her feeling dirty like raw sewage. A stink that she couldn't scrub off hard enough.

Inside the apartment that she knew better than she ever needed to, she glanced around. Sofa bed pulled out. Anticipating her arrival. Sheets wrinkled like someone else had slept there moments ago.

He pushed her down on the bed and wasted no time discarding his clothing. It wasn't a seduction and she knew that. She just wished that she had more faith in her husband. Faith enough to know that he wouldn't leave her if he ever found out her secret. Then there would be no need for her to be here. Giving this man money, sex, and oral favors.

She didn't budge as he came toward her and put his filthy hands on her.

He lifted up her skirt, took down her panties, and pulled her legs apart, satisfying himself and pressing her face into his dirty sheets the entire time.

When he was done she lay there unable to move, think, or cry. He walked to the freezer, pulled it open, and tossed a frozen TV dinner on the counter. Slowly and numbly she became aware of her surroundings again and pulled her clothes on and straightened herself up. Her dirty little secret not so well hidden anymore.

"I had a really good time, Carla," he said. "Next time I'll clean up the place for you." He grinned.

She didn't find the humor in it.

As nasty as she felt, she had a meeting to attend; then she would go home and tell Sam the truth. There would be no next time as far as she was concerned.

* * *

Carla made it to her meeting fifteen minutes after it had started. The women sat around in a semicircle. Two of them huddled together on the other side of the room. Whispering. Probably about her.

Are you and Uncle Sam getting a divorce? kept resounding in Carla's head. She wished he could tell these women about herself. She believed it would make her feel better if nothing else. It might make her feel like she had a support system. Someone to catch her when she fell, and she would fall, eventually.

She sat in her chair mentally sorting out her own thoughts. She wanted to get everything out in the open. She wanted the burden off of her chest.

I cheated on my husband. Only thing is that he wasn't my husband when I cheated on him, he was my fiancé. The guy I cheated on him with wanted more than heavy petting and forced himself on me, and my fiancé, he married me anyway. We got married and I've hidden a terrible secret ever since.

The same woman from several weeks ago started with the same thing about having no money to put on a good show for her husband's family. Carla was cold, hungry, and couldn't concentrate.

"Do you have anything you want to share?" the faciliator asked Carla.

Are you and Uncle Sam getting a divorce? Are you? Are you?

She tried not to imagine Troi and Sam together. Spending the nights and stealing moments that were hers. Carla snatched up her things without a word and bounded out the door with anger burning in the deep recesses of her heart. Troi would not win Sam without a fight. She'd make sure of that.

"What are you doing here?" Troi asked.

"I can't come visit a *friend?*" Carla asked, pushing her way in.

"I'm not saying that."

"Maybe you're expecting someone else this time of night?"

"No, that's not it either, I—"

"You think I don't know what you've been up to?" Carla rested her hand on her hip and backed Troi into the bookcase. "He's been sneaking up in here night after night and you, you're supposed to be my friend and you're trying so desperately to steal my husband."

"That's a lie!"

"So he hasn't been here?"

"Yeah, but not for me. We were talking about you." Troi shook her head.

"Really, now?"

"Yes. I wouldn't lie about that."

"Was that before or after he warmed your bed last night?"

"I don't know what's wrong with you but I care about you, Carla. I would never do that. You've got to know that."

"Nobody cares about me. You want my husband to fill the void you've had aching inside you for years, and since I'm not willing, he'll gladly do it."

"How can you say that? We're friends." Troi was in total disbelief.

"There is no such thing as a friend. Just people who wait around in your life for the opportunity to take advantage of you."

"Let's sit down and talk. This is getting blown way out of proportion, Carla."

"Don't be mistaken, Troi, this is not a social call. Stay away from Sam!"

Nina walked in the door with an antique lamp in her fist and a lamp shade in the other.

"Hey, Carla," Nina said.

"Hi." Carla spoke dryly.

Nina looked from Troi's face back to Carla's face.

"What's going on here?"

Troi looked away.

Carla looked up to the top of the stairs and shook her head as Dakoda sat crouched with her face buried in her hands.

"What kind of example are you setting for you daughter?" Carla spat.

"You leave Dakoda out of it!"

"Just remember what I said, Troi, stay away from him!" Carla stormed out the front door, intent on setting things straight at home the moment she got there.

19

Troi

Last night was unreal. Someone she thought she knew changing before her eyes like a chameleon. Troi was trying to pull her own life together, help her sister reconcile with Tim, and assist Sam with the arduous task of understanding his wife. After Carla's impromptu visit any thought of what she and Sam felt for each other fizzled and seeing him with Shelby draped around his neck hammered the final nail in that coffin. She was done with him.

Right after Carla stormed out the door hurling all types of accusations, Nina consoled Dakoda and the phone rang and it was Sam.

"Sam, I definitely can not do this now—" Troi said and slammed down the phone.

Troi didn't dare tell him that Carla had been there at her place accusing them both of conspiring to have an affair together.

Carla hadn't smiled or exuded any amount of affection on her visit. She just said what she needed to say, leaving their friendship in shreds.

Troi had an appointment this morning to meet with someone from the department store. She was still feeling a little frazzled but they said they would look at her hair product, no promises, but it was a start. Nina said that she would come along for moral support but Troi didn't like the way her sister was reweaving herself into the fabric of the city as if she were back for good.

Troi didn't know what was going on with Dakoda either. Was she missing her father that badly or just going through that teenage privacy phase? She had been shaken up last night with Carla making a scene. She'd try to calm her down by sitting with her and having a heart-to-heart tonight.

Troi put herself out of her misery; she turned her music on low and allowed the rhythm to soothe her. She even thought that after Vaughn's death, his parents would have played a more important part in her and Dakoda's life, but what Troi and Dakoda did for the Singletons was provide a constant visual reminder of the son they no longer had. So Dakoda had no grandparents on either side that were a constant presence in her life. Troi didn't get how people underestimated the power of family. She had to shake these thoughts. They weren't good for her. They were taking her focus off of business.

Troi was neatly pressed in her navy skirt suit that she had worn to church a few times and once for an oral presentation for class. She paced in front of the glass counter in the department store and purposely ignored the exorbitant prices on the pastel sunshades. She stepped aside as two girlfriends tried on shades with pink, blue, and yellow lenses.

"Mrs. Singleton?"

"Yes."

"Come with me." The manager ushered her away from the clothing racks back to his office.

Troi placed a jar on his desk and watched as he slid his glasses farther down his nose and examined the product. He held the jar at arm's length, turned it sideways, raised it up to the light, and rested it back down on the desk.

"I'm not sure that your product is right for our shop."

"You haven't even given it a chance."

"What experience do you have in sales, Mrs. Singleton?"

"I took business courses at the local university."

"But that's education, not experience."

"I ran a beauty salon for several years."

"A beauty shop? What was the nature of your business."

"Hair."

"Mrs. Singleton," he said, smirking, "a hair shop hardly—"

"It was a salon, not a hair shop, but if you feel my product isn't right, I'd rather not spend my afternoon trying to convince you otherwise."

Troi pushed her product back into her case and headed out of his office. He didn't come after her.

"Mrs. Singleton?" The secretary walked out into the hall. "It's politics. Please don't take it personally."

"How can I not take it personally?"

"You want to know what I'd do?" the young black girl whispered.

Troi was somewhat interested.

"Come with me," the woman instructed.

They wove their way through the cosmetic counters and tables. "How many jars do you have?"

"Ten."

"Perfect."

The secretary lined up four jars side by side and placed three jars on top of the four and two more on top of the three like a pyramid.

"Business cards?" she asked.

"I only have a few," Troi confessed and handed her the short stack. "I thought he said it wasn't right for the store?"

"Listen to me. What I've learned is that you have to create demand. That's all they understand. How many jars do you have left?"

"One."

"Okay. Take it to that counter"—she pointed—"and pay the lady at the cashier."

"You want me to buy my own product?"

"It works every time." She smiled.

"Not that I don't appreciate it, but why are you helping me?"

"If you saw how they marked up everything three hundred percent, you'd feel compelled to help a struggling entrepreneur too," she said, humoring her. "C'mon, follow my lead."

Troi stood behind the woman who was next in line.

"I heard all the celebrities use that in their hair." The secretary stood off to the side speaking directly to Troi.

Troi's eyes got wide and she almost bubbled over with laughter.

"I swear by this stuff," Troi said. "This is the only place I can find it."

"I know," the secretary said. "And if you don't get here as soon as the product arrives—you're out of luck."

"What's the name of it?" The two girls who were trying on the shades came up behind her, each with a pair of overpriced items in her hand.

"Hair Joy." Troi smiled.

"Mary, Janet, Jada. They live on this stuff."

"Get out!" The friends looked at each other.

"They have it shipped directly to their home." The secretary urged them on. "It's right over there. Only nine jars left."

The woman in front of Troi glanced at the product that was creating such a fuss.

"Next?"

Troi moved up in the line and the cashier examined the product for a bar code. The sticker price was $9.95.

"Where are the salespeople responsible for marking new products?" she said out loud to herself. "There are no codes on these jars."

The cashier waved down a woman in a smock. "Can we get stickers for these?"

"What's the price?"

"Nine ninety-five."

"I'm going to give this woman here a generic receipt. Can you just label the rest?"

"Okay." The woman walked away.

The cashier bagged Troi's purchase.

"Thank you." Troi smiled and looked over her shoulder at the secretary, who was nowhere in sight.

Troi was cloud-nining all the way home. Maybe she could make the transition from service to full-fledged entrepreneur. The first order of business was to call up everyone who had ordered her product in the last thirty days and see if they needed to restock. Then she'd begin spreading the word that there was a new product in town.

When Troi reached home Nina was still dressed in her robe and whispering into the phone like a teenager. Had to be Tim on the other end. The first step to reconciliation finally. Troi was elated. There was hope for true love after all.

20

Nina and Tim

"Tim Richardson's office."

"Tim?"

"Nina?"

"Yeah."

"I've been trying to talk to you for a week now."

"I know. I just didn't feel like talking," she said.

"Nina, you've got to know that you mean more to me than anything walking around in heels."

"Didn't seem that way when . . ."

"When what? Say it."

"Listen, Troi just came in. I can't do this now."

"C'mon, Nina."

"Tim, the only thing you're concerned with is being a successful filmmaker. You couldn't care less about what you have to step over, on, or go around to achieve that."

"That's not fair."

"The hell it isn't."

"So I'm being punished now for wanting to be successful."

"What was she doing there in the first place, Tim? Answer that."

"There was nothing going on with Michelle. I can't stop her from going wherever she wants."

"Not even for your wife?"

"Nina—"

"No, Tim. Good-bye."

Nina didn't know why she had called him. Troi had encouraged her, but she had never been as forgiving as her sister and, given the circumstances, she probably never would be. She had never learned to fight for what she wanted. Anger had gotten the best of her. There was only one way to remedy this situation and she knew that. She had gotten over her fear of flying when she merged her life to Tim's. Flying was no longer an issue. At this point it was really the only solution.

Tim was tempted to call Nina back but he had to get home, shower, and meet Michelle at this function that she swore would change his career forever. Movers, shakers, backers, and financiers. Alliances he could forge that would get his film distributed, finally, and make him and his ideas more than just a flash in the pan.

After the tedious drive home in silence he arrived and looked around the house and realized that without Nina it no longer had that feeling that made him come home at night and know that he could unwind. There was no buzzing in the kitchen, Monet was moping about in the yard pacing in circles, and there was no one standing around him asking him how his day was.

Tim loved her. For the first time in his life he was going to see something through, and Nina's love was something he needed to feel with all of his senses.

She wasn't just another woman; she had changed him. Took him from lost to found and had only required love in return, but he had thrown in faithfulness for good measure. It's what he had seen his parents do. They loved each other until death did them part. As long as he had breath he'd seek Nina until she was right where she belonged, back with him again.

Even though Tim was supposed to escort Michelle to the function she had shown up at his front door like she had pondered the thought of one day soon inhabiting the place.

"Didn't I tell you I'd pick you up?" Tim frowned, answering the door.

"I just wanted to surprise you." Michelle smirked.

"I bet you did." He nodded.

Tim ushered her into the house so that Francesca wouldn't see and report back to command central . . . Nina.

Michelle thumbed her nose at the decor and was more than likely thinking she'd make major changes in and around his life with Nina's departure. She examined the photos on the sofa table.

"Can I get something to drink, sweetie? My mouth is dry."

She sat on the sofa. Tim was one step ahead of her. He took her arm and ushered her from the room.

"We don't have time." He slipped his jacket on and escorted her to the car before she could sit down and get comfortable.

He spent the entire ride with her hand on his thigh getting too familiar.

Tim couldn't say that he wasn't excited about rubbing elbows with the big boys. He knew that mingling with them would give him the capability of making his dream that much easier. Film made, sitting on the shelf. No distribution deal. No real money unless he was given the opportunity to prove that he knew what he was doing and that his work was good.

The only thing he hadn't anticipated was Michelle tugging on him all night.

"There's someone I want you to meet, Tim." She looked across the room and pulled him in that direction.

"What does he do?"

"He's done casting for major films at Paramount. Some casting at Warner Brothers for *Matrix Three* and he's assisting New Line with convincing the writer to pen a *Love Jones Two*. These are high-profile heads of companies that can make or break a film."

The face was familiar. Tim frowned trying to place him. Older white man. Bald. Like a flash it came. The night he and Nina had gone out on one of their first dates. The curator from the museum.

"Long time." Michelle kissed the man's cheek.

"And you look as stunning as ever. Is this the man who snagged my little tulip?"

"I'm working on that." Michelle glanced over at Tim. "This is Tim Richardson. He's a filmmaker."

"Hey there. You look familiar."

"I believe we met in New York. A gallery opening," Tim said.

"Perhaps."

"Impressive event." Tim smiled.

"Oh, it's not my function. I'm strictly an attendee."

"I'm going to get a drink, sweetie. Would you like anything?" Michelle rested her hand on his shoulder.

Tim shook his head no.

"What brings you to the West Coast?"

"Films."

"Writing, directing, casting . . ."

"All of the above. Seeking distribution now."

"I do know a few people who may be be able to assist you."

"Thank you." Tim gave him his card.

"Here's my card. I'll be back on the East Coast next week. We can do a conference call."

"I will." Tim grinned.

"What's a business contact unless you use it?" the man said and then blended into the rest of the crowd.

Tim looked at the card. He was holding his future in his hand. He had taken no thought to meeting him before; now here he was, at the crossroads of his life and he could very well make it. It had been his dream forever, to direct his own ideas for the passionate love of it. But did he want it at all costs? Did he want to leave Nina and all of their history behind for fame and the dull flicker of being well known? What was a dream without someone to share it with?

Tim walked onto the balcony in the home with the spacious interior.

"What's up, Tim?" Michelle came up behind him and pressed her cool drink to his neck.

He didn't flinch.

"I can't do this with you, Michelle." He moved her hand and the glass from his neck.

"Do what?"

"Be with you. Pretending."

"What are you talking about, Tim?"

"I love my wife. That's what I'm talking about."

"But she's not here." Michelle smirked.

"She's here." He pointed to his heart. "And nothing can replace that."

"So you'd rather be a flop? Because without my help that's what you'll be. That's exactly what it'll be."

"I'd rather be nothing with Nina than be something without her."

"Women are gonna be your downfall, Tim."

"They already have been, but dreams never die, Michelle. You don't have any so you wouldn't know that. Your dream is having me. That's as far as you can see."

"I'm the type of woman you need." She draped herself around his neck.

"Conniving, trifling, and materialistic? I don't think so. That will never happen." He threw her arms off of him.

"If I can't have you—"

He snatched her by the wrist. "Don't play games with me. I've had all kinds. Nina's the real thing. In your wildest dreams you couldn't fill her shoes."

"Tim . . . I'm just trying to help—"

"I'm not for sale!"

"You want me as much as I want you and it's gonna happen." She frowned.

"You are sillier than I ever imagined." He looked her over and walked away.

"Think I'm kidding? Just try me," she whispered.

Tim left the party and made his way to his car. He thought of something his momma had said years ago. She had told him, when he found the right woman and they had their disagreements, not to worry about who was wrong or right, just do whatever was within his power to keep her. One hundred and twenty-eight dollars in his pocket. Nina had the credit card, so with the clothes on his back and a burning desire in his heart there was only one option . . . Greyhound.

Michelle was sorry. Or at least that was what she would say. Anything that would right the wrong between her and Tim. Freshly done makeup, perfume sprayed behind her knees. She hadn't slept for the past two nights. Just sitting around waiting for that 2:00 A.M. "I miss you so come over" call. She had let an entire day go by without calling Tim. She wanted him to cool down. Give in. Forgive her. Move on and work his way around the roadblock that had presented itself in their lives. *Their lives.* That sounded so together to Michelle. She just hoped Tim would buy it.

At 7:00 A.M. she pulled up in front of Tim's place, put her car in park, made her way to the front door, and rang the doorbell. She tossed her hair out of her face and allowed a seriousness to cover her.

I'm sorry. I'm really sorry, Tim. Tim, please forgive me. Tim . . . I know you're upset but . . . Tim, I don't know what came over me the other night. I'm just so sorry. Can you ever forgive me?

Michelle was done rehearsing, and she rang the bell a second time. She pressed her lips together and listened to the door unlock and braced herself as she prepared to lay it on thick and make her acting debut with the grandest apology. She clasped her hands to-gether in front of her and waited to greet the man she knew she would marry eventually. A woman as together as she, there was no way he could resist. The door pulled open and before Michelle could readjust her thoughts, Nina stood in the doorway and spat each word at Michelle.

"What the *hell* are you doing here?"

21

Carla and Sam

"He's from South Dakota. Met her mom at the University of Michigan," his boss told him. "Stocks. I believe that's how he made his money. He wasn't born into it but he has it just the same."

Details, details, Sam thought.

His boss seemed rather inspired by the fact that he had taken up with this woman. He constantly reiterated her worth as if Sam needed reminding.

Shelby had been determined to spend her daddy's money, so with his boss's urging Sam had spent the entire morning showing the rich kid homes. She didn't like anything she saw. Too out of the way, too plain, too weird, and too inexpensive, cheesy, musky, chipping, peeling, eerie, or too avante-garde.

She offered to buy him lunch at an out-of-the-way Italian joint in Suffolk County, so he spent his entire day at her service, explaining molding and assessing the additional costs of installing a skylight in the master bathroom of one of the homes that she was seriously considering. By home number six and a filling lunch of rigatoni pasta and red wine, Sam wasn't feeling shy and she was relishing his constant company. So while opening cabinets and exposing the spaciousness of the kitchen, with a gas stove and convection oven, like a match being struck leaving a sulfuric residue, he accidentally brushed against her and ignited her fire.

Her eyes locked on to his and with her lips slightly parted, she said, "There's nobody here but us."

Nervousness crept over him and her wanton way took flight and gave him the much-sought-after pleasure of feeling desired again.

Her hands roamed all over his masculine body, touching him in places where he didn't realize he still had feeling. He willingly went into her heat.

On the oven range with the exhaust fan going and his belt still in his pants jingling around his ankles, his thirst for his wife was quenched by a five-eight statuesque rich girl who had come prepared with easy-access clothing and enough money to give him a nice commission on anything she decided to buy. Her legs dangling and her flesh willing, he tickled her fancy and said things to her that he'd never say to his wife or any woman he respected. They made their way from the kitchen to the center of the home's living room. Parquet floors, no carpeting, a sexual release that went in with such a mouthwatering anticipation but pulled out with much regret.

No sooner was he back in the office to lock up for the evening than came the avalanche of guilt.

She's not your wife. Carla didn't deserve that. You have a child. How will you explain this? Your wife isn't well. Patience, you need to be more patient with Carla. Two wrongs don't make it right. Shelby will end your marriage.

Then a coworker hanging around the office late came with the disturbing message.

"There's been an emergency at your daughter's school. They called about an hour ago. I tried to call you on your cell phone but you must have it turned off. You need to get over there right away. They can't reach your wife," the receptionist said.

Sam bounded out the door and headed over to Mount Sinai on the east side, believing that if he hadn't been with that woman all afternoon, his child would be fine right now. This was his punishment. His child's life for the seconds it took to satiate his dry spell. What goes around, comes around certainly but doesn't always land in the lap of the doer of the dirty deed.

Doctors huddled in the hall, dotting his arrival with suspicion as they stood with medical records tucked under their arms and an X ray being held up to the light.

"Ashley Singleton . . . is she okay? What room is she in?" Sam barged up to the nurses' station.

"Mr. Singleton, the doctors are in with her now. You need to fill out these insurance forms."

"I want to see my child right now!"

"We need these forms, sir—"

"My child is in there probably dying, and you want paperwork?"

Sam pulled his wallet out of his pocket and littered the nurses' station with dollar bills.

"Here! Take all my money . . . you can have it!"

"Calm down, Mr. Singleton."

Hospital triage and a lengthy registration process later, the doctor spoke over his shoulder and said, "You may need to give blood, Mr. Singleton."

"I want to see my daughter."

Sam handed the woman the forms and the doctor ushered him down the hall to the elevators and they took the elevator up to the intensive care unit and down to the private room.

"Is she gonna be okay?" He stood outside of her room, blinking and trying not to show emotion.

"She needs blood. That's the best thing you can do for her right now."

"Well, what happened?"

"She punctured her spleen."

"Is it that serious? I mean . . ."

"It's serious enough."

Sam pressed the palm of his hand on the door and entered the room with the doctor. He observed as the nurse hovered over Ashley tending to the monitors and the machines they had her hooked up to.

The sun was setting and peeking through the window off in the corner of the room, daring to be a beautiful day. Carla was still nowhere to be found.

"Can I be alone with her for a minute?"

The doctor nodded. "The sooner we get her the blood, the sooner we can reevaluate her prognosis."

"I'll be back, sweetie." Sam leaned over and kissed Ashley on her expressionless face.

Sam went down to the lab. He sat in the chair with his shirt cuff unbuttoned and rolled up his sleeve. The plebotomist was methodical in drawing the blood. Sam was more in a hurry to get back to his daughter's bedside. He wanted to watch over her. Be her protector. He wouldn't leave her until he knew she'd be okay. If that meant sleeping hunched over in a visitor's chair all night, so be it.

That's exactly what he did. Sam tried to take a thin hospital blanket and recline the chair, make himself comfortable, and ignore the beeping of the machines. He was thinking to himself that Ashley just had to be all right. Sam hadn't drifted off to sleep yet when the door creaked open.

"Everything okay, Doc?" Sam squinted in the light that peered in from the hall.

"We couldn't use your blood." The doctor spoke lowly. "I have her medical record in the hall."

Sam flung the blanket off of him and joined the physician outside Ashley's room.

"You couldn't use my blood. What does that mean exactly?"

"Her blood type is AB positive and your blood type is O."

"Yeah. I've always been O. So what are you saying?"

"What I'm saying, Mr. Singleton, is that with her having AB blood, there is no way that you can be her father."

"What?"

"She's not your daughter."

"There's got to be some mistake . . . I mean . . ."

"I'm sorry but there's no mistake. Blood is as accurate as you can get. DNA will reveal the same thing, I'm afraid."

"Can we do the DNA anyway?"

"It will take approximately forty-eight hours. If you want, we can do that," the doctor consoled.

"You know how mix-ups happen. Tubes get switched. That sort of thing." Sam tried to be optimistic.

"I understand," the doctor said. "I'll get the paperwork. We'll need another sample, of course."

"That's fine." Sam nodded.

The hurt left Sam's face and was quickly replaced with anger, but the tears stayed, making their way down his cheeks.

Hospital. Blood work. Not your daughter.

Sam sat and watched his blood leaving his arm. Knowing that this time its results would change everything. It would be the determining factor on whether he stayed with or left his wife. It would determine what kind of foundation their love was ever built on.

"She's stable." The doctor appeared behind him. "You can go home and get some rest if you want. There's a forty-eight-hour waiting period for the DNA results. We'll give you a call."

Sam convinced himself to go home and grab a few hours of shut-eye, then head back over to the hospital later in the afternoon. He was no good to anyone on overload and barely being able to pull his thoughts together, so he pulled out of the hospital parking lot at almost three in the morning and headed home.

Carla sat in the chair in the corner of their home growing more anxious with the rising sun. She heard his keys in the door but before

Sam could come inside and close the door behind him, she lunged at him from across the room like a madwoman.

"Where were you last night and where is our daughter?" Carla shouted, clawing at him hysterically.

Sam determined to offer up information on a need-to-know basis. He pulled her off of him and stormed into the bedroom, pulled out his overnight bag from under the bed, and tossed a couple of days' worth of clothing into the bag.

"Where are you going?"

Sam zipped the bag shut and headed for the door.

Carla's tears coated every word now.

"You can't just walk out on me! Tell me something! I'm your wife, for God's sake!"

Sam looked Carla in the eyes and held on firmly to the bag.

"Where is Ashley?" She fought to calm down.

"She's in the hospital."

"Hospital?"

"Everyone tried reaching you yesterday. School. Doctor. Me. But you were nowhere to be found."

"What hospital?"

"What do you care?" His lips curled up at the corner.

"She's my daughter. Of course I care."

"Mount Sinai. . . ."

"I've got to get there. She needs me and—"

"Carla . . . I want a divorce."

22

Troi

"I'm not particularly concerned with the fact that you fabricated your feelings for me or that woman you're chauffeuring around town. You have torn apart my best friend's life and used me and everybody else in the process to do it. So just tell me one thing . . . why are you here now?" Troi glared at Sam standing at her door with a bag in one hand and a sorrowful look on his brow.

"My world is falling apart. I just found out . . ."

"Found out what?" Her hand rested defiantly on her hip.

"I just need someone to talk me through this."

"Talk you through what?" She was looking at Sam as if he were crazy.

Concern always did get the better of Troi.

"Ashley had an accident in school. I'm coming from Mount Sinai Hospital now."

"Is everything okay?" Her eyes softened.

"She was unconscious and had lost some blood. They're running tests now."

"How did it happen?"

"Who knows? But I've been trying to reach Carla all yesterday afternoon and evening."

"Well, I know she was out of it. And she—"

"Ashley's not my daughter, Troi."

"What? What do you mean she's not your daughter?"

"I thought she was. The doctor said her blood is AB and mine is O. My wife is out with other men at night. I don't know how I'm supposed to stay faithful to her with all of that. There's only so much a man can take. I love her but I'm human, you know."

"Sam, you are not happy with Carla but I can't be that for you. I won't. You have to work it out."

"She's not my wife, Troi! Wives don't lie to their husbands. Wives don't let other men father their child and keep it a secret for years."

"I understand that, Sam. I honestly do, but talk to her. Tell her how you feel but don't let it eat away at you."

"I don't even want to look at her right now. She disgusts me."

"Oh, so now the thought of your own wife disgusts you, but being seen with Shelby doesn't disgust you?"

"I can explain, Troi—"

"Don't explain anything to me. I'm not your wife, so you can dissolve that notion." Troi folded her arms across her chest. "But the thing is that Carla came by here last night asking me if I was having an affair with you. She asked me if you had been coming by here. You know I wasn't going to lie. So she's feeling pretty bad now too. You're not the only one."

"I need to get out of here."

"Where are you going?"

"To the hospital. Ashley is still my number-one priority, whether I'm really her father or not."

Troi watched Sam hurry out the door. She couldn't believe everything that was going on.

She was the martyr of the family. She had always been. Single mom, lost her husband, assisting her sister and Tim in their marriage as well as trying to understand her best friend and the woman her friend's husband was cheating on her with while trying not to fall in love with him in the process.

She threw on something quickly. She wanted to go by the hospital too and see Ashley. She hated when adults put children in the middle and that was exactly what it appeared would happen with Sam and Carla. All that Troi could think was that this accident was timed to bring the entire situation to a head.

"Ashley Singleton's room?"

"Family only," the nurse informed Troi.

"I am family."

Troi waited as the man behind the information desk handed her an orange laminated visitor's pass and directed her to the express elevators.

Troi followed the signs once she was off the elevator. She paused

at the nurses' station and waited for some information so she'd
know what to expect.

"How is the patient in room six B-three?" Troi glanced at the
pass.

"She's stable. Doing much better."

"What happened exactly?"

"She got pinned up in one of those old amusement park rides.
Took a bad gash. Lost some blood. Stitched her up nicely. It didn't
help that she was anemic. You can go right in though."

"Thank you." Troi smiled and crossed the hall, then pressed into
the room.

Carla's eyes met Troi's.

"I didn't know you were in here. I'll just go," Troi apologized

"It's okay," Carla said softly and reached for a tissue.

"She's gonna be okay. She's in my prayers." Troi smiled.

Troi made all attempts to comfort Carla.

"I know she will. But Sam and I won't be the same."

"You'll work it out."

"He wants a divorce. It's destroyed. Everything ruined. The marriage is over."

"I hope you're not still thinking that it's because of me or that I—"

"No. I know. Some spoiled rich girl he's been spending his afternoons showing homes to. And more than that too probably."

"How'd you know?"

"The receptionist and I are friendlier than Sam knows."

"How's Ashley?" Troi glanced at the peacefully sleeping child.

"She's doing better. I just don't know what I'm gonna do without
Sam. He tried giving blood and—"

"And what?"

"He's not her father, Troi. I've known that from the beginning."

"Who—"

"I promise I'll tell you but I need to talk with Sam first. I'll stop by
your place tonight."

"I have rehearsal until about nine."

"That's no problem. I appreciate that you're here. Thanks for
coming."

"You know I'm always there for you." Troi embraced Carla
warmly, then left her to comprehend the moment as it was.

Troi arrived home to find Tim sitting on her front steps.

"Tim?"

"Troi, sorry just to show up like this, but Nina wasn't being rational." He stood up. "She hung up the phone on me so I decided just to show up here. I love her. You know that. We've been through enough. I just want to put an end to all this confusion."

"I understand that, but she's not here, Tim. She left two days ago, back to California to make up with you."

"She left?"

"She went back to Cali to make up with you. To fight for you."

"Why didn't she call me?" He frowned.

"I don't know, Tim." Troi shook her head.

Tim's disappointment was mixed with a little frustration. "Can I come in and use your phone?"

"Sure." Troi nodded.

"Hey, Ma." Dakoda walked through the door just as Troi was about to shut it.

"It's three-thirty already?" She glanced at the clock.

Her little girl was not so little. Growing up daily, but now was much quieter than usual.

"What's wrong, Dakoda?"

"Nothing."

"You sure?"

"I dunno."

"You don't know?"

"I have to tell you something." She tried to be brave.

"What is it?"

"I don't want you to be mad at me." She looked to the floor.

"I may not be mad, tell me."

Dakoda sank down into the chair and dropped her book bag between her feet. "I'm the one who told Miss Carla that Uncle Sam was here."

Troi nodded and hugged her daughter. "It's okay. . . . Sam and I did nothing wrong. I'm not mad, I'm really not."

"I heard you and Miss Carla fighting and I knew it was all my fault. If I hadn't told . . . then . . ."

"Don't you worry about that. We'll do just fine. Okay?" Troi rubbed her daughter's shoulders and looked in her face.

Dakoda nodded.

Tim walked back into the room.

"I'm gonna head out," he said, resting the phone down on the receiver on the table. The phone rang again. "She said she'll leave me a ticket at the airline ticket counter." He rubbed his forehead.

"Okay." Troi stood with her hands on her hips. "You two be good to each other."

"We will be." He hugged her.

"Ma?" Dakoda held the phone away from her face. "It's a Mr. Somebody from the department store on the phone."

Troi held the phone to her ear and smiled as the standoffish department manager reluctantly placed his first trial order. He couldn't deny that her products had sold and after all it was about numbers. Money was all they understood. Troi watched out of the corner of her eye as Tim extended Dakoda's arms, spun her around, and chuckled at how big she had gotten, then kissed her forehead on his way out the door.

With the orders coming in now for her product, Tim and Nina reconciling, and Carla trying to sort through her life, Troi couldn't be sidetracked by anybody, least of all Sam.

Dakoda came up behind Troi, hugged her, and volunteered to cook dinner. Fry some chicken, boil rice, heat up a can of corn. Something simple.

"Can you do my hair first, Ma?"

"I have to get ready for rehearsal, Dakoda."

"Please?"

"Get the comb and c'mon." Troi smirked.

Dakoda smiled, got the comb, snatched up a jar of Hair Joy, and tossed the sofa pillow on the floor and sat down Indian style between her momma's legs.

Troi hooked the comb through Dakoda's cornrows.

"Your hair is so thick, Dakoda."

"You have growing hands, Ma."

"Ain't no such thing, child. Either your hairstylist knows what your hair needs or she doesn't."

"So why do people say that then?"

"I dunno. People say a lot of things. That doesn't make it true."

Dakoda felt around her head to see what her momma was doing.

"You want to come with me to choir rehearsal?"

"I thought you wanted me to cook?"

"We can get some takeout afterward."

"Ma, can we just get a movie instead?"

Troi was by all technical definitions a stay-at-home mom, but being there sitting in a chair when Dakoda rushed in the front door from school, then went to do her homework up in her room was hardly quality time.

"Okay," Troi relented.

Dakoda nodded and smiled with the comb still in her hair, then ran across the room and pushed her feet in her sneakers, twisting them on.

They headed down the boulevard to the video rental place. Dusk had snuck up on them magically. Her neighbor's familiar dog sniffed around her feet.

"Ma, we should get a dog." Dakoda shook Troi's arm as she spoke.

"No dog, Dakoda."

Troi looked at the old man and smiled.

Inside the video store Troi picked out a sappy love story to watch long after Dakoda went to bed and she let her pick out something funny but not morally degrading to women. On the slow stroll home Dakoda asked one of the infamous questions.

"Ma, how do you know when you really like someone?"

"A boy someone?"

Dakoda looked at her mom bashfully. "Yeah."

Troi wanted to shake her just like her momma had done her. She wanted to tell her that she didn't have time for boys. Boys only want one thing and one thing only and once they get it they're gone. Sometimes they stay around for several months so they can keep on getting it, but in the end the same thing . . . gone. She wanted to tell her that books were her friends now. Get a book and read it. Dissect it. Reread it. Discover a world other than boys and hurt feelings. But she didn't.

Another part of her wanted to tell her girl that sometimes you'll marry wrong, date wrong, and then when you least expect it you'll discover a love that is forbidden, taboo, off limits, prohibited, out-lawed. A man that married your best friend. Then you'll discover another lesson. Heartache.

"You just know," Troi told her.

Dakoda motioned to the Chinese restaurant. Troi silently agreed. Anything beat cooking this late at night.

A quart of shrimp-fried rice and an egg roll later they sat on the floor in front of the television talking over the movie that had turned out to be boring and a total waste of money.

"Ma, that man from the department store that called, does that mean that you're gonna be rich?"

Troi smiled at her daughter's wishful thinking. "I hope so. If not rich, at least enough to put away for your college education. So who's this boy?" Troi tried not to seem overly interested in the answer.

"Just somebody. He told his friend to tell me that he likes me."

"So he didn't even have the nerve to tell you himself?"

"That's the way everybody does it. They don't want to make it seem like they're sweating you."

"Doesn't make sense to me." Troi shook her head. "So do you like him?"

"I guess." Dakoda shrugged.

"You don't have to like him just because he likes you, you know."

"I know." Dakoda smoothed down her hair.

"Just remember, you're not grown."

"I know that, Ma."

"And also remember that little boys are men in training."

"What does that mean?"

"It means that they want to play the game but they don't know all the rules yet, so as girls, or little women in training, you have the upper hand."

"Really?" Dakoda looked confused.

"Yes, really." Troi turned around when the doorbell rang.

"I'll get it," Dakoda said.

"You get ready for bed. I'll get it." Troi opened the door, and standing before her was Carla, eyes puffy, mascara running, hair twisted up all over her head, same clothes she had on the other day, just disheveled from head to toe.

"Hey, Carla. Come in, sis. I made coffee. Let's talk."

23

Nina and Tim

Tim was glad to be home. Back in his house. The chill in the early morning New York air made his bones ache. He preferred LA by a long shot. Santa ringing his bell in December wearing Bermuda shorts and a red and white coat in seventy-five-degree weather.

He was glad to have his feet on his carpet. His fridge, his dishes, his sanity all within his grasp again. A domesticated version of what he used to be, and he liked that. Domesticated by love. He was anxious to see his wife and wondered where she was and why she wasn't home, but he was just as eager to get into a steaming hot shower and let the water pulverize him. Brand-new showerhead, seven settings.

Right there in the living room Tim did it. He disrobed. He stepped out of his pants, boxers, and socks and quickly balled up everything and took it to the bedroom and stuffed it down into the hamper. He turned on the shower in the master bath and stepped inside its pleasure letting the reality of things soak in along with the water that was dousing his skin.

An hour. That's about how long Tim was in the shower. Soaping up and rinsing over several dozen times. His fingertips were wrinkled as well as his toes. The bath mat repelled water rather than absorbed it. He tossed a thirsty towel around his waist and made his way to the fridge to hydrate his insides as drops of water dangled from his lashes, and puddles of water pooled under his feet.

Tim looked up to see Nina and Francesca walking in the door with a bag of groceries each.

"Thanks, Francesca."

"No problem," she responded.

Francesca's eyes met Tim's and looked him over. She placed the paper bag down on the table.

"I think I'll go now." She motioned to the door with her eyes. "If you need me . . ."

"Yes, I'll call," Nina said.

Tim smiled.

Nina rested her paper bag on the kitchen counter taking no thought to what she'd say to Tim, but she faced him and the words just tumbled right out of her mouth like a habit.

"I'm sorry, Tim, but—"

"I'm sorry too, Nina." He pulled her close and held her, taking in the sweet scent of her hair that curled against her neck, inhaling her femininity, fingering the cool fabric against her skin.

Nina pulled away and looked into Tim's eyes.

They kissed each other softly and gently, wanting to stay wrapped in the moment until their hearts beat in sync and all the doubts dissipated.

"What?" Tim's eyes got wide.

"Michelle was here yesterday morning." Nina twisted her mouth.

"What did she say?" Tim held the towel around his waist.

"I didn't let her say anything," Nina said calmly. "You didn't have this woman in our bed, did you, Tim?"

"How could you think that? Have I ever disrespected you like that?"

"She came here ringing the bell like she had gotten comfortable doing that. . . . Besides, that's not what she said."

"She's a liar and I'm your husband."

"And?"

"And what?"

"Just tell me it's not true, Tim. I need to hear you say the words. I mean . . . I'm tired of being afraid to say things to you. I shouldn't have to be afraid. I shouldn't be the one always apologizing like I did something wrong, so just tell me . . . I want to know . . . was she in our bed?"

"It's not true, Nina," Tim said calmly, unpacking the navel oranges from the paper bag one at a time, resting all ten of them in the glass bowl.

"What do you want from me?" Tim transferred them in the bowl to the kitchen table.

"Honesty, loyalty, and mutual respect," Nina said.

"I give you that, don't I?"

"Honestly . . . no." Nina eased onto the couch. "You weren't completely honest about Michelle, and while that episode in your office leaves me with several reasons to doubt your loyalty, I can say that I don't believe that you respect me at all."

"Of course I respect you." Tim emerged from the bedroom pulling on a pair of faded sweats and then shoving his head through a holey T-shirt.

He opened the back door and Monet bounded through the house leaping and lunging all over Tim and scrambling across the carpet.

"Down, boy. . . ."

"So why aren't you giving me your full attention now if you respect me so much? I'm trying to talk to you about something important," she said as she watched Tim pour a mound of dog food and send it tinkling into Monet's metal dish.

"I'm sorry, Nina. There's too much on my mind. Work, this film . . . lots of things."

"I guess I have to be a movie starlet to get your attention. I mean, you don't even notice me, Tim. Am I beautiful to you? Repulsive? What?"

"Nina . . ."

"I had a hard life, Tim, you know that. My mother is an alcoholic, my dad . . . well, let's just say my dad is not even worth discussing. Sometimes we don't know how detrimental to ourselves we are. You saved me, Tim, and I'm not afraid to admit it." She motioned to him. "Without you in my life, who knows where I'd be? Probably still feeling incapable of love, not feeling worthy."

Tim listened intently.

"You remember that night in the restaurant on our second date?"

"Yeah."

"Not the times you stood me up . . ."

"I know." He nodded his head.

"I sat there the whole time thinking, now what does he want with me? I went out of my way to look pretty for you. Turn your head. Make you notice me when inside, I didn't feel like any of those things I wanted you to see in me. I didn't feel sexy, beautiful, and I definitely didn't think I'd end up here with you, the ever-elusive prize, within my grasp."

"When I saw you that night, I forgot everything, Nina. You gave me a chance when I didn't know what I wanted. Didn't really know what love was. I still remember you sitting there holding your cup of coffee. Pink slinky dress, hair curly with little clips, and glitter across your shoulders. We had dinner in a Mexican restaurant, a movie, then the Staten Island ferry. It was a powerful night. You are a starlet to me, baby. Can't you see that?"

"I knew you were a player when I met you."

"I didn't run a game on you." Tim chuckled.

"You said, 'I like your shoes.' I mean, c'mon . . . and the wilted flowers." Nina opened her mouth and laughed out loud.

"I keep telling you they were supposed to be like that. Tulips or something. I was trying to be clever."

"Don't I know it."

"What can I say? You stole my heart."

"Pick another phrase," Nina said.

"You touched my soul. . . ."

"Another."

"You are the missing piece I've been looking for, Nina. You saved me too." He sat on the couch close to her. "Let's go outside, baby."

"Outside?"

"Yes, give me a minute." Tim rushed to the kitchen cabinets, pulled two wineglasses off the shelf, and held them between his fingers. He snatched up a bottle of white wine by the neck and motioned for Nina.

Nina followed Tim outside and stepped over the dog that was curled up on the grass and only raised its head to see who was passing. Tim sat in the lawn chair, held the bottle between his feet, and popped open the bottle of wine.

The sun was doing its thing setting on the horizon leaving streaming colors that defied description. Nina nudged her way between Tim's legs. They sipped wine quietly for a moment until the phone rang. Nina stirred to answer it.

"Let it ring," Tim said.

She was tempted to get up and answer it anyway but didn't want to budge and risk toppling them both over.

He put his attention back on Nina. "You know, you really mean more to me than I ever let on." He took another swallow of his wine.

"Why keep it a secret? If you feel it, say it." Nina smiled.

"Easy for you to say."

"I'm serious."

"I know. It's just that with you on that plane, gone, I couldn't spend the rest of my life believing that I lost you because of something so stupid."

"Tell me the truth, Tim. The truth about Michelle."

"I have no idea when or why she came into town. The last time I spoke with her was before we were married. I owed her some money and since I had some I wanted to do right by her. Next thing I know, there I am at my desk in my office and in she walks. The woman's got a screw loose."

"That she does. Just tell me again that you're not sleeping with her. My heart couldn't take it if you were."

"I'm not. That's the truth, but I did want to confess one thing though."

"Go ahead." Nina sipped her wine liberally.

"I considered using her to help advance the film, but I couldn't do it. I didn't want to risk everything we have, not for her. It was bad enough that you had left me, although I knew you were in New York, but she doesn't make me feel like you. She doesn't mean what you mean to me."

"Oh, yeah?" Nina grinned. "Prove it." She shoved him.

Tim rested his glass next to the chair. They sat face-to-face in total darkness now, making their way to their knees on the grass beneath them. Only the streetlights shone from the other side of the fence, leading the way to their pleasure for each other. Tim's hand was on her hip and with his other hand he removed the glass of wine from her hand and placed it on the unstable grass next to them.

"This is a new outfit, Tim," she cautioned.

"I'll buy you another one." He pressed his lips to hers.

Nina closed her eyes and allowed Tim to woo her as he always had. Nimble fingers and lips so deserving she gave him everything she had.

"I want you, Nina. . . ." Tim nudged his nose against her neck.

"I want you too, Tim." Nina shuddered as he undid the buttons on her blouse.

Nina slid over on her elbows. Tim disrobed as quickly as he could. He rested his sweats under Nina's head.

Tim decorated her body with kisses, taking detours in between. His passion was ripe, right here and right now, for his wife. A long time coming.

"I've missed you, Tim," Nina managed between pleasurable pants.

Nina grabbed his hips and pulled him close to her.

"I don't want to lose you," he said.

"I ain't going nowhere," Nina convinced him. "Just don't hurt me, Tim."

"Shhhh. Never that."

Nina rolled over onto her stomach. That was when she felt the first drops of rain. They rolled down between her shoulder blades, then sprinkled her on the back of her neck. She closed her eyes and took her time enjoying every drop until she was bathed in the satisfaction that both the rain and Tim had delivered that night.

24

Carla and Sam

Several days in the same clothing would not do. Carla had to freshen up. It was a must. She needed to do it to salvage her sanity, her pride, and her marriage.

Part of her was happy that the secret was out and exposed for what it was, so she didn't have to drag it around everywhere she went like a burden. The other part of her, however, was terrified by the uncertainty of a marriage that she needed so desperately.

Abandoned by parents, sure she had overcome that trauma, she'd pushed away the thoughts of having to fend for herself while her parents were chasing their highs. She almost convinced herself it hadn't happened. She swindled her mind into believing she hadn't lived in boarded-up buildings or slept on rooftops and spent half the night discovering places to find food that would make the average person regurgitate. That was then and this was now.

She put on a dress that she had back in the closet. Something Sam had bought her when he was always begging her to go out with him. It still had the tags on. She popped them off and dressed herself quickly. She tied a matching rayon scarf around her neck and knotted it. She looked just as she always had back when she and Sam began dating. Her dress was short and clinging. She checked herself in the mirror and then headed out of the house. She didn't want to be late.

"Hey." She pulled up a chair at the table in the restaurant.

Sam sat across from Carla in Hunan House. They both skimmed the menu. Carla sat nervously, hoping, praying, and making futile attempts to discern what was coming.

Sam tossed the menu in the center of the table.

"You want to order now?" she asked.

"It's over, Carla."

"Just like that?" She flinched at the sharp shooting pain his words carried.

"Yeah." He checked his watch and looked around impatiently.

"You don't even want to hear my side?" Her voice cracked.

"Everyone has a side, but does it really change anything?"

"Who is Shelby?" Carla lashed out.

"Who is Ashley's father?" Sam glared at her, making his point.

"Tit for tat? Is that what it's come to?"

"Don't start. I've stood by you, Carla. You know I have. I was here when no one else was. You told me about your mother and father and I loved you anyway. Married you, even though you cheated on me. I took care of you and a child that now I find out is not even mine. What do you expect me to do? Lie down so you can walk all over me some more? You're not—"

"Troi . . ."

"What?" He frowned.

"I'm not Troi. You've wanted her from the day you laid eyes on her. If she hadn't met your brother first, you would have assumed the position with her, I'm sure."

"This is not about Troi, it's about you and me." Sam lowered his voice as he waiter brought two glasses of water to their table.

"Yes, it is about her. She has it *so* together. I'm sorry I can't be as together as Troi."

"What happened to you?" He shook his head. "You used to be so loving. Cared about people. Now you're a cold, dead fish. You don't even look at your own child. Do you even love her?"

"Don't you give me that! You have no idea what that man did to me." She pointed in his face.

"You changed after the breakdown."

"The breakdown was because he raped me, Sam. He forced me to—"

The waiter reappeared and Sam motioned for a few more minutes.

Carla gritted her teeth. "You have no idea what he did. You weren't there. He took what he wanted and when that wasn't enough he demanded money and sexual favors not to tell you."

"Why didn't you come to me in the first place?"

"I was afraid of losing you. Everything I love I lose. Can you understand that? Have you ever lost anything you cared about?"

"My brother. I loved him more than anything and instead of being jealous of Troi you should get a grip and empathize with her. She needs a friend, not an acussor. She's been through enough."

"You think I don't know that?"

"You don't act like you know. Barging up into the woman's house acting like a maniac. No decent woman acts like that."

"So I'm not decent?"

"I have one question." Sam fiddled with a fortune cookie pulling it out of the wrapper and breaking it open with his thumbs. "Did you know about Ashley not being mine before or after she was born?"

"Sam, I—"

"Before or after, Carla?"

"I knew before." She took note of his facial expressions. "But let me explain . . ."

Sam dragged his chair away from the table, stood up, and spoke directly into Carla's face. "Come and get your things. I want everything you own out of my house by this weekend."

"That's only gives me one day."

"That's one day too long." The scowl on his face told her that he wasn't budging on the matter.

"Where am I supposed to go?" Her hands pleaded.

"I'm done caring." Sam placed several bills on the table and gave Carla a pitying look as he walked off.

"Sam!" Carla avoided the prying eyes at the surrounding tables. "Don't walk out on me!" She pounded the table with her fist. "Sam!"

Sam went to the hospital to see how Ashley was doing. The doctor standing at the nurses' station said that she was stable and that she was young and would heal quickly, leaving almost no visible scar. In his mind Sam knew that Ashley wouldn't stop being his first priority just because Carla had fouled things up for them as a family.

Sam walked down the hall and inched into Ashley's room. The tubes had been removed and she appeared to be resting finally. He moved over to the sink and washed his hands and pulled napkins down out of the dispenser and dried them. He examined Ashley's dinner on the collapsible tray next to her as she stirred in the bed.

"Hi, Daddy . . ." Her glassy eyes looked up at him.

"Hi, sweetie. How's my girl?"

"Fine." She wiggled in the faded pink and white hospital gown.

"You hungry?"

"Cheeseburger and french fries . . ."

"I don't know if you can have that. I'll ask the nurse," he said.

Sam chuckled. He knew that anything was better than hospital food. "I'm gonna go downstairs to the cafeteria and get you something. I'll be right back, okay?"

"Where's Mommy?"

"She's coming," he assured her. "Just getting you well, that's first on my list."

He kissed her forehead.

In the hall the doctor stood by the nurses' station reviewing a patient's medical record.

"Doc? When do you think she can go home?"

"Another two days and we'll discharge her."

"She can go home?"

"Yes. And oh, we have the results from the DNA. . . . You have a moment?"

"Sure." Sam nodded reluctantly.

The doctor pulled up the information on the computer screen and printed it out, then tore the paper off and examined it.

"In layman's terms it's like this. . . ." He stepped away from the nurses' station to the middle of the hall and Sam followed his lead.

"There's no way you can be her father."

Sam eyed the doctor.

"You knew that already, didn't you?" The doctor examined Sam's reaction.

"Yeah." Sam nodded. "But thanks for the confirmation."

Sam had a sinking feeling that life for him would never be the same.

"Thank you, Daddy." Ashley reached for the brown paper bag, the grease already seeping through.

Sam sat in the chair next to the bed and watched Ashley's hands wrap around the burger as she took a bite and then reach back into the bag squeezing a bunch of french fries together and then stuffing them in her mouth. He wondered how difficult her life would be now because of what was going on between him and Carla. Would she learn not to see things through? Would she become unfeeling and lack empathy? He loved this little girl with every fiber of his being and amidst all the confusion all he could honestly say was that he absolutely hoped not.

25

Troi

Troi sat in the kitchen with her lips tight sipping her coffee and tallying her receipts. The sun had risen but she paid no mind to that at all today. She hadn't been able to sleep after the phone rang at 5:00 A.M., startling her out of a sound sleep. Dakoda was standing behind her now waiting for her toast to pop up out of the toaster. She was standing in front of the iron skillet on the stove scrambling eggs and tossing strips of bacon alongside them to go with her toast.

"Why are you using so much butter, girl?"

Troi didn't know how to say what she needed to say to Dakoda, a child who had brought so much joy to her life, so instead of making it sugary sweet so she'd accept it she cut to the chase and before she knew it the words bombarded her daughter's wide eyes without warning.

"Your grandparents want to see you. Spend some time with you."

The blank stare on the child's face proved that she didn't understand. *Why now?* her expression read.

Troi tried not to think of all the years that had passed without Vaughn's parents so much as picking up the phone and asking to spend the day at the park with Dakoda. They weren't there when the little girl cried her heart out when the circus came to town and her daddy was no longer alive to take her.

His parents acted as if she were to blame, but she wasn't the culprit, he was. Despite his diagnoses and endless promises to stay heterosexually faithful, Vaughn hadn't. His desires had run rampant and when he had gone out and had his fill he came home apologizing and trying to make Troi feel better about where they were together.

Nowhere. He had said to give him some time. Part of her hated him for it. If he couldn't do it he should have said so, but a lie was just so unforgivable. "Things like this take time," he said. The Madison girls never had the luxury of time. So whenever he left the house she'd lie in bed at night doing a play-by-play in her mind, imagining what in the world she had done to deserve that kind of treatment.

Troi pulled the fork out of Dakoda's hand and took over scrambling the eggs.

"You know I love you, right?" she said without looking directly at the child.

"I know, Ma." Her daughter watched as Troi spooned the eggs onto her plate.

"So what are you going to do about your grandparents?"

Dakoda shrugged her shoulders. "I guess I can go." She eyed her mother nervously.

Troi nodded. "It's your choice, Dakoda. If you want to go, you can go." She hugged her daughter. "I won't be mad, so don't not go for my sake."

"Yeah. I wanna go."

Troi smiled and nodded her head. "Okay, eat so you can get headed to school."

Dakoda pulled herself up to the table in the chair.

Troi had to reflect on her life. The shop she adored had burned to the ground over ten years ago, the culprit Sophie still upstate, already having served her five years for arson, now serving time for something else she'd done. Tracie, the man who had come between her and her husband's affection, had initially tried to jump bail once they charged him with attempted murder for not disclosing his HIV status to Vaughn. Tracie had lost his condo and his innumerous possessions. He was found beaten and bloody in Miami Beach and returned to New York to stand trial. Died two years later from pneumonia complications.

"Ma, what's wrong?" Dakoda asked.

Troi shook her head. "Nothing. I'm fine."

"You thinking about Daddy?"

"Sometimes but not right now."

"If you don't want me to go I won't go." She put the dirty pan down in the sink.

"I'm not like that, Dakoda. Those are your grandparents. If they want to see you it's okay."

"You mean that, Ma?"

"Yeah. I mean that." Troi smiled.

Dakoda hugged her mom, then hoisted her book bag on her back and headed out the door. "I can stay home today if you want."

"Why would I want you to stay home?"

"I dunno, just company."

"Girl, no . . . go on to school. I'm fine."

"Okay. Bye, Ma."

Troi was glad for the child to be gone, out of the house, leaving her alone with her thoughts. Thoughts that Dakoda was too young to understand. Thoughts that weren't for children. Thoughts that Troi didn't fully understand either.

When the doorbell rang Troi laughed and made her way over to the door.

"Dakoda, you forget your key?" she asked, pulling open the door, and stood face-to-face with Carla.

"Hey, Troi," Carla said.

"Carla . . ."

Her friend's clothes were wrinkled. Her face was drawn.

"Where have you been?" Troi asked more out of curiosity than concern.

"At the hospital with Ashley, and I need a huge favor. I need a place to crash for a few weeks. Just until I get back on my feet. Sam said he wants me gone and . . . and . . ."

Showing emotion had been foreign for Carla. Troi had never seen her cry. Didn't think she had it in her.

"Carla, I don't . . ."

"I know I've been a horrible friend. Coming over here acussing you of sleeping with Sam. You have been one of the only ones who has been there for me from the beginning. Since fourth grade."

"Third."

"You're the only person who cares about me . . . the only person I can trust."

Carla wiped her nose with the back of her hand. "All I need is a room for Ashley when she comes home. I can sleep on the floor."

"Okay," Troi agreed.

"I just need to have a place."

"It's fine, Carla." Troi waved her in. "You want coffee?

"Yes. Please."

"Dakoda made bacon this morning. . . . If you like, I can scramble an egg to go along with it or I can heat you up some waffles. I think we have some in the freezer."

Carla reached for the mug and pushed her face into it and swallowed her coffee by the mouthful, nodding. "Waffles are fine."

Troi set the cold, shriveled bacon on the table next to Carla.

Carla reached for a strip and chewed on the bacon as if she hadn't eaten in days. She placed a spare house key on the table too.

"I know you may not be asking my opinion about anything that is going on in your life right now, Carla, but I think Sam needed to know. Eventually that child will need to know who her father is too. You can't have her walking around looking into the eyes of every single man for hope."

"I don't wanna talk about it."

"Not talking about it is what got you here—"

"Damn it, Troi! You think I don't know that? I'm just asking for someplace to stay, not your psychoanalysis."

"Fine." Troi waved her hand.

Carla lowered her head.

"I didn't mean to yell." Carla's voice was low. "I never used to be like this."

"I know."

"But ever since that man forced me against my will, I've just been . . . different."

"Ashley's father?"

"Yeah. I mean . . . he just didn't care. Sam still took me in. He still wanted me, but now that he knows about Ashley . . ."

"Sam's a good man. Give him time for it all to sink in. It's just too much to comprehend all at once."

"You think he'll forgive me?"

Troi set the waffles in front of Carla. "I think he will, but you've got to forgive yourself first, Carla."

26

Nina and Tim

"Something smells good in here." Tim's deep syrupy voice greeted Nina warmly.

"Blueberry pancakes. I thought you were still sound asleep." Nina grinned and pushed the spatula down into the pan to flip the pancake over.

Tim came up behind her. His facial stubble brushed against her neck. "I'm wide awake."

"So, Tim, did you enjoy your excursion to New York?"

"No . . . you weren't there." He made a sad face for her and swiped a strip of bacon. "I didn't get to see my sister either. It was a spur-of-the-moment thing."

"You ever hear from that friend of yours that took over your apartment?"

"Justin? No, but last I heard he was starting up this record label. House Music or something like that."

"Okay."

"What do you do in New York?" Tim asked, putting a pat of butter on his pancakes and rubbing it around until it melted.

"Lunch. Some antique shopping."

"Your favorite thing to do, huh?"

"Yep."

"What about your old neighbor Martha?"

"I didn't see her but I heard she's working as a receptionist at some church. Her daughter's in college on a music scholarship. All those piano lessons paid off, I guess."

"What happened with her and Junior? They still dating? They were keeping late hours back then." Tim chuckled. "Remember?"

"No, I doubt they ever were serious. He rents a room from her sometimes, still selling watermelons, from what I hear."

"What about Shelby?"

"Got a few hours?" Nina looked at him seriously. "Saw her in New York when I was there. I was out with Troi at One Fish Two Fish and saw her all curled up in the arms of Carla's husband."

"What?" Tim rested his fork on his plate. "You see . . . that's why I don't want her around you, or in our house either, for that matter."

"Don't start. . . ."

"Oh, I almost forgot. I've got good news," he said. "Remember back to our first date and we went to that art gallery in New York to appease your friend Shelby?"

"Yeah."

"Remember the guy who was the curator? He gave me his card?"

"Oh, yeah."

"Well, I ran into him last week and he said something about he'd see what he can do in regards to getting distribution for my film. He called to say that he put in a good word at one of the top distribution companies and to give them a call next week. It's hard to get picked up so that your film is actually showing."

"Really?"

"Yeah."

"That's been your dream forever."

"I want you to help me," he said.

"Help you how?"

"Work for the company."

"You're hiring me?"

"Your doctoral thesis was on advertising, right?"

"Yeah."

"Think we can have a marriage and a business?"

"It isn't unheard of." Nina pulled her chair up to the table.

They both turned to the light tapping on the door.

"Hello?"

"Hey, Francesca." Tim grinned.

Her eyes were wide and cautious.

"It's okay, girl. Aliens abducted Tim. This is a clone, a people-friendly one at that," Nina kidded.

"Funny." Tim excused himself with his plate.

"So how are things?" Francesca asked Nina.

"Never better."

"I bet."

"Coffee?"

"No, thanks."

Nina poured herself a cup.

"So what happened?" Francesca asked.

"I came home and when I got here he was in New York looking for me." She rested her hand on her hip. "Things will be fine."

"I'm certain."

The telephone rang and Nina ignored it as she listened intently to what Francesca was saying.

"What about the woman in his office?" Francesca spoke in a low voice.

"We're working it out." Nina smiled.

"Great. Glad to hear it. Well, I've got errands to run. Want to go to the market?"

"Sure. Let me get dressed. I'll be over. Give me about thirty minutes, okay?"

Nina headed down the hall to their bedroom and stopped halfway as she heard Tim on the phone in a conversation that sounded like a hushed argument.

"Look . . . why are you disrespecting my house by calling here? I'm married. I never told you we would be together. I love my wife," he said, then slammed down the phone.

Nina tiptoed past the doorway to the bedroom and wondered why women who say that they can get any man they want always find it necessary to invade the sanctity of someone else's marriage.

"Honey," Tim called, "I'm going into the office."

"Okay. I'm going to the market with Francesca." She tried not to let her suspicions trick her into saying the wrong thing. "Who was that on the phone?"

"Nobody." Tim let out a sigh.

Nina rolled her eyes and turned to leave.

"Okay, okay, wait . . . I want you to hear something." Tim pulled the desk drawer out and reached for his minicassette recorder and pressed PLAY.

"You need to go."

"Throwing me out so soon? I'm only here to help."

"Help what?"

"*A friend of my dad's can get your film distributed, no questions asked.*"

"*That's what you want, isn't it? Makes no sense at all to make movies that no one gets to see. So I'm here to help make you famous. Behind every great man . . .*"

"*Is a woman, I know.*"

"*And what's in it for you?*"

"*I just want you happy,*"

"*That's it? My happiness?*"

"*And make it like it was before. . . .*"

"*And how was that?*"

"*Me needing you and you satisfying me and my needs. Whenever and wherever.*"

"*So if I sleep with you—*"

"*Exactly.*"

"*And if I don't?*"

"*Dozens of films go straight to video every month.*"

"*I see. . . .*"

"*I've got my Blockbuster card. I can rent your latest.*"

Tim pressed the stop button and rested the cassette recorder on the desk.

"That's Michelle." He looked at Nina. "What do you think I should do with this little piece of information that I just happened to secure on tape?"

"I think you should turn her in."

"Really?"

"Yeah. And not just because I'm your wife but because she's probably used her influence to manipulate others. That has to be illegal, right?"

"You know something?" Tim pulled his wife close and sat her down on his lap. "You're absolutely right."

27

Sam and Carla

Carla sat in the principal's office. Never thought this would be a room that she'd frequent, only somewhere they threatened to send her unruly students. She looked around and fidgeted in the chair trying not to think about how her entire life was falling apart.

The door opening behind her startled her and she turned and faced him trying to figure out what his request to be in his office at 8:45 A.M. was about.

He shuffled through some paperwork and a few files until he found the one with her name on it and slapped it down on the desk.

"Mrs. Singleton—"

"Carla is fine."

"We heard about your child, Carla, and we're sorry about the accident. Our decision regarding your status at this school, however, was made before the unfortunate accident that Ashley had a few days ago. And we hate to have to add to your grief, but you haven't called us, you haven't completed your anger management sessions. Therefore we have placed you on administrative leave without pay."

"Fired?"

"No. On leave, Mrs. Singleton."

"But why? I love the kids. My whole life is this school. I've been here for what, eleven, twelve years?"

"I'm sorry but the decision wasn't mine. Take some time off—"

"I don't need time off."

"Policy says that you—"

"I need to work. I can't support my child with no income."

"When the board reconvenes in two weeks I'll bring it up, but as it stands now—"

"Save it for someone who wants to hear it!" She stormed out of his office slamming the door behind her.

She stood outside the door. Her head resting back against the words PRINCIPAL, she watched the children in the hall filing into their homerooms. They were hugging their notebooks and toting colorful book bags on their backs. Girls huddled in corners talking about boys, and boys stood around in the hall making their presence known by laughing rambunctiously.

Unpaid leave. No job, no Sam. Now what?

Carla's life was now reduced to a list of things she used to have. A job, a husband, and a father for her child. There was only one thing left for her to do now.

Carla showed up at Sam's house in the middle of the day looking like an alley cat. Her clothing rumpled and hair that would make Troi cringe. She needed to talk to Sam. She desperately needed him to take the edge off. Make some sense out of what was happening to her and her life. He had always made her feel comfortable, wanted. But she hadn't always reciprocated.

With a few steps up to the house she did a double take and stared in disbelief at the FOR SALE sign pressed down into the grass out in front of the house. She looked around the street before she rang the doorbell but as she anticipated, he wasn't home so she used her key that thankfully still worked.

She stepped into the house. A place that she used to call home. A place where she and Sam were raising a child and had planned on spending the rest of their lives together. She eyed the foyer. Still the same. Table by the doorway piled with mail. None for her. He was already having her mail forwarded to Troi's place in Brooklyn. She couldn't believe him. What nerve. Her things had been stuffed into cardboard boxes near the front door and labeled appropriately. Three boxes that simply said *Carla's* and two other boxes, one marked *Ashley's* and the other *Ashley's Toys*.

Carla couldn't deal with any of this right now. Not the boxes, the divorce, and the ultimate message that he was sending loud and clear. She locked up and headed to Brooklyn. Someplace where she could get some peace of mind and rest. Someplace where she didn't have to see the evidence that she and Sam were over for good.

*   *   *

Carla was completely frazzled. Her hands trembled trying to unlock Troi's front door with her spare key. She looked up and down the street suspiciously.

"Troi?"

Carla called throughout the house.

"Troi?"

Carla closed the door behind her and was only a few feet away when the doorbell rang. A frown covered her face as she peeped through the side pane.

"Mrs. Carla Singleton?"

"Yes?"

"Are you Mrs. Singleton?"

"Yes, I am."

"This is for you." The process server motioned to her with the folded papers.

Carla opened the door and grabbed the papers, thanked him, and closed the door behind her again.

She stood there in the hall and unfolded the papers. They were a legal document from an attorney. White papers stapled to a blue backing. She looked out the window at the man who was halfway down the street now. She took the papers with her into the kitchen and sat at the table in disbelief.

Divorce papers? Already?

She was glad to be alone, as her tears came on purpose this time and she tried not to weep too loudly.

Carla felt a presence and looked up long enough to see Dakoda in the doorway looking at her. Carla dried her tears with the back of her hand, pushed the folded paper down into her bag. She fumbled around and pulled out a business card. It was the card that the therapist at the sessions had given her. She had said, *"If you ever want to talk just call me."*

"Come here, Dakoda." Troi motioned.

"Huh?"

"Where's your momma?"

"Making deliveries," she said.

"How are you doing?" Carla sniffled. "Did you hear anything about me at school today?"

"No."

"You sure?"

"Yeah. I'm sure. I wasn't feeling well, so the nurse let me come home."

"You know that I'm not mad at you for telling me what you told me about Uncle Sam. You were just trying to help and I know that."

"So you and Uncle Sam aren't getting a divorce?"

"I don't know." Carla shook her head.

"How's Ashley doing?"

"She's good. Coming home tomorrow. She's feeling much better. We'll be staying here with you and your mom for a few weeks if you don't mind."

"It's okay." Dakoda shrugged. "I like Ashley."

"What about me?" Carla kidded.

"Oh, I like you too, Miss Carla."

Carla smiled. "I like you too, Dakoda."

Carla picked up the card and examined it. She had tried everything else to save her marriage and nothing worked. Maybe this would. "Hand me the phone, Dakoda."

Dakoda handed Carla the phone and walked out of the kitchen. Carla dialed the number not knowing exactly what to expect; the only thing in life that she knew for certain was that she wanted her husband back.

28

Troi

Troi had finally adjusted to having just Dakoda to worry about and now she was readjusting to Carla and Ashley being there underfoot. She didn't mind the company. After it just being her and Dakoda for the past few years it was just all so new to her. Like living back at home with Nina and her father and mother again. Cooking for four, empty orange juice container, crossword puzzle poorly done in the daily paper. Dakoda wanting burgers and fries every night just because Carl was giving in to every one of Ashley's whims because she was still healing.

Dakoda was happier with Ashley around though. A more pleasant child altogether. Someone to talk to, someone to teach, someone to goof around with. Troi guessed that was it. Never taking the place of her dad but still giving her something to partially fill that void.

Toying around with onion rings, dragging them one at a time through ketchup on her plate at the kitchen table, Carla continued making confessions that Troi never saw coming.

"You know that Sam has always had a thing for you. And I've always been jealous of that . . . that thing he has for you, that is."

"I've never fed whatever it was Sam had for me, Carla." Troi sipped her coffee. "Honestly, you've been first and foremost in my mind . . . always will be. Our relationship has always been important to me. Sam *is* fine but so was Vaughn." Troi smirked.

"I know." Carla nodded her head. "And I know we're not as close as we used to be but I wanted to ask you something, Troi."

"Ask away."

"Since Vaughn died, how come there's been no one else in your life? I mean, don't you miss having someone?"

Troi nodded. It was time to talk about it. "Sometimes. Sometimes I think I may not be ready for it all over again. Not knowing how long the love will last et cetera. Then sometimes I realize how important being single is. Getting to know yourself. I have learned to stop rushing into things. Even though I know I loved Vaughn, I probably wouldn't have raced into the arms of the first man who proposed, if I were surer of myself back then."

"I suppose."

"I started using my maiden name again." Troi lowered her head to her cup.

"Why?" Carla asked.

"Vaughn is gone." She shrugged. "His name is only a constant reminder of something that no longer is. Some memories good, some forgettable."

"I bet." Carla took up another onion ring. "You still doing hair?"

"Sometimes, but when I want. I'm trying to get away from all of that curl and relaxer stuff and focus more on the business aspect of hair care."

"Sounds like while I was in Jersey stressing, you were over here hashing out a plan."

"Let me ask you something, Carla."

"Okay."

"Why didn't you just tell Sam what that guy did to you? I mean, why did you hold it inside all these years and allow it to eat away at you? It's just making matters worse."

"I dunno. My entire life is a haze, really. My parents, the drugs, and school. Lord, being treated like an outsider was the worst. It really does affect the rest of your life."

"Only if you let it, Carla."

"It's the only reason I became a teacher."

"So." Troi shrugged.

"So? In the light of all that, I still found it necessary to allow myself to gravitate toward any man who would show me the time of day and even though I held my head up high and felt like I could do anything and that I had risen above what my parents were, I still cheated on Sam and I knew that I wasn't worthy of him."

"You know better than that, why would you think you weren't worthy?"

"No, I don't mean that I wasn't worthy because Sam was so special, but because of what I was. I couldn't hide it. I didn't even know I was pregnant and when I found out I figured it was Sam's. I thought I had miscalculated the dates or something. That's when I pinpointed it. Ashley's real father, I didn't even have to tell him. He knew. Like he had planned it. He promised not to tell as long as I paid him."

"Pay him? You didn't pay him, did you?" Troi frowned.

"I did. I paid him because Sam had just forgiven me for sneaking away with this man after choir rehearsal. I knew he wouldn't forgive me for being pregnant by him too."

Troi shook her head.

"I loved him. I couldn't take that chance, Troi. So, I paid him. Sometimes a hundred dollars, sometimes fifty. Sometimes I didn't have any money and he swore he'd march over to Sam's office and tell him every detail over lunch unless I . . . unless . . ."

"How could you let him make you do those things? There are so many people you could have told."

"To keep my secret, I needed to, Troi. I would have lost everything. And who was I going to tell? You? That wouldn't have saved my marriage."

"Have you spoken with Sam?"

"I went by the house this afternoon and it's up for sale."

"Sale?"

"Yeah, I don't know where he is. A process server dropped these by this afternoon."

Carla pulled the papers out of her bag and slid them across the table to Troi. "He didn't waste any time."

"Sure didn't," Troi said, unfolding the paper.

"Sometimes I wonder why all the hype about marriage if this is all you end up with." Carla twisted her mouth.

"Well, I know waking up alone is still taking me getting some used to . . . and even though I promised to wait until Dakoda is older, I want that again. I miss it. I miss sitting on the bed asking questions while he's getting ready for work."

"But Dakoda's a teenager, Troi. You have to live too."

"Yeah, but she needs me now. . . . I don't want her to feel like I'm choosing someone else over her. Or worse yet, replacing her dad with anybody who happens along."

"Sometimes I think we give men too much credit."

"It's not men," Troi said, "it's love. Good, bad, ugly, love gets all the credit. All of it. Every time."

29

Nina and Tim

Nina and Tim curiously enough started sharing more. Talking about business, she becoming more familiar with the industry, happy to be able to put her university mind to good use again. Elated to have something to talk about at the gatherings he used to frequent alone, sometimes with her. Now she accompanied him more often. Working together had been a good move for them.

As she sat at her desk helping finalize the distribution deal for their first Richardson Film, Tim walked into her office, hands pushed down into his pockets, eyes looking around her office suspiciously as if he were up to no good. He positioned himself by her window, toying with the blinds. Nina looked at him and frowned, waving him away. Tim stroked his goatee and inched in closer to her.

He eased up behind Nina and brushed his fingers lightly on the hairs on the back of her neck. She shrugged him away and pressed her ear closer to the phone and widened her eyes at Tim. He stood directly behind her swivel chair and unclipped her barrette from her hair and ignored Nina as she gripped the mouthpiece of the phone with one hand and mouthed for him to stop.

Tim proceeded to seduce his wife in the chair, hugging her from behind and reaching around to the front of her blouse, undoing several buttons, slipping them through the eyelets one at a time, arranging her hair on her shoulders.

"Umm, I'm sorry, that's my other line and I need to take that call; can I give you a call back?" She spoke professionally. "Five minutes?" Nina hurried the man off the phone.

"Twenty minutes then," she said. "Thank you."

Nina smirked at Tim.

"Are you okay?" she kidded.

"I'm fine." He pressed his lips into her neck and welcomed the way her body responded.

Nina had no logical choice but to go willingly with the passion that was sizzling inside Tim. His love found its way behind her ears, tiptoed its way down her spine, and made its way around her hips, following his hands that were destined to seek out mischief right there in the office.

"Reese might come in, Tim." Nina squirmed in her chair.

"Reese ain't thinking about us," Tim said.

Tim was right, Reese wasn't thinking about them until Nina's office door opened and they both found themselves scrambling to hide their nakedness behind Nina's desk.

"Sorry." Reese backed out of the office and then Nina looked at Tim and dared him to finish what he started.

In the chair that afternoon Tim made Nina feel like a goddess. Every inch of her validated and made to know that marriage hadn't put a damper on things, not one little bit. He had quite a time trying to convince Nina that when he said that he loved her *as is,* it meant nothing added, nothing taken away, no preservatives, nothing.

With the sunlight streaming into their office Nina and Tim made their way over what some would call a dry spell. A patch of simplicity that made them realize why they married each other in the first place. Now they were back in that safe space again with each other. Knowing, loving, and caring so very deeply.

Now everything was out in the open. No more going to lunch every day at noon when Tim thought she was at the gym. Things were changing. Now she was walking around outside for lunch, walking up and down the stairs when the elevator took too long. She was stimulating her mind reading again. Working together actually gave them time apart that they both relished, a balance that didn't leave them smothering each other twenty-four hours of every day but instead, put distance between them to create some type of longing.

Though Tim loved her as she was, she wanted to be happy with herself. She needed to be. She diligently tried the diet shakes thing but had major issues in determining what a *sensible meal* was. She vowed she wouldn't stress about it, and with the stress went the pounds, almost unnoticed until she was in the bathroom one morning and kicked the dust off of the scale and climbed on top of it.

Working with Tim at the office made it easier, giving her some-thing to do, a reason to get up in the mornings. She felt as if Richardson Films were a part of her now, not just Tim's dream but a collaborative effort that they both enjoyed.

Opening night for the film was more spectacular than Tim could ever have imagined. The bright white lights, paid escorts, and private whispering saturated the place. Congratulations all around the lobby, his entire career was riding on this thing. There was a huge difference between writing a script, only to have someone else direct it, and becoming the proverbial writer, slash director that gave your name some real power in this industry.

Tim had waited an entire lifetime for this. His film, counterculture actors, newly minted MDs, and women from LA's red-light district, all buzzing around wanting to see the glamour and prestige that the premier brought with it. No inclement weather anywhere to be found.

"Let's go on that vacation," he said, amidst the beaming lights.

"We can do that but I have one request."

"Anything," he said.

"Okay, well, I know we can't really afford the vacation but . . ."

"But what? Tell me."

"New furniture. . . . It's not that I hate your furniture, it's just that I have never really felt like I live there too."

"Okay."

"I mean, it was yours and—

"Nina?"

"Huh?"

"It's fine. We can pick out furniture together."

"Really?"

"Yeah, it's no big deal." Tim smirked.

"Thank you, baby." Nina held Tim's face between her hands and kissed his lips then brushed wrinkles from his shirt.

"You want a snack? Something to drink?" he asked.

"No. I'm fine."

Arm in arm they made their way through the crowd. Across the theater's lobby he felt eyes on him. The lobby was full of glamorous women with hair, hips, and sex appeal, but he had Nina. The men had confidence. Tim took it all in stride. He looked through the crowd and couldn't avoid Michelle's persistent gaze. Her eyes were burning a hole in him. Undressing him layer by layer with her patented power of persuasion from way across the room, on the arm of another man as equally unsure of where he stood with her as Tim had been.

Michelle made all men feel like that. Pursued them with a vengeance and then left them dangling in her absence like bait. In that moment he did what any man in his situation would have done, he pulled Nina closer, under the bright hot lights, and kissed her so feverishly that any hope Michelle had of ever again getting close enough to breathe the same air as Tim were dashed.

Her spell over Tim had been broken the moment he reminded himself how much he loved Nina. Michelle had lost the upper hand. With his conscious choice he put her power of manipulation to rest.

Tim had sent their little private conversation they were having in his office that day about getting his film distributed to the VP at her father's company. The gentleman was only too eager to meet with Tim over lunch and divulge the fact that Michelle had methodically mangled and mishandled many men on both coasts that had an ounce of influence in the arts. The VP assured him that her father would be informed of her antics. The VP didn't mind hanging something over Michelle's head especially after she had shunned his advances. But that didn't stop her from showing up for the release of Tim's feature film.

At that moment there at his opening his smirk from across the room did exactly what it was supposed to for Michelle, injure any pride she had left. Tim said what he wanted and here it was. His name in blinding lights luring the entire city. The whole shebang before he was forty. Now Nina was by his side. She wasn't a distraction.

Nina stood in line for a Diet Coke and an order of nachos with cheese.

"You want anything?" Nina asked.

"Yes," Tim said. "I'll have what you're having." He kissed his wife's cheek.

Nina smiled at the concession girl and then he and Nina snuggled into two vacant seats in the last row of the theater just as the lights around them were being dimmed.

30

Sam and Carla

"I'm seeing a therapist now."

"That's good." Sam sat on his bed listening to Carla on the phone. He didn't know if he would ever trust a word she said again.

"She's helping me cope with all of these recent changes in my life. She said that no matter what I did with him in that car, no means no."

Sam was silent. He held the phone close to his face, listening and vowing to believe it when he saw it and not a moment before.

"Are you there?"

"I'm here," he said.

Carla tried effortlessly to convince him to let them come back together as a family.

"You know she only likes it when you take her to school. . . ."

"You're in the city now, Carla."

"I don't want to be. Not without you."

"It doesn't make sense to have her coming from Jersey just so you can have things your way."

"She won't mind. Honestly."

"Did she tell you that?"

"No, I just know. You act like you don't want me there. Why are you being so mean to me?"

"You knew when we met what I'd been through. You know how seriously I took marriage because of it. Yeah, I made mistakes too but you pushed me away, Carla. I told you I couldn't take the way we were before I found out about Ashley."

"What are you saying?"

"I'd rather not have Ashley growing up trying to adjust to our dysfunctions."

"So that's it?"

"For now, Carla. It has to be, whether you like it or not."

"What about that Shelby woman? Is it because of her you're giving up your family so easily?"

"This is not because of her. She means nothing to me," Sam said out loud. "You are still blaming everyone else for what you've done. You brought this on us."

He'd stop Shelby from calling. Eventually. The last thing on his mind was a woman. Any woman. Carla had no idea how deeply her deceit had affected him.

"I'm sorry, Sam. What else do you want me to say?"

"I guess that's all you can say."

Carla was staying with Troi so Sam hadn't spoken to Troi in a few weeks. His parents had gained a granddaughter by spending time with Dakoda and had lost a granddaughter when Sam sat his parents down and finally told them what Carla had done.

"Can I call you again?" Carla asked.

"Carla, I need time. I really do."

"Well, how much time?"

"I don't know how much time. I'll just call you, okay?"

Carla reluctantly let him go, and he found temporary relief.

Everyone's life was going on and here Sam was not able to find a woman among all the self-professed *good women* out there.

Sam tried not to upset Carla. He understood that her condition was even more fragile now but so was his. He had lived years of a lie that she had spun and woven tightly to keep what she wanted. It was always about her. He had wasted his life on her by being patient and understanding of his wife even though she never gave him the same consideration. He just wouldn't put up with it anymore. He didn't have to, and he didn't appreciate visualizing his wife with another man. Rape was one thing but her going willingly to this man was downright sick and, from his point of view, unacceptable.

The phone stole him from his train of thought the moment it rang. It was the young man whom he had spoken with the day before at his office. He wanted to stop by with his wife and have another look at his home.

Sam had a few more people who wanted to see his house. The seemingly loving couple with no children and an artist from SoHo who wanted to be away from the whole scene to focus on his craft, and then there was an older woman who was evasive as to whom she'd be living with.

Sam just thought he'd be raising his family in this house. Saturday outings, camping trips, and backyard barbecues. Part of him knew he deserved better, was worthy of more than Carla had given, but he didn't have the heart to try again any time soon.

When his first wife, Brenda, left him for another man, he never thought he'd marry again. Carla came in and changed his mind about that and a lot of things, but here he was again, a good man that women said that they had trouble finding. He had a good job. Financially stable. He was a welcome catch, and here he was alone.

31

Troi

After another weekend with her grandmother, Dakoda didn't seem her usual self. Walking through the door, she headed straight up to her room. Troi was caught up in something she was watching on TV. Ashley came downstairs and spoke softly.

"Excuse me, Miss Troi."

"Yes?" Troi smiled at the child.

"Dakoda won't talk to me."

"Don't pay Dakoda any mind. She's moody like that." Troi waved her hand.

"But she's crying."

"Crying?"

"Yeah. She's all over her bed and won't talk to me."

"Tell Dakoda to come down here for me, please."

Ashley scampered up the stairs and Troi could hear her tell Dakoda exactly what she had said. Ashley came back downstairs and stood by Troi's chair.

"She's not coming."

Troi moved the newspaper off her lap and made her way upstairs with reprimand on the tip of her tongue. Troi peered into the room and pushed the door open.

"Dakoda?"

Troi moved closer to her daughter on the bed. She turned and told Ashley to wait for her downstairs.

"Baby? What's wrong?" Troi sat on the bed next to her child.

Troi looked around the girl's messy bedroom. She didn't want to get started on that. So she focused on the matter at hand.

"Did something happen at Grandma's?"

"No." Her lips trembled and she wiped her eyes with her hand.

"So what's wrong? You can tell me."

"I saw . . . Grandma . . ."

"I know, but what happened over there."

"No." Dakoda shook her head. "Not Grandma Singleton, Grandma Madison."

"You saw her?" Troi frowned. "Saw her where?"

"I was coming home walking down the street . . ." The tears continued to fall from Dakoda's eyes. "Then I heard someone call me, saying that I must be little Troi all grown up. She was dirty and had a bag of cans pulling behind her on her back. She had holes in her shoes. Men's shoes. She smelled really bad and she made me hug her."

"Come here, baby." Troi hugged her child. She rested her little girl's head on her shoulder. "Now just because your grandmother chose to make friends with alcohol doesn't mean that has any reflection on you. We tried to help her. She didn't want our help."

"Why?"

"I can't answer that, baby. She was doing good. She was clean and sober for months. She had stopped drinking and was pulling herself together even after my father left her for good. All it took was one time at a holiday party for her to stop going to her meetings. She started drinking again. Didn't want a thing to do with us. We couldn't help her. You can't help someone who doesn't want help."

"She knew who I was, Ma." Dakoda's tears were still coming.

"She's not crazy, Dakoda. She's just an alcoholic. She knows her own blood when she sees it. She can still function. Maybe being that way makes her feel safe. Just remember her in your prayers. Okay?"

"Okay."

"I'm gonna let Ashley come back in. You can tell her what's wrong if you want. Just get some sleep. We got church in the morning." Troi kissed her daughter's forehead and made her way downstairs. She told Ashley not to push Dakoda, and for her not to ask what was wrong but to let Dakoda tell her.

"Let her tell you if she wants to, okay?"

"Yes, Miss Troi."

Troi hated that her mother wasn't any different than she was years ago. Made up her mind to drink and didn't think to care one iota how it affected other people around her. That had always left a bitter taste in Troi's mouth, and it still did. Probably always would.

* * *

It took almost all morning to convince Carla to go to the service with her and Dakoda.

"Service starts at eleven, Carla. Whatever it is, you have to face it, sis. . . . I'll be there with you."

Part of Carla's therapy was to face the things she was afraid of. She hadn't done an effective job when she spoke with Sam. She was still irrational where he was concerned, but she did think that to sit in church and face all of those people might help.

Dakoda looked pretty in her skirt and blouse for a change, putting to rest those dusty blue jeans just for a day.

"How you feeling, Dakoda?" Troi smiled, mixing a pot of oatmeal and browning biscuits in the oven.

"Fine." She sat quietly at the table.

"Troi, can you do something with my hair? I can't make heads or tails of it." Carla walked into the kitchen and spoke nervously.

"Can you do this?" Troi asked Dakoda, handing her the spoon.

Dakoda took the spoon from her mother and continued mixing the oatmeal so it didn't stick to the bottom of the pot.

Troi stood over Carla as she sat in the chair with the brush in her hand.

"You know those people don't want me in their church," Carla said.

"They don't even know what happened, Carla, so why are you saying that?"

"Not one of them called to find out why I had stopped coming."

"They have almost two hundred members, Carla. Don't take it personal." Troi brushed Carla's hair up and twisted it into a bun.

"Troi, please don't make excuses for them. They could have called."

"I'm not saying they couldn't. I'm not even saying they're right, but you're not going to church for them. Do it for yourself."

"I'm going, I'm going," Carla said.

"You want a bang?"

"No."

"You hungry?" Troi brushed the wayward hairs on Carla's hair.

"My stomach's in knots." She waved her hand. "I can't eat. I'll put on my shoes, get Ashley ready, and . . . then we can go."

Troi and Carla were well dressed. Troi and Carla in their Sunday-polished faith, just like they used to be. Troi held on to her friend's arm as they filed into the church.

Carla wondered what the people around her had heard about her, about Sam, about the incident in the car that night all those years ago with a former choir member. Those hallelujah girls would use their mouths for good one of these days, Carla was certain of it.

Dakoda and Ashley followed behind them in the church. They all sat on the right side of the sanctuary in a pew that wasn't too close to the front.

Troi was a friend. She held Carla's hand as the choir sang, and after the service as people approached Carla inquiring as to where she had been, she held her hand even tighter knowing that Carla's first instinct might be to run. Troi was determined to help see her friend through. Baby steps, until she could do it on her own. That was the way friends should be, and that was the way it would be between them. After all, God put them in each other's lives for a reason, maybe even all those years ago God had known that this was it.

32

Nina and Tim

Music, electricity, magic. You name it, if it was spectacular, flashy, and flamboyant, they were both feeling it there on the shores of Belize. Pretty cotton-candy-blue skies, and clouds billowy white and picturesque like angels' wings. Nothing like the gray New York skies or the smog-filled horizon of LA. The heat was unforgiving but Nina didn't let it bother her much, as she stood on the hotel balcony of the split-level villa in awe of how pure Belize was. More culture than you could decipher from a glossy travel poster. An occasional jogger keeping an uninterrupted pace, a pair of spotted dogs chasing each other through the mounds of sand, and huge man-sized seagulls out-waddling the incoming waves as they snuck up on the shore, then retreated back to the sea. The sun's brilliance was impressing early risers and inviting them to fall in love.

"Are you glad we took this trip?" Tim lay in bed with his arms stretched out and his fingers laced behind his head.

Nina walked back into their room from the balcony and grinned.

"Yes. I am." She pushed her feet into her sandals and made her way over to him.

Tim reached out for Nina but she pulled away.

"You've gotta get ready. The tour group meets in the lobby at ten." She smirked.

"What time is it?" He looked over on the night table, squinting.

"Nine-fifteen."

"We have time, don't we?"

"Time for what?"

"You know what." He flexed an eyebrow and grabbed Nina, making her tumble onto the bed.

On top of her now he smothered her with feverish kisses. He pecked her forehead, her chin, the crevice of her neck, her cheeks, and saved her sweet lips for last.

"You know what?" She looked up into his eyes.

"What?" He rested on his side and studied her.

"I just want you to know that I trust you, and that no matter what, I'm here to support you."

"Do you mean that?"

"Yes, I do, Mr. Richardson."

"I was thinking of doing something different." He looked at her.

"Like what?"

"Teaching at the local college. Film or just production, editing, something."

"Yeah, and drive all those college-age girls crazy, right? With your *fine* self."

"I ain't the only one who's fine." He squeezed his wife tight.

Tim kicked off his checkered boxer shorts, and Nina, in sync with his mood, undressed herself as well. First her sandals, then her shorts. There they were, lying there, caught up in the moment that wouldn't let them forget what they meant to each other. Something that reminded them of late-night drives into Brooklyn and the chilly rides back and forth on the Staten Island ferry. Sunday morning church services. Late-night snack runs for coffee and danishes. Something that allowed Tim to appreciate how sincere Nina was and had always been and in turn allowed Nina to see past Tim's bad-boy exterior, no longer doubting her husband.

It was delicious, something that had them tangled and mesmerized in the moment, satiating each other's minds and hearts as they lay up in the tropical atmosphere, yearning, enjoying, and relishing the looks on each other's face, as they took their time, there in Belize, making the sweetest, most everlasting love ever.

33

Sam and Carla

Carla finally agreed to dissolve their marriage if that was what Sam Singleton wanted. She wasn't up to the stress or strain of fighting him on it, or fighting for him. She had one request, and one request only; she wanted to sit down and talk with Sam, cordially. No yelling or name-calling, just talk. Rationally.

Sam refused to come by Troi's house and made excuses as to why he couldn't meet her at a restaurant that would be neutral territory for both of them. All she wanted was to bring closure to her mind.

Carla pleaded with Troi to drive her to Jersey to talk with Sam, and after much pleading she did. Troi took her to the house she used to share with Sam. A place that used to be their haven, a place that she could no longer call home. The possibilities were uncertain.

Troi dropped Carla off at the front door and said that she'd be back in an hour or two and they embraced in parting. Sam pulled open the front door.

"Carla and I have nothing much to talk about, so an hour won't be necessary." He stood at the door. He wanted them to have their conversation standing there with neighbors walking by. Out in the open. So Troi agreed to wait in the car for however long it took.

Carla began the conversation asking if he thought about her at all and if he would be willing to consider reconciliation.

"I can't do it, not even for us."

"I know that, I'm just asking because I've got the papers in the car and before I signed them I wanted—"

"Give it time. A lot has happened, Carla."

"I just need to know how you feel and what you think of me. I mean, what are the odds of you totally forgiving me?"

"I can't say." Sam shook his head and stood with his hands shoved down in his pockets.

"I know you must hate me." Carla lowered her head. "But I think that we both went into this marriage for very different reasons."

"Like?"

"Well, you were trying to forget your ex-wife and getting another shot at it. Me, not wanting to be alone, I guess."

"I'm not serious about anybody, Carla. That thing with Shelby was nothing. I don't have any feelings for that woman."

Carla looked at the man she was technically still married to. She wanted to believe him. She needed to believe him, just as much as he needed to believe her and find some validity in all they had been to each other.

"You never know what might happen," he said.

"Mentally I just need to straighten things out, that's all. That's the only reason why I'm here. I mean, Ashley is asking questions and you are honestly the only male figure in her life."

"It'll work out." He pulled her close and hugged her.

Carla smiled for the first time in almost a month. His thick strong arms were a comfort. When Sam let her go she walked over to the car; she returned and handed him the signed papers in an envelope.

"I'm not sure what'll happen; you aren't either. Here are the papers, do what you feel led to do," she said, before she inhaled the fresh headiness of nature and walked over to the passenger side of Troi's car.

Carla got in the car and was determined not to break down. As Troi pulled off, Carla looked back at the house. Sam standing there watching her go down the street. She didn't wave. He didn't move. Things still unsure but something deep down told her that, together, they might get over this hurdle yet.

Carla looked forward to resuming her teaching career in the spring. The principal wanted to meet with her right after the Thanksgiving recess. Sam and Carla spoke several times; he said that he'd help her find an apartment of her own. Something affordable for her and Ashley. He agreed to sit down and talk to her before too long. No matter how much she didn't want to accept a life without him, she'd take his help, she had no choice. Accepting his help just might have been the next step in getting them back together.

With or without Sam she needed to go on, not just for her own sanity, but for her daughter as well. Troi said that letting go of someone that you love doesn't mean relinquishing the memories. Troi was always saying something and giving advice. It was almost always on the money too, Carla thought, nodding to herself.

Up late one night, sitting in the kitchen talking, Carla asked Troi how she had gotten so wise.

Troi stirred the sugar in her coffee and said, "Trial and error."

Carla was certain that she'd learn the exact same way.

34

Troi

The air got noticeably cooler as winter neared. On her daily paper run dressed in a gray wool jacket and a scarf that was wrapped around her neck to keep the cool air off of her chest, Troi encountered the same limping dog that she always had on her outings. The dog inched up to her and smelled her new shoes, then began yapping at her feet.

"Pay him no mind. He's just showing off," the stranger said.

"What happened to the older man that always walks with him?"

"He's my grandfather. I'm Damien. I just help him out sometimes. He's been feeling a little under the weather, so I decided to do the honors." He chuckled at the prospect of cleaning up after a dog.

The well-dressed man in his beige seersucker pants and beige shirt stood still and allowed the dog to circle him and tangle him up in his leash.

"Oh, I see." Troi nodded.

"He sniffs your shoes to get to know you better."

"Oh, is that what that was?" Troi smirked. "It's been years, he should know me by now."

"Maybe he can sense that I'd like to get to know you better too." The man flashed his boyish smile.

Troi waved her hand.

"Dinner?"

Troi shook her head.

"Lunch? A movie?"

"I don't think so," Troi said.

"Coffee? A walk in the park? An art exhibit? We can sit some-where quiet and talk."

"I can't."

"The theater? Miniature golf . . ."

Troi giggled.

"I'm going to keep on until you pick one," he said.

Mid-thirties or thereabout, good-looking, but I'm not ready, Troi thought to herself. *This isn't easy for me. I wouldn't even know how to act on a date.*

She looked over at Dakoda standing there in front of their house sucking on a red Ice Pop.

"Go ahead, Ma." She waved her hands.

"Okay." Her eyes found his. "Coffee."

"You sure?"

"As sure as I'm ever gonna get." Troi nodded, putting her hand over her face and shielding her eyes from the sun.

"Friday. Coffee it is. I'll pick you up here." He pointed to the side-walk.

"Right here?" She stepped on the line.

"Yeah." He chuckled.

"That sounds fine."

"What's your name?"

"Troi . . . Troi Madison."

"Until Friday, Troi Madison."

Damien untangled the dog's leash from between his legs and made his way down the street.

Troi and Dakoda stood on the steps and didn't say a word to each other. They just watched Damien walk down the street in the nippy weather and enjoyed the moment and what it had just done for both of them.

"Ma. You really gonna go out with him?"

Troi was determined to have a little happiness in her life, even if she had to make it a self-fulfilling prophecy.

"Yes. . . ." She closed her eyes and smiled, relishing what felt like a religious experience. "It just might be the start of something good."

FEVER

BY

LINDA DOMINIQUE GROSVENOR

About This Guide

The suggested questions are intended to enhance your group's
reading of Linda Dominique Grosvenor's FEVER.
We hope you have enjoyed the sequel to
LIKE BOOGIE ON TUESDAY.

DISCUSSION QUESTIONS

1. How much of Carla getting out of control in the classroom was a reflection of her childhood?

2. Should Carla have told Sam that Ashley wasn't his child from the beginning?

3. What are your thoughts about the rape that led to the conception of a child? Should the child ever know?

4. Do you believe Nina was or wasn't content with her life? Did her discontent have more to do with herself or her husband?

5. Do you feel that Troi was right to urge Nina to return home?

6. When Nina walked into Tim's office to find his ex-girlfriend and him in a compromising position, what do you think Nina should have done differently?

7. Should Nina have given up her dreams in lieu of Tim's?

8. Would you say that Troi and Dakoda had a good mother/daughter relationship?

9. What do you believe was Troi's biggest fear for her daughter Dakoda?

10. Sam was a good man; do you think that Carla owed him an explaination for her behavior?

11. Sam's desire for Troi was obvious. Do you believe that it was there all this time or something that just surfaced?

12. What are your thoughts on how Troi handled Sam's advances? What would you have done differently? Would you have told his wife?

BONUS CHAPTERS INCLUDED

In case you missed the exciting novel that started it all, LIKE BOOGIE ON TUESDAY, we have included the first six chapters for your reading pleasure. Don't miss the exciting novel that has garnered critical praise from reviewers and fans alike.

"From the beautiful, thought-provoking beginning to the climactic ending, as unforgettable as the sunset and hotter than the hinges on the gates of hell!"
— Timmothy B. McCann, author of *Until, Always* and *Emotions*

"Grosvenor has written a beautiful novel that touches the deepest, most tender moments of your heart. She's created characters you'll come to love and hate to leave."
— Jacquelin Thomas, author of *Singsation* and *The Prodigal Husband*

1

Nina was the director of a newly formed company, Dartmouth. They put together the literal demographics that businesses used to decipher who was buying what product, how much they were spending on average, and the income bracket into which they helplessly fell.

Their PR and advertising department then constructed vibrant sales pitches for products and used the subliminal advertising her thesis spoke of to get people to buy items that were manufactured and sold by several companies that made up their client roster.

Nina managed a staff of ten in a small neutral-colored office across town where there were hardly any trees or a pleasant view. It was a close fit, but lawfully comfortable. Four women and six men. She oversaw the smooth operations of the sometimes hectic office efficiently. Her rose-colored Formica desk wasn't cluttered with Post-It notes, files, paper-clip chains, or rotting rubber-band balls. She was a neat freak and relied only on the daily necessities prearranged in an orderly fashion.

She had a photograph on her desk in a handmade sterling silver frame of her and Troi in Cozumel four summers ago, an oversize coffee mug that said, DON'T MESS WITH ME, YOU KNOW HOW I GET, and a red crystal heart-shaped Elsa Peretti paperweight that was given to her by her father last Valentine's Day, which now held down a few wrinkled receipts and miscellaneous papers.

Her daily planner sat neatly in the center of it all. She enjoyed being tidy. She also enjoyed the freedom of running an office that virtually ran itself, and the occasional sunshine that came in through the window to nurture the plants on the windowsill and reflect off the Ansel Adams black-and-white print that graced the wall.

She felt a twinge of guilt sneak across her conscience about that. His work didn't fully express who she was as a person. She wasn't one to get caught up in what the rave was. But, like most things in her life, she would allow it to do for now. Even a barren forest with shriveled trees in a frame was better than a blank wall.

Nina didn't date much. She hadn't dated much in college either. Romance was as foreign to her as a trigonometry and calculus high. And she hadn't had time lately for more than a cappuccino, latte, or espresso on the run with any one person in particular.

She was educated, creative, and the type of woman who could shower and get dressed in less than thirty minutes. That was a noteworthy achievement in itself. She lived alone in a huge brownstone in Brooklyn Heights.

She spent most languid Saturday afternoons decorating the upstairs apartments one room at a time, with pieces she'd siphoned from friends and family, and the remnants of which she'd discovered strolling in and out of the antique shops along Atlantic Avenue. She enjoyed finding rare treasures and castoffs in the shops at which her friends and family turned up their regal noses.

They gladly emphasized that it was used furniture, and wanted a round of applause for their insight. But Nina got a natural pleasure from browsing through the antiques with their musty smells, swollen wood, affordable price tags, rusted latches and knobs that you could polish up like new. She didn't mind the teasing; antiques were something she had relished for years while they had all only gotten hip to decorating and home furnishings by watching cable.

Nina adored the quaint little shops that transported her through time and the wares of what were left of the art and book vendors in the city. She loved soft billowy fabrics, too. Moleskin was something quite peculiar. Sort of like the kid in school that nobody understood. It's the closest you could come to that suede feel without having to worry about permanent stains and enormous dry cleaning bills, although Nina couldn't fathom dropping her lounge chair off at the cleaners and having it back in an hour.

Moleskin. She'd fallen in love with it the moment she'd felt it against her skin and wrapped it around her waist and shoulders, then draped it behind her, trailing through the fabric store like a queen making her way to her throne. A little on the expensive side per yard, but the softness of the fabric soothed the back of her hands, her neck, and her wallet.

Nina closed her bashful eyes and imagined herself sitting naked in the middle of her living room swathed in this luxurious fabric, sipping coffee that warmed her hands as she turned the pages of the book she was reading with her toes. Turning pages with her toes was a trick she had learned in college while always trying to do three things at once and realizing she only had two hands.

She had bought several yards of the supple fabric in a rich moss green hue that, on second thought, she would use to refabric her favorite chair. If she had any left over, she would make a few throw pillows to make the room even more conducive to reading. Nina liked to read with her feet propped up on several pillows, too, four to be exact.

"I'll take some fringe, too. Gold," she'd spoken confidently to the suspicious salesclerk, who hadn't been too pleased that she was dragging the expensive fabric across the dusty floor.

Nina was definitely what some might describe as a walking catastrophe or an accidental mishap, but she prided herself on being unique, and got a kick out of colorful art that grabbed you up by the collar, held on, and shook you until you bought it. It was like learning to hula. It was fun while it lasted. Not many artists lured her like that. She could name several unknowns, but couldn't have a conversation about it with the people she knew, and that was a sad fact.

Nina figured that one day she would actually be able to rationalize spending two grand on a canvas delicately smeared with a few tubes of acrylic paint. She agreed that up-and-coming artists needed more exposure and that people needed to appreciate art as much as the money-laundering presidential elections.

Most natives or foreigners couldn't name three living artists off the top of their head. Degas, Dali, and Picasso didn't count. They were overrated and dead. Nina agreed with Shelby that a house was not a home or decorated properly if it only had movie posters taped up on the walls over a four-poster bed and a leaky radiator off in the corner hissing and making a mess.

She also agreed that right here in the city, people were starving, too. Two thousand dollars could feed a whole family for months. One day she'd get something to replace that substitute that hung on her office wall, something more soothing to her spirit and reflective of her heritage. Something that had depth and had to be explained by the artist himself. Something she could relate to intellectually.

Nina also was a fiend for music that leaned more toward classical and jazz. She liked to tap her feet, clap her hands, and bob her head a little too much for most people's taste. Kim Burrell was a serious singing sister. Listening to her crooning melodies in minor keys was sure to get you caught in the worship of it all.

Nina also had a thing for horns. She relished the fervor with which the musicians played. She'd never been like other kids, listening to that boring music that had everyone learning the latest dance steps and forming a Soul Train line right in their living rooms on Saturday mornings.

She preferred jazz and classical to the Top 40, and she couldn't care less about Billboard. She'd lean out of her window sometimes in the evening, resting her elbows on a goose-down pillow, and listen to her neighbor across the street playing his submissive instrument like his next meal depended on it. He blew aggressively into that horn like a rite of passage, and Nina overindulged herself on it all.

His melodies were tranquil, and ivy framed his window like a trellis. She often saw the sun setting in the evening, full and rested, and she would swear musical notes were floating from his parted curtains, inviting her to dance and play footsie.

Her neighbor's comforting tunes caressed her and took her mind someplace where she felt rocked to sleep with her favorite doll and pacified with her thumb, grinning because she didn't have to answer to anybody.

She was blissful as she enjoyed a place where she had a daddy but no mother, and she and her sister could swim in the lake under the noonday sun, and Daddy would fish and catch them something that he would slather with cornmeal and fry up nice and crisp and serve with some fresh-squeezed, slightly tart lemonade.

Nina could see the seeds slowly sinking to the bottom of the glass every time she took a sip. She loved lemonade. Ice-cold. She wondered if her neighbor played in a band and thought if not, he should. His music took her to faraway places that only existed in her mind and invited her nightly to come and pretend over and over again.

Nina wasn't a difficult girl, really. She often hung out in joints like Sweet Basil, which was supposed to be New York's hippest jazz club, and the Blue Note. She loved live music and the atmosphere of it all, although she could do without the smoky haze.

She loved jazz clubs not just because they were the happeningest places in town, but because music did things to her that people hadn't managed to do thus far. Nina didn't care about friends. She often found herself desiring to be alone, listening to the sultry sound of Nina Simone.

Too often she'd press Play and Repeat as Nina Simone crooned something about dying and despising a man she once called father. Nina remembered how she would lie on her crisp powder blue sheets in the autumn breeze with her eyes closed as the large earth-hued maple leaves brushed near her window, calling her, and she'd rediscover the sound that often serenaded her as she drifted off to sleep.

Music was Nina; she had known that ever since her freshman year at Cornell. She would listen to the guys from the school rehearsing in the courtyard. They'd warm up and exercise their lips for a nonstop jam session that lasted way into the wee hours like a church revival. Everyone sat out in nearby complexes reading and enjoying the free music that helped them escape having to study or write research papers.

Nina's passion for music almost prompted her to change her major in her sophomore year, but she didn't. She refused to ruin her desire of it by overindulging in it. She also didn't want to know about B-flat and off-key; she just wanted to enjoy the sound that tickled her ears and made her believe she was sexier than she actually was. Her mother was pleased as peaches that she reconsidered changing her major, although Nina insisted, "It's my life, you know."

Nina had her dreams and aspirations, but often thought of things that she never wanted to be. She never wanted to be one of those women who read *Shape* but was never physically fit, she never wanted to be a guest on a talk show, she never wanted to become a product of her environment, and she never ever wanted to be still single at forty.

One out of four wasn't that bad. She didn't crave a man or the presence of one, she just wanted to have someone with whom she could share and communicate the little things. Things like a district-manager-of-the-month certificate, or maybe even just the regurgitated details of the annoying assistant at the office who refused to clean the food particles out of the telephone receiver when he was done munching lunch while talking on it.

She needed someone to tell, even though Nina made a silent pact with herself to deny it to the death. Having a love interest surely beat coming home and talking to her fish and plants. Heck, they could talk to each other, she thought with a laugh.

She just wanted to know that her holidays would not be spent alone sitting in her favorite chair watching her prestrung reindeer with sparkling white lights sitting in front of the house twinkling. She also didn't want to end up drinking so much thick prepackaged eggnog from the carton until she wanted to vomit, or calling up people she no longer liked just to prove that she still had someone to talk to around the holidays.

Nina could appreciate mittens, snowballs, holding hands, and having to pick up someone from the airport even on a late-night transatlantic flight. She wanted to expect a birthday card from someone besides her sister. Valentine's Day needed to find her dining at Maxim's in a red dress with a French manicure and being served like a goddess by a waiter named Jacques.

She wanted to be excited about something more than just Alvin Ailey American Dance Theater. She was elated because she had gotten tickets ahead of time. They had once performed at her school, she'd joined their mailing list, made a donation, and was now what they considered a sponsor.

She wanted things to be different this year. They ought to be. She just needed to find a comfortable place and reside in it.

2

Tim was silent. He scribbled his notes and buried his head as his classmate stood at the head of the class and acted out her dialogue within the guidelines that the professor had set forth from the textbook. His professor had written the textbook, so regardless of the fact that Tim hadn't had enough funds to purchase the book in time for the start of class, it was smooth sailing, as the professor went over each chapter verbatim. Tim was thankful enough for that. His class was made up of approximately eleven men and nine women. Age range was between nineteen and forty-six.

"Can you see how important dialogue is?" his professor asked, gesturing, then applauding at his student's efforts. She made her way back to her seat, smiling all the way.

The woman sitting directly behind Tim nudged him in the back, then passed him a folded-up piece of paper. Tim looked over his shoulder and smirked as he unfolded it and read the words. The letter made him feel like a grade schooler with some girl diggin' him, too shy to say it. The note read *Let's do dinner @ my place.*

Tim turned around and eyed the woman, then leaned back in his chair and ignored her. He knew it was just a matter of time before some woman would be overeager and hit on him. It never failed. From time to time he had to take inventory, check himself, and make sure he wasn't sending mixed signals by staring too long or trying to be overly helpful. He wasn't. Women were just a trip.

His hair cut close, his silk sweater courting his muscular frame and baggy khakis assisting, he was being smug, and he knew it. She leaned forward, put her lips to his ear, and whispered, "You looking good, Tim, so when?"

"Dialogue makes our scenes come to life." The professor paced the floor.

"When what?" Tim spoke over his shoulder.

"You, me, dinner and . . ."

Her words left him hanging.

"C'mon, Tim, we can work on our projects together," she said, ignoring the professor's gaze.

"This is important, and you both need to be paying attention." The professor glared in their direction.

"Go over your syllabi this weekend to see when the project is due and make a note of it. There will be no late papers, no makeups, and no exceptions. Class is dismissed." The professor nodded.

Tim lifted his bag onto his shoulder and hurried out of the classroom to his comfy ride, old faithful. He tossed his books in the backseat and headed over to the beauty shop, looking behind him only once to make sure his classmate wasn't hot on his heels.

Rochelle needed a ride home because Carl was working late. He hated the thought of going into that hair place, because women always sat around gossiping about nonsense. When he walked in they'd glue their eyes to him as if he were their last supper. He could think of better things to do than fighting to keep those man-hungry women off of him. He could go by the fish place, get some takeout, kick back, and listen to some tunes, or stir his creativity by toying with his Magnetic Poetry set. He enjoyed sliding the magnets around on his fridge, discovering new phrases and being prolific. It often gave him fresh thoughts and a new direction for his ideas.

Tim grudgingly pressed his way into the salon anyway and offered smiles all around as he spotted his sister near the back of the shop and made his way to her.

"Good evening, ladies." He eyed them one at a time.

"Oooh, good evening, young man. What can I do for you?" A middle-aged woman with clothes two sizes too small squirmed in her seat, rearranged her breasts, and got comfortable.

"I'm here to pick up Rochelle." He slowed his pace.

"Oh, umm, uh-huh, I see." Another woman eyed Rochelle over her specs.

"That's my brother, if you all must know." Rochelle smirked.

"Good-looking young man," the old woman agreed.

"Yeah, he needs a date, some love in his life, though." She shoved her brother.

"So does my sister," Troi interjected while making change for Rochelle, counting out singles.

"Tim, this is Troi Singleton. She's been doing my hair forever." Tim nodded his head and acknowledged her.

"Don't pay your sister any mind. She's always trying to set someone up." Troi waved her hand at Rochelle.

"I'm trying to help him, Troi. He does need love. We all do," Rochelle added.

He couldn't believe his sister was practically saying that he was desperate in front of all these strange women—women she had to know had granddaughters who they were probably eager to pawn off on him.

"I need a little love myself." The woman with the tight clothes and protruding breasts pursed her lips.

"You ready, Rochelle?" Tim spoke impatiently.

"Yes. I'm coming." She gathered her things up.

"Nice meeting you, Tim." Troi smiled.

"Likewise." Tim nodded.

Rochelle waved and tripped out of the salon. Tim held the door open for her and gave her an icy glare.

"What?" she asked.

"You know what . . ."

"If I knew, I wouldn't ask, Tim."

"You know I don't like that."

"It was innocent. They didn't mean anything by it."

"I didn't mean them, I meant you."

"C'mon, Tim, lighten up."

"You're always telling me to lighten up."

"That's because you won't listen."

"I'll find someone when it's time, Rochelle." He slid into his car.

"How do you know it's not time now and you're not just blocking it out or something?" She pulled the door closed.

"Because when it's time, I won't need you to tell me, I'll know for myself."

"Fine then. End up old and gray with no one to tuck you in at night." She raised her hand toward him.

"I'm sorry, Rochelle . . ."

"No, you're right. It's your life. I can let you wither away if you want. I just thought that I was helping."

"You're my sister. Your love is help enough."

She glanced over at him, not sure if she wanted to accept the truce.

"I love you, too, Tim."

"I know you do." He smiled. "I know you do."

3

Nina Madison was a nonaggressive Pentecostal woman in her midthirties who observed Easter and Christmas in the more traditional sense. Not that others didn't; it was just that she had managed to incorporate the spirit of it all into her celebrations. She'd deck her halls, but she didn't offer chocolate bunnies or give into the blasphemy of Santa Claus, not even for the kids.

She never could get the correlation of Christ to a bunny rabbit, and ho-ho-ho was hardly the same as Noel. She did, however, enjoy the luxury of jelly beans, though it had absolutely nothing to do with the holiday itself. She had a sweet tooth. Jelly beans were her sugar of choice.

Nina took frequent pleasure in giving to the homeless by volunteering her time at a local soup kitchen on Thanksgiving, Christmas, and other nonoccasions in between with her sister, while others who were abundantly provided for sat around, ate like gluttons, and beached themselves like harpooned whales in front of the television, watching football and being thankful for nothing more than clear reception.

She imagined that most people normally felt compassion for the homeless in their hearts; they just didn't take the initiative to get up and do something or otherwise show it. Volunteering made her feel useful, needed. There was much to be said about those who were selfless enough to give.

As of late, Nina had been in and out of the halls of sanctification and wore no labels that were perpetuated by mere men. She wasn't estranged from her faith; she still prayed, and she was even more comfortable now without the accusing look-who-decided-to-come-to-church stares.

Her face was fuller, although her lips always were. She had matured quite handsomely and was often told that she was mentally stimulating and energetic.

She loved laughter and paid close attention to her weight, which was now teetering between 190 and 195. She didn't care who laughed at that. She was as content as a kid in a double-feature matinee with a large popcorn and a family pack of Milk Duds.

Nina was comfortable being a size fourteen, sometimes sixteen, and dressed modestly unless it was one of those rare occasions that brought out the diva in her—for instance, when she'd take in an evening performance at the Met dressed in sequins or a stunning bugle bead number with a slit that bared a little thigh.

Renditions of *La Boheme*, Elgar, or Chopin were equally entertaining, although her enjoyment of it all depended more on who was performing than what she was wearing. She led a rather voluptuous life.

Nina's family, on the other hand, was something she was less vocal about. Her father was a melancholy man nearing sixty who had left the contracting company that had drained his entire life and sucked the fabric out of his family bond and started a small contracting company of his own.

Remodeling kitchens was one of the rare things he enjoyed. Nina could swear that when she'd stop by a job and find him working without a lunch break and trying to meet his deadline, she saw the residue of a smile every now and then. Her mother had reluctantly agreed to take out a second mortgage on their house to fund his construction company idea. It was a long time coming and barely thriving. He was too smitten to notice.

Nina's mother was a head nurse at Mount Sinai in the city and had made financial plans to retire in two years. It was straining, watching her parents disagree and circle like vultures above the carcass of what they'd managed to scrape together and still call family. She loved her father, though Nina and her mother had never really been close. Mother would tend to smother her creativity by criticizing everything Nina adored. Nina often resented it out loud and made vain attempts to be as flamboyant as she could be without being considered ridiculous.

Nina's sister, Troi, did hair. Troi did wraps, scrunches, finger waves, box braids, goddess braids, Senegalese twists, and any other style in *Black Hair, Style Q* or *Hype Hair* magazines. She had her own shop and spent endless hours in her haven listening to the chatter of the unfulfilled lives of women as far away as Jersey and Connecticut.

She attended the Beauty, Barber & Supply Annual Convention, the Big Show Expo, and the Summer Madness Hair Competition faithfully, to keep all of her customers up on the healthiest and most stylish alternatives for hairstyling. Troi was content. She always doted on her husband and child. They were staples in her life, along with God. The shop just fit neatly into the equation. All she needed now was a tidy red velvet bow so she could peel off the backing and stick it right on top of her gift-wrapped perfection.

Owning a beauty salon had been Troi's dream since she was a child. As far back as Nina could remember, her scrawny little fair-faced sister had said, "I'm gonna have my own shop. I'm gonna do every style there is and I'm gonna do it better than everybody."

"You've got to know what you're doing, or you'll be out of business in a heartbeat," Mother had chided.

Shangrila had materialized just as if Troi had spoken it prophetically into the wind.

Nina remembered how, growing up, Troi would style her doll's hair just like hers. She would go to school every morning with a newly created hairstyle that would be the envy of every girl in her homeroom. She'd have all the girls staring at her all day long and then running home anxiously trying to imitate her latest coiffure.

Troi would come home, plop down at the kitchen table, whiz through her homework, mix a noisy glass of chocolate milk, and then pull out her worn drawing tablet. She'd sketch up hairstyles that she envisioned a sleek model would wear on the fashionable Paris runways or at a brightly lit photo shoot on location in the Caribbean. Whimsical thinking. It came rather naturally for Troi.

Twisted locks fastened with colorful barrettes, loops, pins, woven braids that looked more like a hat than a hairstyle, and fanlike Patti Labelle things swaying more than the hips of the woman for whom she fantasized she had created the style. She was only fourteen years old then. She was curious and creative, an interesting combination. Mother had resented the fact that Troi chose hair styling as her profession. "She'll grow out of it," everyone had said.

"Doing hair? It's so limiting and common, child," Mother had said, never once taking into account what desires her children had stirring inside them or what dreams fueled them to breathe.

As a mother, she could have been more supportive, but then, their mother wasn't your run-of-the-mill June Cleaver type. There were no kisses, hugs, or congratulations. She didn't bake brownies, and they were never Girl Scouts, but she was their mother, like it or not, even if she was barely tolerable.

Mother lived to voice her opinion and could cut you down to the nubs with her words, gag you, and then cast you aside like a mule that was too useless to cart a load. Mother hadn't necessarily seen what Troi did for a living as talent, but Troi's career was definitely paying the bills now. The family felt safe.

Nina, on the other hand, wore self-imposed labels from her past. She thought from the inside looking out that she was boring, a little too chubby, and had a lisp that was slightly noticeable only to those looking for something to criticize.

Nina remembered the school functions where she was always the one standing in the corner, leaning on the wall, waiting to be asked to dance. She'd drink watered-down punch until her tongue and lips were blood red. In junior high she was jokingly voted most likely to become a wallflower.

The kids had thought it was funny, but they didn't know how deep wounds buried themselves. Labels peel off, she often thought. But with her self-image, her mother's concept, and everyone else's thoughts about her buzzing around all the time, no wonder she was a walking mishap. She just wanted the peace and quiet to live a fulfilling life.

Nina had become a compulsively private person over the years and kept to herself more as she got older and wiser. She had maybe three friends, if you counted the one who barely called her. She shredded her mail, even the sweepstakes.

She refused to put return addresses on envelopes, made sure to blacken the address label on all of her magazines before she lent them out or gave them away, and denied her heart the overwhelming joys of love. She'd never love someone who would eventually end up leaving. That would be absolutely too much for her jaded heart to bear.

Nina was a rules queen. She had tons of them. She never argued in public. She locked the doors and windows and checked them again before she turned out the lights to retire for the night (although her therapist warned that that type of behavior bordered on compulsion). And although Nina lived alone, she still went to the bathroom with the door closed and the flap from the roll of toilet tissue facing out.

She was made paranoid by the "what ifs." Always creating scenarios in her mind of a masked man with green teeth running through the house and surprising her on the toilet or in the kitchen. He'd probably tell her that the door was open so he just came in, but she'd know he was lying. She could spot a liar at least half a block away.

The fear of the unknown kept Nina a virtual prisoner the majority of the time. Friends who made futile attempts to try to get her to lighten up also offered that she needed to enjoy life, open up, and feel free. It was easy for them to say. They blossomed like ripe tulips in the spring breeze, with the sun beating down on them and releasing the fragrance of who they were, while Nina felt more like a weed that a passing dog lifted his leg to pee on.

Nina wasn't svelte and she was always self-conscious, especially since her mother found it necessary to remind her that she was fat every chance she got. In school, Nina had been teased about her butt being big, fat, and hanging over the chair. Some of her classmates had been way past fat, but they'd joined in with the name-calling to take the focus off of themselves.

The kids would say Nina sounded like King Kong coming down the hall. They'd embarrass her by holding on to their lockers as if there were an earthquake and they were trying to save each other's lives. She'd swallowed one too many doses of pride and sat on one too many tacks.

It had been because of those episodes in school that Nina had always acted out at home, releasing all of that repressed hurt and anxiety. This was no surprise. Home was the only place she felt she had any power. Her father let her have her way most of the time, and it was more fun than a roller-coaster ride. She relished the attention of being heard. She felt invincible for the most part, although she was growing more and more uncompromising, like her mother.

"It's expected of a child," people had said, but she didn't know how her father put up with such behavior from her mother.

Nina had a calculating personality. She was always up to something, if not with her hands, then in her mind. The preacher stood on the pulpit and said, "Woe unto them who let an idle mind rule them."

But even Nina herself was glad when she outgrew her mean streak.

"It's useless and self-defeating," a counselor at school had told her parents. "It may stem from feeling estranged from your mom," the counselor had added to Nina. "How is your relationship with your mom, Nina?"

That was the last appointment Nina remembered them ever having with that counselor.

"I don't need some high-heeled diploma-toting woman with a razor-sharp tongue interfering with how I raise my kids," Mother had spat.

Nina was a little girl then, she hadn't a clue, but she understood what her mother was now. Even then, with continued weekly counseling visits that eventually became monthly and a therapist they all almost agreed on, Nina had been allowed to realize that her anger wasn't so much a part of her personality as it was rage directed toward her mother.

"You need more interaction with your children, Mrs. Madison."

Mother hadn't liked this new therapist either, but Daddy had refused to go scouting for another one. It was always like a tug-of-war with Nina and her mother from birth. When Nina was a knee-high child of almost ten, people couldn't help but chatter, "Watching you is like looking at your mother, child."

Nina would stand, hand on hip, as children should never do. She would plug her ears with her fingers, tired of people telling her the same thing over and over again.

"Stop telling me that, I can't take it," Nina would say.

I'm nothing like my mother, she thought. She wasn't useless. In hindsight, she realized that her mother had stolen enough from them. She was such a clumsy thief.

"Cut it out!" her father would yell when her mother would go on and on about Miss Nina being too fast with her mouth. "She got it honest." He'd frown.

He didn't take sides. He just rustled the paper, folded it over to the sports section, and refused to get involved. He demanded peace in his house. Occasionally he got it.

"You can't say everything that comes to mind, Nina," he'd plead. "You have to respect your mother," he'd request, his arms extended like a pauper in utter despair.

Nina hated when her father scolded her. Nina would nod as if she understood, her head full of beads with aluminum foil at the tips, shaking her head wildly and rolling her eyes, making the beads jingle. Her bell-bottoms always made her feel dangerous. Girl power was nothing new. She was a child and was supposed to be rebellious. It was what was expected. It had never been her intention to disappoint.

Nina was a homebody. Even as a child, she enjoyed the time she spent at home more than school. Home was more than four walls closing you in and warding off evildoers, home was where her music was, all shiny and vinyl. She loved some of the songs from back then when she was growing up, too young to know all the words or apply them. The *Daily News* was a dime, and the songs, they were more like anthems for life.

She was just a baby, so "Love the One You're With" was hardly something she could live by. Nevertheless, she loved to ignore people and get under their skin and stay awhile, especially people who wanted to teach her lessons. She would hear her father go on and on about how she needed to try more with her mother. But her mind drifted consciously to more musical thoughts. Thoughts like how she could convince her daddy to start giving them an allowance again so she wouldn't have any problems getting those new 45s she wanted so badly played in her mind.

"I won't tell Mother, I promise," Nina had convinced him.

She didn't purposely manipulate people; she was a kid herself. But those who she couldn't manipulate, she'd ignore. Antisocial was an understatement. She hated everyone in her school, every single teacher and even most of the nosy fashion-tragic people in her church. On the rare occasions that her father took her mother's side, it made Nina want to hold her breath and count to three hundred.

Her mother would feel as if she won any little debate she and Nina were having once her father put his two cents in. Her mother would smirk like a spoiled-rotten child, pushing her chest out and chin up, being sure to keep her upper lip stiff, as if to say, *I told you so*. Nina would mumble something under her breath that only her mother could hear, pretending she was singing it. It was always a game to her.

"See, she's starting now, Charles. When I finish with her, she'll be sorry, hear?"

"Sadie, you can't be so sensitive. She's a child. Quit acting foolish."

Her mother would huff off to a secluded part of their yard-sale chic house when she didn't get her way. Nina manipulated her daddy because she was his favorite, although she denied it every time Troi was nothing new. She was a child and was supposed to be rebellious. It was what was expected. It had never been her intention to disappoint.

Nina was a homebody. Even as a child, she enjoyed the time she spent at home more than school. Home was more than four walls closing you in and warding off evildoers, home was where her music was, all shiny and vinyl. She loved some of the songs from back then when she was growing up, too young to know all the words or apply them. The *Daily News* was a dime, and the songs, they were more like anthems for life.

She was just a baby, so "Love the One You're With" was hardly something she could live by. Nevertheless, she loved to ignore people and get under their skin and stay awhile, especially people who wanted to teach her lessons. She would hear her father go on and on about how she needed to try more with her mother. But her mind drifted consciously to more musical thoughts. Thoughts like how she could convince her daddy to start giving them an allowance again so she wouldn't have any problems getting those new 45s she wanted so badly played in her mind.

"I won't tell Mother, I promise," Nina had convinced him.

She didn't purposely manipulate people; she was a kid herself. But those who she couldn't manipulate, she'd ignore. Antisocial was an understatement. She hated everyone in her school, every single teacher and even most of the nosy fashion-tragic people in her church. On the rare occasions that her father took her mother's side, it made Nina want to hold her breath and count to three hundred.

Her mother would feel as if she won any little debate she and Nina were having once her father put his two cents in. Her mother would smirk like a spoiled-rotten child, pushing her chest out and chin up, being sure to keep her upper lip stiff, as if to say, *I told you so.* Nina would mumble something under her breath that only her mother could hear, pretending she was singing it. It was always a game to her.

"See, she's starting now, Charles. When I finish with her, she'll be sorry, hear?"

"Sadie, you can't be so sensitive. She's a child. Quit acting foolish."

Her mother would huff off to a secluded part of their yard-sale chic house when she didn't get her way. Nina manipulated her daddy because she was his favorite, although she denied it every time Troi insinuated that. Her mother would sit at the tiny lopsided kitchen table and lose herself in a choice of gray haze: a game of solitaire, or three shots of vodka.

Mother would sit with a lit cigarette dancing on her bottom lip, licking the rim of a shot glass. The careless cigarettes burned holes in the peeling contact paper that was supposed to cover up the fact that they were long overdue for a new kitchen set. This had gone on as long as Nina could remember. Bickering and family outings that never were as perfect as they appeared to those on the outside looking in.

"What pretty little girls you have, Sadie," friends, neighbors, and church members said.

It sounded lyrical when they made that statement. It made you think that Nina and Troi should be on top of music boxes. Ballerinas. Twirling.

"They're absolutely adorable."

Her mother would give them dry dirty looks, only half-masking the statement, *you want 'em you can have 'em*, as she nudged them forward.

Nina often wondered if Mother would really let them pack up and go, and possibly salvage some of the life they had left. Snide remarks like that cut right through little children and made them feel like they had grubby hands. Never feeling wanted, needed, or good enough to sit on what Mother considered the good furniture was all either of the Madison girls remembered.

Nina couldn't even imagine hugging or feeling her mother's warmth. Nina had held a snake once, down South when they had spent the summer with the only living relative that remained on the Madison side. She wondered if Mother felt like that.

Nina remembered vividly when she'd made her mother an ashtray in the third grade. She'd painted it royal blue and green because the plaid sofa had green stripes in it. She had pressed down on the clay when it was soft, making sure that it had more than enough spaces for mother to rest her cigarettes. Nina had missed recess that day because she'd wanted so badly to finish her gift for her mother. She'd felt revived, almost yearning.

She'd been attempting to be more useful. In her mind, she'd seen her mother's joy when she unwrapped the gift. Her mother would give her kisses for the first time ever and hug her so tightly that Nina wouldn't be able to breathe. She'd imagined that her mother would say that she was sorry for everything and wanted them to be like normal families. Nina would ignore the stench of alcohol that seeped through her mother's pores, leapt off her breath, and lingered in her clothing, and they would be on their way to something good. Finally.

When Nina had actually brought the ashtray home, proud and willing to try being nice as Daddy had asked so many times, Mother had laughed hysterically.

"What is that?" She'd pointed at the ashtray as if it were a creature.

Nina had swallowed hard. The lump in her throat wouldn't move past her chest. She'd fought the pain and dared not let it lead to tears. Mother had rejected the truce.

"Please get that contraption off my living-room table, Nina! You don't think I'm gonna display that, do you?" Mother had been falling over with laughter, and had waved Nina away when she'd tried to assist her to her feet.

People on the outside looking in didn't know how much of a joke it was being one of Sadie's kids.

4

Sharon bought Tim delicate silk shirts in brilliant tropical hues. Fuchsia (which he probably would never wear), lime green, aqua, and a pale yellow. Michelle had been paying Tim's overpriced tuition for his continuing education classes faithfully for the past year and a half. It was too expensive, and he knew she only did it to show him that she didn't care how much it cost. It was the name that he was paying for more than anything. It was the best. She wanted him to have the finest, so she provided the means even if it cost her everything short of breath.

He had met them both right after he'd found out that he had been accepted to college. Now he was enrolled in New York University's film school. It had been two days shy of a month since he had spoken to either one of them. He tried not to allow women to distract him. He needed to focus on his screen plays and completing his film assignments in a timely fashion without being interrupted by someone craving attention—unless it was him who was craving. He smiled slyly to himself, licking down the corner of his mustache.

Getting his films to stand out and catch the eye of major studio executives was the priority on his list. He was weaving a plot so tight that it would snatch them within the first ten pages, and slap them in the face with the last. But it seemed that the two things he was most passionate about often clashed. Filmmaking and women, in that order. Filmmaking always came first, but women hardly ran a distant second.

Women always admired Tim's towering height and muscular frame.

"He can change a lightbulb without standing on a chair," he once overheard a sister say.

He was six feet even. His smoldering complexion and dark eyes left women claiming that he was exotic looking.

"Where you from?" they'd ask.

His eyes drew them in, they said. So, it was only inevitable when they fell for him.

"You know what you do," an ex-girlfriend once told him. "You set women up for the kill."

He smirked. It was almost true.

Women adored Tim's sleek sideburns and mustache that always had a slight sheen, and he had to curb their constant urges to touch his face. He had sensitive skin, and women were always putting their hands in his face. They wanted to prove that he was theirs. He didn't like that.

"Love is a game," Tim said, "and I don't want to play it."

He was talking to his reflection again, brushing his goatee and checking between his teeth, doing that little thing with his tongue.

He wasn't vain. He just didn't have time for love, a relationship, or someone who would be there in his apartment trying to get him to eat what they thought he should eat, playing wifey, planning his weekends, and making smug attempts to redecorate his urban suite.

They called him a pretty boy, but he was pretty tired of the game is what he was. He wasn't God's gift to women. He wouldn't allow himself to believe that. He was charming, intelligent, and most women just believed they needed someone, namely him. He'd been told more than enough that he was pleasing to the eye, captivating even, and granted, he loved women, but his head wasn't up to the emotional game of tag that usually ensued shortly after becoming involved with them.

He believed that men limited themselves by dating exclusively.

"If you aren't married, then you're single," he was famous for saying.

Most women walked around with a leash dangling from their clutches, and as soon as they found someone whom they'd remotely consider, they'd chain him up and walk him home. Tim said it and it was true; he had seen it happen.

As a single unattached man with a vivid imagination, he found that he could swing with a theory that was founded on moral truth. Women wanted to possess men. They were beautiful and came in various shades and ethnicities, but he wasn't buying.

He imagined that eventually he would settle down once he was es-
tablished and possibly do the family thing, but he reneged on the
thought of it for now. It was a far-fetched notion that for now was
only feasible on the way-too-distant horizon. He was concerned that
his love of filmmaking would be hindered by any type of relationship
that he'd try to cultivate, and something had to give.

Women didn't want some of your time, they wanted all of it. They
didn't take no for an answer, and they interpreted *I'll call you* to
mean, *tomorrow morning I'll be there for breakfast, eggs over-easy.*
He didn't play that money game with women either. He didn't have
any. He was living grant to grant, and if he did come into any cash,
he wasn't about to blow it on hair, nails, or Nine West. Women had
to learn to support their own habits. The minute you started giving
women money to shop, they relied on it, and worked it into their
monthly budgets. He was sweet, but he wasn't about to be anybody's
sugar daddy.

Tim didn't have a harem of women, but he wasn't a loner either.
He thrived on the constant feedback from women he labeled "friends."
They hated that term. If you called a woman a friend they'd get in-
dignant.

"What do you mean *friend?*" they spat with snakelike attitude.

They wanted another label. *My boo, my baby, my woman,* or *my
girl.* Even *my stuff* was better to their ears than *friend.*

The constant drama that the women in his life provided stirred his
ideas. He loved the female perspective, and he knew exactly how to
portray them: merciless. And that wasn't necessarily a bad thing. But
he had surely enjoyed the time he had been alone for the past few
weeks. He could focus, and that was a marvelous thing. His thoughts
were clearer and his dialogue flowed from the tip of his tongue right
onto the paper. He was pleased with his progress.

Michelle was out of town on a promotional tour with a group she
was managing. She believed that they were destined for the big time,
like so many other four-guy groups that were but a flicker. They
crooned and woo-wooed, and she shopped for them and spent hours
rehearsing the poses that were most photogenic. She had a life besides Tim, and that was cool. He dug that. He was too busy priori-
tizing anyway.

He had spent the past few weeks dodging Sharon's answering-
machine messages, sorting out storylines, and doing background research for the characters in his script. He loved the fact that like,
women, a filmmaker could give birth to something extraordinary. A

creation that had been fed by their ability to conceive an idea, carry it to term, and bring forth life. His dream had always been to make films. He was barely surviving on the small stipends that he had been given to complete at least one of his amateur films. The money they gave wasn't enough to produce an episode of *Mr. Bill*, but he made it rubber—it stretched.

Sharon kept calling and calling, sunup to dusk. She wanted to come over and lounge in the newness of his personal space, and she always used gifts she had bought Tim as bait. It was no secret that he liked nice things. All you had to do was look at his shoes, his apartment, and his fingernails.

But he didn't want any woman taking care of him. He refused to be a kept man. Women's money and gifts came with strings attached that rendered you a puppet. He wasn't about to be strung along.

Women were creatures bent on instant gratification, always wanting their desires fulfilled immediately. Michelle was a prime example.

She was always too occupied for him, but when she wanted Tim in the middle of the night, she expected everything on earth to stop and succumb to her. And it did . . . he did. But it wasn't a forever thing. He figured he'd leave it at that. It wasn't a constant struggle in his mind to think of something other than Michelle.

He preferred her to Sharon, that was true. She wasn't needy. Her voice sent him to near hyperventilation, though he tried to be nonchalant about it. His sweaty palms always gave it away. Most of the time she pretended not to notice. She was the only woman who did that for him. But if he had to leave her alone, he could. He wondered if she knew she had an edge, however slight.

Tim didn't have time to date exclusively, or go out much, but women all but insisted. Men had to keep in mind that anywhere you appeared with a woman in public was construed as a date. They wanted him to drop them off, pick them up, help them move, drive them to the mall in Jersey, help them do research, put up shelves and bookcases, or program their VCRs.

And when he resisted and all else failed, they offered their cleavage while leaning over reaching for something imaginary. He was raised to be the perfect gentleman; women loved it and hated it at the same time. They were attracted to the gentle courteous nature of a man who had enough willpower to compliment without overwhelming, but not the gentleman who refused to take advantage of a situation.

Women had their tricks. They wanted to buy Tim things and feed him like he was new to the neighborhood. Their motives were fueled by the old adage that the way to a man's heart was to feed him to death. Women showed up with crumb cake, oxtails, paella, peach cobbler, pasteles, curried shrimp, and a host of other dishes that decreased the amount of time he would actually have to spend in the kitchen.

Michelle's specialty was braised lamb chops with wild rice, but with her constantly traveling, he hadn't savored the taste of that in awhile. He did miss her cooking, though it was her presence he missed more. He'd never tell her that. Then she'd really have the upper hand and manipulate him into submission or beyond.

Sharon, however, was a take-out kind of girl. She knew all the best places in the city where you could get mouthwatering takeout that left you licking your fingers and digging your teeth with your fingernails. Dallas BBQ, Cabana, Jerk Chicken House, Sabrosura, Wedge Inn, and Gonzalez y Gonzalez. It didn't matter how far out of the way the restaurant was, as long as she didn't have to mess up her silk-wrapped fingernails to cook.

Many women came in and out of Tim's life, each equipped with their own talents, and although he had never met a woman who had come to his door wearing only a fur coat and a pair of black patent leather stilettos, he knew that it wasn't long before someone acted out the tired scenario.

Tim was doing a good job. He was balancing. He had to fight to make time for himself. Working at school, needing a better place to live, trying to work at odd jobs to fund his ideas, and going to the gym kept him strapped for personal time. He didn't work out obsessively, but his body was prime. He was twenty-eight and still young. He lifted weights when he was kicking around with friends at the local health club, but he knew that he needed to do it more often. Especially now that he was getting older.

Besides, it was a mental release. Exercise stimulated the mind and started the creative juices flowing. He needed some creative juices. Things had been going well, but a dry spell was inevitable. He knew this was like the pseudo-cool after the torrential rain—the sun would come out and dry up every flowing drop of juice. He hated when everything he wrote began to sound like something he had written before. He hated being redundant as much as he hated having to repeat himself, which was the same thing, but not technically. Tim made a mental note to call up his boy Justin to see if he wanted to do this workout thing on a regular basis. Two heads were better than one, he imagined. If Tim made a commitment, he knew that Justin would hold him to it. Always did, always did.

Tim ate voraciously, and though he wasn't a vegetarian, he did limit his meat intake and ate lots of roughage. It wasn't his fault. Women showed up at his door with food. Tupperware, aluminum pans, and pots from their own kitchens just so they'd have a reason to come back. He knew the deal. But he was entertained by eating. It was his favorite thing to do besides creating memorable scenes and overindulging in women.

He favored pasta, and was especially fond of garlic. He ate it raw. It was good for a lot of things, healthwise. He laughed to himself, thinking that it also kept the vampires away. His mother had taught him early on to nourish the inside with food and knowledge. Read. He didn't read nearly enough. He had been focusing on school for the past year and change, and was desperately trying to develop his own niche. He'd get there eventually. He saw himself a household name in less than five years, surpassing Mr. Clean and the Ty-D-Bol Man.

When the phone rang, Tim closed his eyes and scrunched up his nose. Flashbacks of him faking excitement played in his mind. He knew it was none other than Sharon attempting to leave her sixth message. He wondered what she found so fascinating about him, and he smiled, figuring that she hadn't had a man treat her like much of anything. He did feel privileged to give her a standard by which to measure other men.

She was pretty, just a little abrasive for his personal taste. It was unfortunate that some men treated women like a gooey wad of gum that they couldn't get off the bottom of their shoe. But it made it that much easier for the brothers who had a little finesse to get a fair shake or the time of day.

Women loved attention. When they had a man, they felt like they were on stage. Sharon was lonely and desperate; it was obvious by the way she couldn't let a day go by without calling. Their affair had been in its final weeks for months now, but she didn't have a clue. She wasn't budging. She had left five consecutive messages and was attempting to leave her sixth. Tim listened to half of his outgoing message before snatching the phone off the hook and telling Sharon he was busy.

"Oh, so you don't want me to come over?"

"I'm not saying that," Tim said.

"I picked up a few nice things for you and I just want to drop them by, that's all."

He could hear her prerehearsed sexiness emanating through the telephone. He wished she was that feminine all the time and not just when she was trying to get her way.

"You can come by, Sharon, I'm just working on something for school. It has to be completed by tomorrow though."

"So, Tim? Can I stay the night?"

"I don't know, baby. Do you think that would be a good idea? You know I wouldn't get anything done with you looking good sprawled all over my sofa. You know how you do," he teased.

He didn't understand his incessant need to lie to her.

"Uh-huh, I see."

"Seriously . . ."

"You sure you don't have someone else coming over, Tim? Because you know I can find out."

"Baby, when do I have time for that?"

"Uh-huh."

"You know how serious I take my work."

"Yes, I know."

"Tell me where I would fit another woman in my life?"

"I know, I know." She laughed. "I was just testing you, that's all."

"Still playing games, huh, Sharon?"

"No games, honey, you know me. But I'll be over with some Chinese. Shrimp chow mein?"

"Sesame chicken for me, with plain fried rice. Thanks. And no MSG, okay?"

"I'll be there in less than a half."

Tim placed the receiver on the hook, looked around the room, and began to prepare himself mentally for another evening of playing grin-and-bear-it with Sharon, who would taunt and tease him into performing how much he really cared. Tim never had a problem getting women, but it had become a bit unnerving at times trying to get rid of them.

His only major rule was that no one spent the night. He had broken that rule twice with Michelle. He didn't label women trash or objects that needed to be discarded, but they just needed too much. They wanted your time, your money, and sex in compromising ways that was supposed to convince them that you were theirs or vice versa. He didn't have a dime or a flashy car, but surprisingly enough that hardly mattered to most women.

Tim had the look, and he had been getting by on that for years now. Women had been a mental challenge for Tim since he was thirteen. They had a knack for weaving themselves into every aspect of your life. They would do your homework, buy you lunch, sneakers, and pay your homeboy's way to the movies if you told them you left your wallet home. They'd tell their grandmother that you were coming to the family reunion before you even knew a thing about them or their grandmother.

They wanted you to meet their gigantic older brother who drank a gallon and a half of milk everyday and was a quarterback at the local college, as if it was some sort of collateral measure that would assure them that you wouldn't break their heart. The Nina, the Pinta, and the Santa Maria, they just wanted to rush off of the ship like Christopher Columbus and stake their flag deeply into you marking you as conquered territory. Claiming something they hadn't discovered. It was like a game of tag, and Tim was the one being chased.

Tim agreed that his life was promising but wasn't without its fair share of tragedy. Some women literally brought the devil out of you. He wanted to be kind and generous, even a gentleman. But they wanted you to take everything they were and ravage through it. They threw it at you and made you take it and then lay helplessly declaring, "Look at what you've done to me." They wrote songs about it, told their friends about it, and even wrote books about it. You'd think they'd learn something by now. Sisters didn't need rules, they needed boundaries and scruples.

And from a brother's point of view, Tim would offer that "it takes more than a plate of collard greens and some ham hocks to get a man." Each woman he encountered spent her life pretending to be a glass that she demanded was full and then tried convincing you that you drank from it, when she knew she was half empty coming into the relationship.

Estella was a prime example. She was psychotic and possessive. She got a kick out of showing up unannounced and rifling through Tim's medicine cabinet and dresser drawers, counting condoms and searching for a reason to cry and become hysterical. She was famous for working herself into a frenzy.

When Tim had decided to move from 135th Street and sublet his brother-in-law's apartment on 62nd Street, he'd told Estella that he was relocating to North Carolina to stay with his ailing grandmother. His grandmother needed him. She had raised him in the absence of a mother, and he needed to be there for her. She was all alone and had no one to lean on in her final years. He could help her with odds and ends around the house, shop for groceries and help her keep track of her bills so she didn't end up in the dark burning candles for light. It had hurt him to make up stories about his grandmother. Women made men lie.

Tim was tired of the never-ending auditions he constantly encountered with women. Estella hadn't been pleased in the least when Tim had said he was leaving. She had mustered up all the theatrical drama she could and insisted that the real reason he was leaving was because she was too skinny, her breasts weren't big enough, and she was too short. True, he fancied a thicker woman, but she'd insisted, "I can get implants, baby, tell me what you like."

Tim didn't have time to nurture a woman with low self-esteem. He wanted a woman who had goals and didn't wait for a pat on the head. A woman doing tricks to keep a man brought him no gratification; it only gave him the urge to toss her to the lions and out of his life. He wanted a woman who could stand on her own without toppling over and getting distracted the moment he said something that she couldn't look up in one of her self-help books. Estella had a one-track mind. She wanted Tim, but he wasn't about to become her life preserver, or anybody else's for that matter.

From the moment Tim had said he was leaving New York, Estella had begun harassing him daily. He'd been working at a local video store labeling videos and eking out a living that he was sure would bring him closer to his goal.

Estella would show up and wander around the store for hours, rearranging the videotapes and trying to persuade Tim that she was the woman he had waited for his whole life. The thing he remembered most was her mannerisms changing. She developed a nervous condition where she kept rubbing the left side of her face with the palm of her hand as if she had an addiction.

She'd been drawing attention to herself, and their nonexistent relationship, but she hadn't cared. Integrity had forced him to quit his job there. One, because his manager hadn't been too pleased that Estella created a daily scene and constantly distracted the customers whenever she came by; and two, because as long as he was working there, she'd always know where to find him.

Tim had wanted to make a clean break. And although ruthless wasn't a word that characterized his nature, he and his boy Justin had packed up his room full of things—mostly clothes and records—and put them in the U-Haul while Estella stood curbside making a fool of herself, pleading, "Baby, you don't have to do this. We can work it out. I need you, Tim."

"I'm not one for scenes," he'd said, as he pulled her arms from around his neck and threw them down at her sides.

She'd been persistent, clutching for any shred of hope. He'd rolled the window down, pried her fingers from around the driver's-side door handle, driven off, and left her weeping loudly on the corner of 135th Street and 8th Avenue.

He had decided shortly after settling into his new apartment to apply for the film school. He was three days away from missing the deadline. He'd been accepted a month and a half later and enrolled in a summer 101 course. Finally it seemed that his future had direction. He never saw Estella again.

5

Mornings always found Troi deep in wonder, helplessly daydreaming. She had a thriving business that she adored, a husband who was in for the long haul, a healthy baby girl, and God as the head of her life. She felt in sync with the hum of the refrigerator, the second hand on the ticking clock, and mentally punished herself for even conjuring the thought that something was missing.

God was supposed to fill the void, but honestly, sometimes she felt incomplete and unsure. It was those nooks and crannies that had her bothered. She thought that things were perfect, but often felt as if there was more that she couldn't see. A door marked number two behind which would be a fabulous prize to tempt her to trade in what she already had. The myth of the greener grass wasn't going to catch her out there.

Troi shuffled around the bedroom in her fleece robe, trying to snuggle her toes deeper into her slippers and get a few minutes to herself before Dakoda woke up crying for cereal. She definitely needed to do the heap of smelly laundry today, but she knew she wouldn't have time.

Saturdays were the busiest days at the shop. *Hair* and *Saturdays* were synonymous. And Vaughn was still asleep. Besides, he was busy. He was always busy. So the pungent two-week-old pile of laundry that was almost up to the doorknob wouldn't get done. Not this weekend. She didn't know what time he had managed to come waltzing in last night. He was always light on his feet. They had been married for three blissful years, one thousand one hundred and twenty-five days, and she didn't find it too hard to compromise or learn to share her world with Vaughn.

He was attentive and giving. She just wished that he'd dedicate more time to the things that needed to be done around the house and take the initiative with doing the mounds of laundry or sinkful of dishes and not just sit back and wait for her to do it all. She had spent her whole teenage life playing house and cleaning up after grown folks. She was dog tired.

Troi took a deep breath and let out a long exaggerated sigh. She made a conscious effort to be open and receptive to Vaughn's needs. He was a man. "Yes, he is," she said aloud.

Personal space and time to himself were part of that, and she understood. He needed to be around his friends, not cooped up in an apartment every day just so she could keep an eye on him, making sure no one else was sinking her teeth into his heart. Male bonding, he needed that. It was some tribal thing, her father said. She didn't see why he had to go out with friends during the week and every other weekend, and she wasn't too enthused about it, but she let it go.

The last things she wanted to be were possessive and jealous. Women everywhere had been batting their eyes at Vaughn, but Troi wasn't really the jealous type. She had the ring, a firm tug on his heart, and he paid the bills. Furthermore, they respected each other. It was a rewarding relationship. Vaughn was giving, and she was grateful.

He loved his little girl. She was his princess, Koda. He took her to the circus, balancing her all the way there and back sitting atop his shoulders as she spent the entire adventure smacking him around and playing patty-cake with his head. "He's an ample husband, too" she thought aloud, covering her sly grin with both hands.

He wore his wedding band prominently on his third finger, and didn't offer excuses about the ring being too tight just to get out of wearing it, like some men did. All it took was an absent wedding ring to set the process in motion for a man to forget he was married. But they were open, honest, and fair with each other. She told him when she wasn't pleased, what she was thinking, and tried to always put herself in his shoes when they had a disagreement. Being fair was important.

Troi vowed going into this marriage that she wouldn't be the proverbial ball and chain that weighed a man down and made him feel in his heart that he had made a mistake marrying her, so she wasn't.

She also said that she wouldn't nag him. That was a hard one. She had to literally bite her tongue more often than not. Her tongue was her best defense. She had inherited it. It was a Madison trait. She was working on it.

She began her morning routine by making coffee, putting on a worship tape, and sitting cross-legged at the breakfast nook in the kitchen to read the Word. She liked grinding her coffee beans fresh; they tasted better than those freeze-dried tasteless crystals. The flavor of the Brazilian blend would dance on her tongue and make her feel like she was really drinking something special, instead of a mouth full of decaffeinated wash water.

Troi flipped the pages over to Proverbs, as the coffee made itself and soothing music confirmed what she already knew—she was blessed. Spiritually, some never got it, some managed to fumble and lose it, others never thought they would have it so they didn't. But she had it, and although a frayed thread got loose every now and then, she and Vaughn both managed to tighten it up quite nicely.

Troi thought back to a childhood where she was raised with so much negativity and criticism, and wondered how it didn't affect her more obviously. Why wasn't she insecure, fearful, or one of those angry black women that men always wrote in to relationship magazines about? Her father only swept everything under the rug or glossed it over, never getting to the root of what the problems were in the house.

She vowed that she would never be like him. She would deal with issues head-on; but she knew she had seeds from her childhood planted in her. She refused to water those seeds and all the negative things she grew up with. That was the key. The hard part was destroying the roots.

Troi also mentally relived the fact that her mother was unbearable, and she knew for a fact that it was only her dream of one day owning her own beauty salon that had sustained her in that depressing house of torment. She never let the things her mother said affect her, never. Her sister Nina always did. Nina let words plant themselves in her, creep into her blood, and mar her personality.

Mother would water every seed, causing anger and strife to flourish and bloom. Troi thought that Nina's level of tolerance was the only way she was glad she wasn't like her sister. One day she knew for sure that she'd conquer that Madison tongue. She just refused to take on any of her mother's other traits.

Mother was an alcoholic, to put it nicely, or alcoholically challenged, to make it politically correct. Troi had to face that fact finally. She had to look it in the bloodshot eyes, see it, smell it, confess it from her own mouth, and swallow it. They all had to. Enough of the charades and pretending that her mother just needed an occasional drink to calm her nerves or help her relax.

Her mother was 151 proof 98 percent of the time. The other two percent of the time, Mother was in transit to get a drink. And the fact that she had managed to keep her job for as long as she had was a miracle in itself, like the parting of the sea. Mother said that she was planning on taking early retirement, but Troi had overheard Daddy talking one evening late after she and Nina both should have been deep in REM sleep.

Mother had confessed that it wasn't so much wanting to retire from her job as a nurse as it was the higher-ups giving her the choice of taking early retirement or facing the consequences of her slipups. Slipups that included falling asleep at the nurses' station, nondocumentation of progress notes, mixing up patients' medication, and mishandling equipment. The job should have been held accountable long ago for allowing Mother to work in that condition. Spare the patients the trauma. But no matter where you worked, there were always those who found a way to get around the administrators, directors, and their own job descriptions. There were those who could make a single task last a month and a half, and then there were those who didn't even bother pretending. They just preyed on the kindness of others to cover up for them long enough to sign the back of their paycheck, cash it, party all weekend, and then come in to borrow twenty bucks first thing Monday morning from one of their more responsible coworkers. Her mother's job and life with Daddy were just the fuzzy little culprits that enabled her mother to stay intoxicated. Whenever her father was around, all Troi remembered him being was either too tired, too bothered, or too zoned out to care. Pretending was his modus operandi, and the whole family suffered much longer than any normal person should have had to.

But, in spite of that, Nina adored their father, flaws and all. It had been a mystery as to why for years. Troi, no matter how disillusioned, did thank her mediocre parents for giving her roots in the church. Hallelujah! It was the only remnant of sanity that they had managed to offer her dismal and pathetic existence as a Madison. Troi had always gravitated toward truth, so she gladly held on to the promises of God. It was all she had. She grasped His truths tightly and clutched them with bloody hands as if they were a rope hovering over a ravenous crocodile's pit, because she knew her deliverance was coming. She could see His hand in the midst of their situations.

When it came to faith in God, whether it was borderline malnutrition, twice handed-down clothes in September for the first day of school, or no oil to heat their ice-cold feet in January, Troi believed. Mother didn't get it, her father was too far removed to get it, and Nina acted like she got it sometimes but she didn't really. Troi felt that God had been more reliable than her own parents. Truly he was Lord, for only the Creator of life could sustain it.

Troi never thought that anything was worth doing halfway. If you were gonna go to church in the snow and rain, smack around a tambourine and scuff up your new shoes, you might as well receive what was being said and apply it. Make it manifest in your life. Don't just sit there and wait for a tragedy and then call on Him with a snotty nose and tears. That's how too many people she knew were. Seasonal. But then, going to church didn't make you a Christian any more than going to McDonald's made you a hamburger.

Troi remembered vaguely how distraught she had been when Nina had prepared for and finally gone away to college. When Nina had left, she'd been what Troi longed to be, free. Like a field slave in the underground looking back only to motivate his feet to move faster. Nina had packed up every memory that had been acquired since childhood that day. She'd taken with her the reminders of warm milk with too many marshmallows, shiny red apples only around Christmas time, and details about how Troi said the cute boys kissed with their mouths open.

Nina had tried to comfort Troi with a hug that day, but it had been rushed and awkward because of the anticipation of the moment. It was Troi who'd begged her on both ashy knees to stay. Troi had given Nina ten unsurpassable reasons off the top of her head why she should stay. She was her sister, she was the oldest, she cooked better than Mother did, she'd allow her to play her favorite song all day without complaining, she needed her, her daddy needed her, everything she learned she learned from her, she loved her, she missed her, she appreciated her, and dozens of other reasons. Troi had really needed God then. Before the door had closed behind Nina on her way out into a world that welcomed her with open arms, Troi was already missing her sister, who was more like a mother to her than anything.

Sure, Troi had spent a few sacrificial weekends with Nina on campus in her antiseptic and sparsely decorated room, but she hadn't wanted to interfere with her studies, especially when Nina had an exam and was adjusting to being on her own and finally, for once in her life, making a few friends. Selfish was something Troi never was. Being alone. It was all so new to her. Novel yet painful at the same time. For both of them.

So, Troi had prayed, cried, and travailed until she felt a release that allowed her to know that it wouldn't be long before it was her turn to leave. Her turn to escape the hell that so many thought was limited to the afterlife. She wouldn't be in that house forever. The stench of melancholy wouldn't last always. She'd needed to believe that with her whole heart. She'd just needed a little more faith to believe that far. Enough faith to believe past the front door.

Troi had been especially devastated with her home life since, in Nina's absence, she had now become the focus of everything that her mother was angry about. Every dirty dish, every overdue bill, every empty bottle, and every argument her mother and father had. She'd been alone in that asylum of family madness that seemed to leave her no room for a crisp clear thought. She was, however, never one to let a situation overtake her. So she'd had no choice but to recognize when God's hands had definitely stroked a few situations that found themselves brewing in the Madison home, like the college fiasco.

A few years after Nina's departure, Mother had told Troi that it was never too early to start looking at colleges. Troi never wanted to go to college; she just wanted her shop. She thought that if she did go to college like Mother wanted, she would only be wasting money and precious time, both of which the Madisons had only in short supply.

"Who goes to school to open a beauty salon?" Troi had asked.

"Ladies, please," is all Daddy would say when the bickering started.

He was more interested in anything that was going on outside of the house than anyone who actually lived there. It hadn't mattered that she'd been the only child left at home. Troi was convinced that Daddy had other shapely interests. It hadn't mattered much, because once she was eighteen and got a loan, she'd be gone, too. History.

It was a strange, unnatural feeling to be ignored. At one time her father had participated in their well-being and carefully cultivated their minds to utilize the thought process. But the more Mother drank and their marital relationship deteriorated, the more Daddy cast the whole family aside like damp shoes that made your feet itch.

He skimped on time and created situations that would keep him away from home for hours on end.

He and Mother both had already become like the seasonal saints who only came to church on Easter and New Year's Eve decorated from head to toe in overpriced, low-quality clothes. Troi didn't understand how Mother thought that those women in the church couldn't smell her coming around the corner. The alcohol oozed through her pores and discolored her lips, stripping them of pigment and muscle control. Her daddy, on the other hand, was too passive for his own good. Mother's loud mouth demanded a balance. Her daddy often said that he didn't know what all the fuss was about.

"I'm a hardworking man," he'd say, sounding more ridiculous than he looked. As parents, her mother and father were one major disappointment after another, after another, after another.

For instance, Troi, being a stickler for details, remembered the time when Nina almost died of heartbreak. She had graduated from junior high and prepared her walk, bow, smile, and speech three weeks in advance. She had saved her record money to buy stockings that were a shade lighter than coffee. She'd been pretty in her fluffy dress, polished shoes, and Easter gloves. The parents, friends, and family members in the audience that day had eagerly applauded every child as each made his way across to the podium.

When Nina had walked across the stage and looked out into the auditorium, all she'd heard with her heart's ear was her sister clapping, proud and alone. It had been as if Troi's presence wasn't enough. Nina had felt shortchanged. Daddy had been unable to make it to the graduation. "Overtime," he'd said. Mother hadn't made it either, but that hadn't mattered as much to Nina as Daddy's presence. Nina had bawled the whole way home, tossing her things to the ground as Troi watched helplessly. First she'd tossed her gloves, then her diploma. Her nose had been running, her ears hot, and her head . . . Troi was sure it had been throbbing, too.

When Nina had gotten home to her room, Troi remembered how she'd begun screaming and throwing things around like a crazy girl. She'd thrown books, dinner, her collection of 45s, and her favorite Archie jelly glasses. They'd crashed on and around the wall, leaving nicks and scratches that were telltale signs of the misguided childhood they'd both had. Mother had stumbled up the stairs to investigate the commotion, and she and Nina had literally gone at it in a verbal tango. Nina'd gone on boisterously about how other parents knew how to love their kids and how they respected them enough to show up to their graduation. Nina had made a fist, pounded the table, and demanded respect but Mother had said she'd have to get a job and pay some bills first.

When Daddy had come home, he'd just stood motionless and devoid of feeling. He'd stared at the food on the wall, shards of glass on the floor, and directed Troi to clean it all up. He'd been disappointing them all ever since. He'd tried to make it up to Nina for weeks after that with a record here, a package of silver hair beads there, but by then it was as if her heart had become icy and cold enough to disown him.

Nina hadn't eaten for almost a week, and she'd stayed in her room listening to music all day, staring at the ceiling as if it were the sun and refusing to go to school or even take a shower. She was never the same really, especially about trusting people. It seemed from that point on Nina just hung on to her perfect idea of Daddy in her mind, because she knew he'd never actually live up to it. Deep down, Troi hoped that Nina knew he was no longer that man she idolized; she had to know. Troi prayed she did.

Growing up, Troi was a different child altogether. She wasn't disrespectful, although any child might have been, given the circumstances. She wasn't promiscuous either, but she sure was elated when she met Vaughn. He was like a chocolate sundae with extra caramel syrup dripping down the sides, bidding her tongue to catch every drop. Vaughn was delicious-looking and had courted Troi for all of six months and then proposed. Everyone thought it was sudden, but for Troi it had taken way too long.

"Child, you don't even know this man," Mother had said. "What does he do for a living? How much money does he make?" Mother had gone on and on.

"Mother, I love him," Troi had said, "so just be happy for me for a change, okay?"

All the women in the church had turned their noses up at Troi, as if she thought she was better than everybody because she'd unwittingly caught the most sought-after fish in the sea. She couldn't help it if her lure caught big fish and theirs just sat there dragging the bottom of the ocean, snagging uneaten pieces of chum.

"Don't hate me because I'm Mrs. Singleton," she'd said out loud. The Hallelujah Girls hadn't thought that was funny, but she'd sure gotten a kick out of the way they'd expected her to follow

Vaughn's every move. She wasn't that kind of woman, and wasn't about to become that kind now. The less attention she paid to what Vaughn was doing and who he was doing it with, the more he became hers.

They all needed to know that true men of God wanted a woman who had a genuine love for God. Every woman in the church wanted to become a preacher's wife, so they performed and acted out their faith in God openly like women in a beauty pageant trying to win a crown that, for all they knew, was made out of papier-mâché. Some of them hallelujahed their way down the aisle to the altar only to shuffle their way into divorce court a year and a half later.

Vaughn had been watching Troi from the third pew for months. Troi had been a member of Zion Missionary for several years then. She felt led there. She was a down-to-earth sister, and didn't feel the need to wear big fancy hats or have a loud mouth to amen everything the preacher said just to be noticed. Vaughn told her that he really did cherish that about her. "Girl, I know that's right," and other religious lingo were not phrases Troi uttered to prove how religious she was. They called her stuck-up and pious, but the truth was that they didn't know what to make of her, so they talked about her instead, she thought, sitting at the breakfast nook sipping her coffee.

There were times in their courtship when Vaughn had been rumored to be messing around. Several people had told her that he had a baby on the way by another woman that lived across town and that the woman attended his mother's church. It was humorous how all of a sudden they'd found it necessary to look out for her best interest. By the time the rumor had circulated around the entire church twice and made its way back to her, Troi had been negotiating a lease for the space that was soon to be christened Shangrila. She'd been determined that she wasn't going to get pregnant to keep him, and she wasn't about to give in to sex just to woo him into marrying her. If he wanted her, he would have to wait or hit the road just like all the rest who had tried before him.

She hadn't believed the rumors being whispered about him, and wasn't about to try retaliative tactics either. They'd wanted to see her squirm, so she didn't. The Hallelujah Girls wanted her man, the man God had promised her, and if they couldn't have him, they didn't want her to have him either. But Troi and Vaughn had a connection, and he was a provider, she'd known that much about him. Endless nights they had spent together in his little beat-up ride talking...

those discussions had revealed to her that in a million years he wouldn't let his seed lack. So the lie about him having a baby that he was keeping a secret had to go back from where it came: the pit of hell.

"Mah-meee, ceweeal," Dakoda mumbled sleepily, stumbling into the kitchen with her favorite Winnie the Pooh blanket dragging and tripping her up.

"You want cereal, baby?"

Dakoda nodded and raised her arms for Troi to pick her up.

"What kind of cereal you want, boo-boo, huh?"

Dakoda pointed to the Fruity Pebbles, and Troi shook her head in disbelief. All the artificial coloring and dye. She knew Dakoda only ate that cereal because she knew her daddy did. Vaughn was hooked on Fruity Pebbles and Cocoa Puffs. Sometimes she wished he'd grow up. Sometimes he just had too much kid in him for her.

Troi's day began slowly as she sprinkled the cereal in a red bowl, added some milk, and flipped the worship tape over to the other side. Since she was feeding the baby, she thought that Vaughn needed to dress Dakoda and take her to Virginia's. Mrs. Singleton spoiled Dakoda rotten every chance she got by giving her everything she ever pointed at in a store or a supermarket.

Vaughn was still asleep, but he usually got up and played ball early on Saturday, while Troi prepared for a day of women craving to look like something in a magazine.

"Can you do this with my hair, CeCe?" they would ask her.

"Girl, you ain't got no hair." She'd laugh.

"Why you gonna dis me like that?"

"Girl, please, you know it's true."

Troi popped some waffles in the toaster and caught the milk that was running down Dakoda's chin with the spoon.

"No, mahmee . . ."

"Yes, Dakoda, I'm gonna feed you," she said, smiling at Dakoda, who would take too long if she fed herself.

Troi wanted to be dressed and out of the house by ten o'clock. The phone rang. Troi glanced at the wall clock that was struggling on a dying battery. It was about ten minutes after nine. On the other end of the phone was lame Sofie calling in the sickest, most pathetic voice she could conjure, telling Troi she couldn't make it into the shop today because she had an emergency, which sounded more like a hangover than anything else.

"Girl, you know I'm stuck, right?"

Sofie apologized profusely and Troi imagined Sofie's dilemma. She probably just rolled over into the arms of the man who was the dish she'd served the evening before. She hadn't changed.

"These women need to stop letting men come between them and their money," she yelled.

By the time Troi hung up the phone and made a mental list of what she'd have to do in Sofie's absence, the waffles were cold and hard and Dakoda had milk all over the place. Troi poured Vaughn a cup of coffee. Black, one sugar.

"Vaughn, can you help me?" Troi asked, barging into his sleep. She flipped on the lights, holding Dakoda with one arm and rummaging through the dresser drawer for something for the baby to wear with the other.

"I'm sleeping, CeCe."

"Come on, Vaughn, I have to go in early, Sofie's not coming in today."

"Why don't you fire her?" he mumbled from under the pillow, peering at her like a one-eyed zombie who needed just an hour more of sleep to be fully reincarnated.

"And who's gonna do hair in her place, you?"

"Okay, okay," he grumbled.

"I'm sorry to wake you, baby, but don't you have to get up anyway? You usually play ball with Anthony on Saturday," she smoothed over with a hint of sympathy.

"No, not today, he's on lockdown."

"Coffee's done, Vaughn," she tempted.

She hoped he wouldn't be in a bad mood because she'd woken him up. She sat Dakoda on the bed. The baby fell back on the bed, smiling and contorting her body because her daddy was playing peekaboo with her from under the blanket.

Vaughn threw off the covers, stretched loudly, spread his toes, arched his back, rubbed Dakoda on the head, then shuffled into the bathroom. He came back with a damp washcloth in hand. He undressed Dakoda, then wiped off her face first and saved her toes for last to play the counting game as he always did. Vaughn always looked sexy without a shirt. Not too much hair or muscles, but just enough cuts in all the fashionable places. He was mouthwatering, like succulent fruit you took your time to peel and placed delicately on your tongue. He always left Troi feeling as if she had honey on her palate.

"What?" he said, catching Troi's eyes undressing the rest of him.

He always slept with his pajama pants, and sometimes Troi wore the top, but not often. He had on the blue satin ones. They clung to his rear and his lips were as thick and irresistible as the liquid in a chocolate-covered cherry. She never could curb the urge to kiss them, not even with Dakoda sitting between them on the bed mumbling, "Ma-ma-ma-ma."

Morning breath didn't matter; after three years she was used to it. Their kiss lingered and he smoothed down her braids, which were always shiny and neat, and looked her in the eyes, taking her to that familiar place in her mind; then he whacked her on the butt.

"Come on, girl," he said. "You said you had to go, didn't you?" He grinned.

Troi was confident that the shop could manage an extra thirty minutes without her.

"Come on, Vaughn, don't do that to me." She frowned.

"Do what, girl?"

"You know," she pleaded, pulling him closer to her.

"Tonight, CeCe."

"I don't want tonight, I want now." She pouted.

"No."

Troi sucked her teeth long and hard, rolled her eyes, then got up and rummaged through the closet for something to wear. Begging was beneath her. She pulled out a green T-shirt and a pair of faded jeans.

"I need the car, baby," Vaughn said, "so I'll drop you off, then Dakoda, and come back for you tonight, okay?"

"Sure, whatever, just be back by nine to pick me up, I don't like spending money for cab fare when we have a car, Vaughn."

She was obviously agitated. Vaughn admired Troi's facial expressions. He always got a kick out of her frowning and trying to be nonchalant. He smirked as Troi disrobed, kicking off her panties and twisting her arms behind her back to unhook her bra, and made her way into the bathroom. She reached through the curtains to turn on the shower. Vaughn knew that men were always expected to be in the mood. He wanted his wife to be content. They had issues that arose, but he wanted to make his marriage stronger, not weaker.

Vaughn buttoned up Dakoda's jumper and placed her in the playpen, gave her her favorite toy, and turned on PBS so she could watch the blue fuzzy thing that ate cookies. He slipped out of his pajama pants and strode into the bathroom, thick and tall, determined to give his wife a scene she would play back in her mind all day long.

The bathroom was damp. The mirror was clouding over with steam; it moistened him, too. He startled her as he parted the shower curtains to enter. It had been too long, he thought, as the warm water beat down on his back, calling not only his name but hers, repeatedly. Troi's eyes said *thank you*. Vaughn's body said *you're welcome* and his arms assisted.

Her shoulders glistened under the hot streams of water and her soaked braids spread apart and clung to her back as he worked her favorite soap into a rich frothy lather. He slathered her with a bubbly fragrance, smoothed it slowly over the contour of her hips, her knees, and her toes, then patiently made his way back up again. The water soothed them both as he moved her hair to the side of her face and sought a spot where she'd never been kissed.

She managed his name as unidentifiable words followed, escaping her and allowing her mind to reassure her that she loved her husband more than anything. Eyes closed and water that would have obscured their view dripping from their noses, they faced each other, gasping and allowing the moment to remind them both that they had each other and that, despite what people said, there was truly beauty in submission.

6

Nina had a magnificent green thumb, which her mother sarcastically suggested she must have inherited from her grandmother. Nina never knew her grandmother. She hardly even knew her mother, but she couldn't help but think that her mother did suck the life out of anything she came in contact with. A tile hung on Nina's wall in the foyer insisting that MARTHA STEWART DOESN'T LIVE HERE, but Nina's window boxes were always full of exotic flowering annuals. Begonias, chrysanthemums, sweet Williams, carnations, pink coreopsis, black-eyed Susans, and the like.

They often brought butterflies and neighborhood children with itchy fingers who wanted to show their mommas what they had found blowing in the wind. She didn't need gardening shows on HGTV to know what she was doing. The array of colors from the flowers comforted her each time she peeped out of her window, looking onto the streets where passersby were always agitated and in a hurry. She believed that tending to nature was a way of feeling closer to God, although she didn't necessarily believe gardening or appreciating it was a replacement for a relationship with Him. Birds singing, clouds wafting, and the sun beaming just made life more bearable, was all.

Nina could sit in her window and hear the rapturous bells chime from the church that was four blocks over. The air was damp and the birds chirped, fluttered, and played hopscotch on and off the trees above briskly moving cars that, by day's end, would be a traffic jam on Nostrand, Atlantic, and every other major street in Brooklyn.

A slow-moving station wagon tossed the *Daily News* wrapped in plastic into the yards of the same six residents and hurried through the block, making a slushing sound on the wet street. The bus at the corner stopped as it did every morning around seven forty-five, letting two people off who, arm in arm, shared more than normal people should at seven in the morning. And although it was still early and half the neighborhood was probably still curled up comfy, a roaring plane overhead tried to convince Nina that she should be on a tropical island somewhere seeing her world through hot-pink lenses, fantasizing and digging her toes in the sand.

Nina opened the front door and squinted in the sun's brightness, which hadn't given her a chance to adjust. She squinted as she often did when people thought she was frowning. She picked up the paper, which had made its perfect landing in the large clay flowerpot at the base of the stairs, took the plastic off, and unfolded the slightly damp paper.

She waved at Junior, the neighborhood vagrant who actually didn't even live in the neighborhood, but rather just roamed up and down the street looking for something to get into. He was dressed in his everyday gray polyester work pants with evidence of static cling and cat hairs skimming the hem. His sneakers had Velcro flaps and he was sporting an Afro mustache. He gave a semitoothless grin, tipped his oily red hat, and was on his way.

The newspaper headline read HANG TOUGH—FIRST LADY URGES BILL NOT TO CHANGE STORY. Nina thought how she never wanted to be in the president's shoes, or his wife's. Their lives were too public, too showy, too theatrical and dramatic, and Nina craved privacy. The limelight truly wasn't for her. No one ever had to worry about her stealing the stage.

"Morning, Nina." Martha waved with an overused broom she was using to sweep down her scantily littered steps.

She wore a pink paisley housedress, blue striped tube socks, and brown men's house slippers.

"Hey, Martha, girl, what you got planned today?"

"Just some shopping. What you got planned?"

"I have to pick up Shelby. We're gonna take a ride up to Shangrila. Just look at this mess," Nina said, pulling off her navy bandanna and running her fingers through her hair.

"Yeah, I know, I have to do something with mine, too, but not today."

Martha had plaits sticking up all over her head, and Nina thought, *That girl better come and go with us now!*

"I have to take Glenda to her dance class at eleven. What's doing tonight?"

"I don't know, maybe going by the country club with Shelby, I'm not sure. I'll call you?"

"Don't you have to be a member or something?"

"Martha, you know if you wanted to go, you could get in with us," Nina said, almost scolding.

"Child, that's okay, I don't have a baby-sitter and Gerald might come by. And besides, I don't have a thing to wear." Martha made excuses, as if she wanted Nina to run out and buy her something quick.

"Well, let me know if you change your mind."

"I sure will," Martha said, still fixed on sweeping the debris down to the last step.

Martha and Nina had gotten friendly mostly because they were the only women who lived on the block who weren't shacked up or married. They hung around on Saturdays and talked a bunch about nothing. Married people became reclusive. Nothing existed for those codependent couples except their world of marital bliss, a world she thought people fooled themselves into believing was a never-ending honeymoon. Martha was great company. Open, honest, and never bit her tongue. Always said what she felt. Didn't matter whose feelings she hurt.

She made Nina laugh often. She would tell stories about the men who came in and out of her life. Nina lived her life vicariously through Martha's, just as she had done through Troi's her entire life. Martha would tell Nina about the men who wanted to be a part of her life so badly they'd do whatever she said.

They'd arrive with groceries, bootleg videos, jewelry, and money, expecting to sleep over and get a little something extra. If she felt like it, she let them, but only after Glenda was asleep. She didn't want Glenda to get the wrong impression or end up like her, though she couldn't care less what the nosy neighbors thought. Everyone had bones in their closet. Skeletal remains. Some people had so many they couldn't open the closet or their mouths for fear of an avalanche.

Martha and Nina would chat for hours and just sit looking out the window, seeing who was doing what with whom. They made plans for things they wanted to do with their lives once they either found someone significant enough to share them with or made their first million; both were sure the million would come first. Martha liked to talk about all this New Age stuff, which Nina explained to her was really Old Age stuff since it had been around since before Jesus came.

Martha would go on and on about feng shui's negative chi and what a harmonious life you could have through the arrangement of furniture, mirrors, and such. *If her life is so harmonious, why can't feng shui bring her a husband, a job, and a father for Glenda?* Nina thought, trying not to sound too judgmental.

People wanted answers right now, Nina imagined as she lit her honey-colored twenty-wick candle sculpture. It had taken almost two years to burn halfway down and was too big to hug. She always spent Saturday mornings lounging in her newly upholstered moleskin chair.

Nina enjoyed the natural oils that wafted from the candle and mingled with the April breeze that blew through the sheer muslin curtains. Her door was slightly ajar. It excited her senses. The wildflowers on her windowsill danced a little in the sway of the morning air. She sipped on café vianetta, watched the sun reflect off of the wood floors that she was accustomed to walking on barefoot, and played a little jazz to clear her head of déjà vu clutter until it was time to go uptown to Shangrila.

Troi had promised to twist Nina's hair or do something to it that would make it more wash-and-wear. Nina required maximum potential with minimal effort, and didn't have time for pin, curl, and wrap. She had outlived that preoccupation with her hair in her twenties.

Nina was hungry. The marble tiles in the kitchen were cool on her feet, so she tiptoed over to the counter, toasted a slice of cinnamon raisin bread and buttered it, then took a bite. She puttered around the closet, deciding what she would wear today. Something comfortable, she thought, pulling out her favorite pair of jeans and a belt. Any top would do, so a navy acid-wash tee did. She didn't want to get too dressy. That was Shelby's job. And far be it from her to upstage Miss Shelby.

Nina wasn't hard to please; she was just determined. A friend had once called her cold-natured, which may have been true, but the only fact that bothered her remotely as much as that comment was that she was never as hard on men as she should be. It was a fact. Kevin, for one, had never been reprimanded. He'd trampled on her, leaving footprints that were noticeable and dark, yet she'd taken him back countless times until she swore off men for good a few years ago.

She couldn't deal with the distractions or the bitter taste the masquerade left in her mouth. Nina had always been a strong-willed child, but like a horse being whispered, she'd mellowed considerably. She was still vocal about everything except men. She allowed them to come in and rob her blind. They stole her self-esteem, which was flimsy to start. Sure, she came on strong and tough, but everybody knew that once they got past the icy exterior, she was Silly Putty.

Growing up, it was a constant that Nina had an opinion about everything.

"She'll grow out of it," her daddy said, but she wasn't buying it, even if it was on sale.

"Never talk about politics or religion," she remembered hearing in a multicultural America course.

"People have opposing views when it comes to religion and politics," the professor had explained, "and it's not worth the debate."

"Politics and religion are crucial issues that should be discussed," she demanded. No one would refute that fact with her. They might have labeled her a wilted wallflower or even a Wall Street bore, but she always had her say. Nina had many beliefs, though they nearly consumed her in their contradictions. She had things that she didn't believe in, too. She didn't believe in the skinning of animals for the beautification of man. And although she had since graduated, was working making more than enough, and could waltz into any thrift shop and purchase one, she didn't own a fur coat.

The fur coat issue was a controversial topic, especially in the church, where outdoing and upstaging was the prerequisite for acceptance into the religious cliques. There was the fur coat clique and the "I've-got-the-latest-hairstyle" clique. There was also the "I've-got-a-brand-new-car" clique, but they didn't really count because the repoman could come just as quickly as it took for them to say, "Fill 'er up." It was senseless, she thought. A sick society of people who wore all the money they had on their backs or on their fingers and then lived somewhere reminiscent of a crack den. Many people offered that her antifur campaign was her opinion, and they were right, it was.

She wasn't an activist or anything remotely obnoxious. She was however, peculiar in a sense and determined to have her say. She was almost novel, in fact, and found herself leaning more toward eclectic than cool on the popularity meter. Her friends didn't care, they swung their pelts about as if to say, *look at me, see me, envy me.*

They couldn't care less about the torture and bloodshed it took for them to wrap themselves in fur that was skinned off an innocent animal foraging for food. It was like stealing the covers from a malnourished child in a third-world country on a blustery cold winter night. Trifling.

Nina often thanked God that she was nothing like her friends. She didn't know why she thanked Him, she wasn't much like God either—something that she vowed to rectify each New Year's Eve. Her friends with their opposing views were a constant distraction. She had grown to care about them, but she hadn't picked them; they chose her.

Her friends wanted to know the boyish girl who seemed unafraid to say what was on her mind. They wanted to observe her when she went head-to-head with the dorm mother, who was fighting to shorten the curfew, and the dean of students, who was eagerly going along with the program because he didn't want to be responsible for any promiscuous teen girls in New York City after eleven P.M. on weekdays.

"We're women," Nina had reiterated, and, clipboard in hand, she'd started a petition fighting to stay the current curfew.

"We're all over eighteen years old, and we pay to attend this college, it's not free."

Five thousand twenty-three signatures and a board meeting later, the curfew had been stayed and Nina had become a hero of sorts for initiating the fight. Neighbors, store owners, the man in the cleaners, students, and their parents had signed the petition, only reinforcing the fact that there was strength in numbers, and that the pen was indeed mightier sometimes.

These friends that Nina had acquired were so different from her and the life she was allowed to lead. They crowded their weekends with faceless men whose names were never remembered, for the sole purpose of not appearing to be dateless. Nina never understood their dating dilemma or the urgency. It was as if they had an imaginary deadline to meet. There was nothing barbaric about not having a date. It didn't make you less of a woman. If that were the case, Nina thought, her femininity would have been shot from day one. "I can do bad all by myself," came to mind. But the men she knew were just as tired as that old cliché.

She never really meddled in the love lives of her acquaintances and scattered friends. But she still couldn't relate to these people. It was like comparing airplanes to boats. They both got you to your destination, but one glided through the air unscathed and the other sort of dredged through tepid waters against the current.

The only person Nina had to confide in when she was growing up was her sister. It's why she and Troi were tight. There was no parade of schoolmates in and out of the house; Mother didn't allow that. Mother had to keep up her royal front. She wanted to be held in high regard. She played numbers, chain-smoked, swore relentlessly, belittled only those directly related to her, and drank like a fish in purified water, but sure, she still wanted people to see God in her. It was the longest stretch of the imagination.

If Mother didn't go to hell for sinning, she'd sure go there based solely on how she treated her kids. But looking back, Nina was sure it was God's doing really, because Nina and Troi had been there for each other in ways that only strengthened the bonds of sisterhood.

"Family business stays in the family," Mother said quite often, as if either of them wanted to pull out a chair, get on a bullhorn, and broadcast their family life.

Nina and Troi had relied on each other for everything. They were each other's confidants and worst critics. Boys never came between them, although Troi was the prettier one and the one with the endless suitors. But if it ever came down to a boy or each other, they knew that they were stronger than that.

As adults, their lives were aligned differently. Troi had run to the church and the saving grace of God, and although Nina had followed, Troi practically lived there. She had consumed herself, immersed her heart in redemption and salvation. Shelby was considered part of the family, too, but she'd run as fast and as far from the church as she could, which wasn't a surprise.

"I have more entertaining things to do," she'd said, dismissing the women as frumpy and plain.

Martha, on the other hand, allowed the theory of reincarnation to comfort her into believing that if she didn't get it right this time, there'd be other lives to try again. Troi had said of Martha, "Maybe she'd come back as a guest in a hotel and get a wake-up call." Troi seemed so confident in her beliefs.

"Girl, I wish I had your faith," Nina had commented one evening over three-cheese lasagna.

"In God?"

"Yes . . ."

"It's something that comes in time, Nina. It's a process. You know how we were raised; I am a miracle, a testimony. I mean, even if salvation were a hoax, I'd rather be safe than sorry."

Nina had nodded, wishing she was more like her sister.

And so, Nina sat in her favorite chair that matched her fondness for nature and watched the weekly visitors file into the block. The Jehovah's Witnesses were like teenage boys with raging hormones begging for sex. They kept coming and laying the pressure on, telling you how good it was for you, and how you needed it. Paradise, bliss, they named it to lure you in. They didn't take no for an answer.

They opened her gate, trespassing, and walked patiently up the stairs. They nudged the little girl ahead of them. She was their sales gimmick. A mile away you could spot them with their plastic cases.

"Just tell them politely, no, thank you," Mother slurred whenever she overheard Nina complaining about it.

Troi understood. But everything seemed simple from the seedy haze in which her mother was perpetually vacationing.

Nina opened the window and rested on her elbows as she dug around in the window boxes, propping up her flowers and discarding fallen leaves, squinting again in the sun. She managed a smile and shook her head no, as they approached the top step and began to tell her something about good news. She refused to hide behind her door like a guest at a hooky party. This was her house, and they would just have to respect that. From the smallest to the tallest, they had to learn that they couldn't just come probing and prodding around in her space.

Nina watered her plants more sufficiently than the morning mist had and pondered how she would spend the day. She thought about how people didn't respect each other or relationships. "It'll be okay," she said to herself, realizing that some plants got more faithfulness than people. She still hadn't decided if she would go riding with the girls tonight at the uppity little country club that allowed them all to become members. In clubs like those, it wasn't about having money, just about having enough.

Shelby loved it. She fit right in, poor little rich girl that she was. Shelby didn't care if she was token. Nina wasn't looking forward to the facade. It wasn't what she'd call an enchanted evening. Shelby was caught up in the prestige of it all. When the valet smiled and took Shelby's keys, she would saunter in like royalty, plop down poolside, and snap her finger for something cool that would slide down her throat and give her a slight buzz. Nina wasn't amused.